THE
MASKED LOVER

J. BRACKEN-RUSSELL

THE MASKED LOVER

Copyright © J.Bracken-Russell (2022)

The right of J.Bracken-Russell to be identified as author of this work has been asserted by him/her in accordance with section 77 and 78 of the Copyright, Designs and Patents Act 1988.

About Author

 J. Bracken-Russell hails from South Wales, United Kingdom, leading to spending a part of his childhood days in Co Meath, Southern Ireland. From a young age, he admits to being creative and interested in just about everything; he was able to fill in life's repertoire. I am elated to be supporting Galop who, provides advice and support to empower anyone in the LGBT+ community experiencing Domestic abuse.

Table of Contents

Chapter One

Being stuck in this dreary sales office day in and day out is just not how I had imagined my life. I feel like a hamster stuck on an endless wheel. My office phone rings for the hundredth time today. Should I answer it, or just let it go through to voicemail?

I look out of the office window. The puffy white clouds are changing colour, and my mind floats away with them. They look solid enough to walk on, and I bet they would be so soft under my bare feet …

Suddenly, I feel a pair of eyes stabbing me in the back as the phone continues to ring. My work colleague and best friend, Mandy, softly says, "Brayden, are you going to answer that?"

I slightly turn my head. "No. I can't be bothered."

Mandy tuts and shakes her head at me as the ringing of the telephone stops.

1

I move my mouse to continue with the sales account I am working on. Nothing happens when I click. I jam my finger into the mouse button incessantly, but it refuses to open the file. "Great!" I mutter. I wiggle the mouse, but the cursor has frozen. Tapping like an ape at the keys for a few seconds might fix it. No, no it doesn't. Frustrated, I bang the keyboard of my computer. What the hell is wrong with this heap of shit now?

"Brayden, I can hear you grinding your teeth from over here. Let me help," Mandy says.

"Here she is—super Mand to the rescue!" I say.

She chuckles as she hustles over to my desk with a swish of her floral skirt. "It will not work if you bang the keyboard like that. She taps my shoulder. "Stand up, then."

I rise from my cushioned chair and step to the side of my desk. Mandy gracefully lowers herself into my seat and taps a few keys. Just like that, she has my computer purring like a kitten.

"There you go. It just needed a little TLC." Mandy's smile matches her warm, comforting tone.

"Thanks, Mandy!" I say. She vacates my chair, and I plonk myself back down in front of my computer. "Speaking of TLC, I am waiting not so patiently for the intimate details of what went on this weekend!"

Mandy blushes. "Oh, well…"

"So? Come on, how did your weekend go? Did you meet the man of your dreams, or was he a troll?" I giggle. "Come on, show us a pic! He can't be that bad."

Mandy sighs and shows me a picture of a man on her phone. I give my signature nod of approval. "I am sure I have seen that guy somewhere before in magazine or the on the web." Mandy rolls her eyes at me, so I make my smirk wider and kick my teasing into high gear. "Mmm, he is definitely strawberries and cream! He would be at the top of my dessert menu."

Mandy chuckles. "Every man you see is at the top of your dessert menu."

"Only the ones who have a satisfying lunch box on show hun."

We both dissolve into a fit of laughter. I do love these conversations with Mandy; we are both hopeless romantics at heart, and sharing in each other's dating highs and lows are honestly the highlights of my dreary days stuck in this hellhole of an office.

"So, did you get his number?" I ask. "When are you seeing him again? Come on, Mandy, don't leave me in suspense. You know I need this to get through the day." I give my friend full puppy-dog eyes, which I know she can't resist, and I walk over to her desk to hover over her until she spills the beans.

She lasts about ten seconds before she cracks. "All right. Well, he told me that—"

Mandy stops talking abruptly as the office door flies open. "Here she comes, the witch with more awful shoes than her attitude," I whisper before our office manager, Corinna Gotobed, gets within earshot. She is the reason my heart sinks every time I enter this ruin of a workplace.

Corinna's nasal voice pierces the air. "Mr Willoughby and Miss Harris, how is it remotely possible that you have time for gossip when the deadlines for the accounts are this afternoon? Get it done! I expect the report on my desk by 3 p.m., not one minute later!" She clips away on her high heels to go nag somebody else. I walk over to the office door to check Corinna is out of sight, and close it decisively behind her.

As I walk back over to my desk, I shudder. Doesn't Corinna know she would get better results from her employees if she was actually nice to us? Perhaps she just likes being awful. I'm pretty sure she was the inspiration for Cruella de Vil. "She needs a bloody good shag, not the accounts report," I say to Mandy, who still looks shaken from Hurricane Corinna's brief, but no less destructive, visit to our desks.

Once my humour wears off, I quickly realise my workload just got a lot heavier. Thanks a lot, Corinna. I put my head in my hands and sigh so loudly that I could swear it makes the windows rattle.

"Come on, Brayden, let's go get some lunch. My treat." Mandy, my angel, always knows just what to say.

I look at her and flash her a weak smile. "Aha, you thought you were going to get off without telling me if you got the guy's number!"

She stands and swipes her bright crimson lipstick across her mouth. Her lipstick was already fine—she's obviously stalling.

"Well?" I prompt.

She pauses for a moment longer as she dusts her face with powder. Eventually, she says, "No, I didn't get his number. He said he would call me." She sighs.

Unfortunately, I am a person not blessed with a brain to mouth filter, so I blurt without thinking, "Yeah, the call that never comes. Maybe you weren't igniting his flame!" Shit! Why did I say that? Come on, Brayden, think, think. "I mean … aw, hun, you know you should never say goodbye until you have their number." That's all I can muster.

Mandy doesn't reply, and I wish a hole would open up in the office floor for me to fall through. The last thing I want to do is upset my best friend.

Luckily, a smile beams across her beautiful painted lips. "Oh well, I wasn't sure I liked him that much anyway." She throws her makeup into her bag and grabs her coat from the back of her chair. "Come on. Lunch."

I grab my coat and we both head out of the office. As we walk along the corridor to the lift, I ask, "What do you fancy for lunch?"

"I really fancy a sausage," she says.

"So do I, but I don't think either of us is going to be able to have one of those this lunch time."

She laughs. "No, Brayden, I mean a sausage with chips, and gravy soaked all over it."

I shrug. "Not exactly how I like my sausages, but whatever floats your boat, I suppose."

"Shut it, you." Mandy presses the lifts button. Luck is on our side—the lift door opens immediately. As we stare at the blank steel doors on our way down, she says, "But seriously, what do you want for lunch?"

"Don't know. I'll see when we get there, I suppose."

The lift stops on the ground floor, and we both walk out into the fresh air. The sky is covered in dreary clouds, but being outdoors makes me smile. Now I can be free from the place I call hell on earth for an hour or so. We walk down the concrete steps, Mandy's shoe heels clipping each one as we walk down.

We arrive at the chip shop, only to find there is a queue that stretches around the corner. I look at Mandy. "I am not waiting in that. We will be here all day, and Hurricane Corinna won't be happy. I'm not sure even a sausage is worth getting torn to shreds by that witch."

Mandy purses her lips. "I think you're right. Come on— let's find someplace else."

We walk a few doors up from the chip shop, and our eyes lock onto a new coffee shop. If luck is on our side, they might serve takeaways.

Mandy says, "It's going to have to be a sandwich or nothing, Brayden."

I nod, and we push the glass panel of the coffee shop door. A wooden sandwich board greets us with the words "Welcome to Cappuccino's Coffee House!" Mandy pauses to read the sign, and I gently nudge her to keep walking. I don't want to spend my entire break queueing.

When we arrive at the counter, Mandy asks, "What do you fancy? I can't decide—there's so much to choose from."

I start to peruse the menu, but my eyes are drawn a very handsome assistant, who is arranging a fresh batch of cakes in the counter display. My reply is out of my mouth before I really have a chance to think. "Well, I'm thinking five feet eight inches, blue eyes … a large lunch box."

6

Mandy follows my gaze and laughs. "No, Brayden! Not the eye candy assistant. I meant food. Come on, I'm starving."

The gorgeous sales assistant finishes his task and asks Mandy and me what we would like to order. I can't focus— my eyes are drawn to his fit body, and I imagine him naked standing there in front of me. I am pulled back to reality when Mandy nudges my arm. The sales assistant says, "If you can't decide, I highly recommend the chicken club sandwich. I'm Jack, by the way."

Mandy takes his advice and orders a chicken club. I try to speak, but my tongue has stopped working. Jack is so mesmerising. I imagine us on a beach, with me rubbing sun lotion on his back.

Jack says, "And what can I get for you, sir?"

My mouth finally decides to function. "You. I mean … I will have the same thing she is having!"

Jack walks off to the other side of the shop to prepare our sandwiches. Mandy grins. "Maybe it's for the best that I didn't get that guy's number this weekend. I quite like the view I am seeing now!"

I laugh and nudge Mandy. "Piss off, bitch, I saw him first!"

She snickers and looks at her watch. Her expression drops into a frown. "Shit, is that the time? We are going to be late back to the office. Corinna will be foaming at the mouth if you're late with those sales reports!"

"Oh, forget it," I say. "We give half our life to that place We don't even get a thank you—we are just seen as a number on the payroll. Besides, being late once in a while is not the

7

crime of the century. Ever thought of having a career change, hun?" I think I'm saying that last sentence to myself as much as to Mandy. When I was younger, I wanted to run a toy shop. I should've done that instead of accepting a dreary office job.

Mandy says, "But if you had taken that path, you would not have met me. And what would you do without me?"

I pause for a moment and chuckle. "Yes, that's true. I'm not sure what I'd do without you."

Jack returns, and my ability to form words disappears once again. I take the sandwiches out of his warm soft hands, looking deep into his eyes. He gives me a wink; my body tingles all over. Mandy thanks Jack, but her voice sounds distant. Everything except Jack fades into the background. Mandy has to practically steer me away from the counter.

As we are about to leave the shop, I take one more glance backwards, hoping Jack does not see me staring. Our eyes meet like two strangers in the dark. It's electric—I never want to stop looking at him. In my distraction, I bump into Mandy, then fall over the sandwich board, knocking it to the ground. Mandy tries to help me set it back up, and Jack leaps from behind his counter to assist. "Hey, don't worry. People are always knocking this thing over." He chuckles. I feel as if I could just die of embarrassment on the spot.

A loud clap of thunder splits the air, and a bolt of lightning lights up the darkening sky outside. "Come on, Brayden, we are going to be so late!" Mandy snaps me to my senses.

"Just one second, Mand." I stare at Jack as he bends over to repair the sandwich board I knocked over.

Mandy easily works out why I'm staring. She pokes me and whispers just loud enough for me to hear: "Nice underwear, Jack"

She's right. His bum is so tight in his trousers that it indents his underwear lining. I imagine what the size of his lunch box really is. He's been behind the counter most of this time, but I bet the view from the front is spectacular.

Mandy drags me back to the office, but I can't get the image of Jack's underwear out of my head. Or the image of what might be underneath his underwear. I have to hide the sudden movement in my trousers. When we finally return to the shelter of the office building's foyer, soaking wet from the thunderstorm, Mandy stares down at my damp trousers. "Someone got all excited!"

"Piss off. You're just jealous that he is most likely on my bus, not yours!"

We both laugh as we scoff our sandwiches down in the entryway. As I bite into the chicken club sandwich Jack's hands made, a glob of mayonnaise flies out of the bread and into Mandy's face. She screams and glares at me, her face and parts of her blouse covered in mayonnaise. "Brayden!"

I can't help it; I burst into laughter. "Not funny," she says, but she smiles too. "Not the worst thing I've had all over my face."

I snigger. "I can only imagine." I dig a pack of tissues out of my pocket. "Here."

She wipes the mayonnaise off her face and begins to dab at her blouse, but it just smears it around. She sighs. "Can you grab me some water?

I fetch her a cupful from the water fountain, but as I hand it to her, she fumbles and it spills all over her blouse. Mandy's bra appears like a magic trick through her shirt. She gasps so theatrically that I can't control my laughter. "I'm so sorry, Mand! I'll get you some paper towels."

"You had better, Brayden! Now my breasts are on show for all to see."

As I walk off to the gents' toilet to retrieve some toilet paper, I hear voices coming from the top staircase, getting louder and louder. One of them is horribly nasal and familiar. The Wicked Witch of the East, Corinna, with her shoes clipping down the stairs as fast as a machine gun.

"Shit!" I dart into the gents' toilet and pull the door closed, listening through the door until Corinna's voice fades away. Everything falls silent except for my heart hammering in my ears. If Corinna caught me out here, when I was supposed to be back at my desk two minutes ago, it would not be pretty.

I manage to find Mandy a roll of toilet paper—not as good as paper towels, but it'll do. I return to the foyer to see Mandy looking in her makeup mirror, apparently checking to see if she has any further mayonnaise down her blouse. I hand her the toilet paper, and she uses it to soak up the worst of the water. Luckily, her clothes are mostly dried by the time we finish eating without further incident.

We'll need lots of energy to face the Wicked Witch of the East during the sales meeting later this afternoon. Mandy sets her bag down on top of the metal umbrella stand and takes out her makeup. It seems that powdering her face and applying even more lipstick to her lips is her way of protecting herself from this cutthroat work environment, like some kind of armor. Why else would she touch it up so much?

My eyes catch sight of the clock on the wall, which is showing 3:05 p.m. "Oh, shit! I am late for the meeting. Corinna will have my balls on a spear. Can you take this back to my desk?" I whip off my coat and throw it at Mandy, who is still admiring herself in the mirror. It settles neatly over her head.

She pulls the coat off her head and glares at me. "What did you do that for?"

I hold my hands up, pacifying. I don't know whether it's worse to have Mandy or Corinna angry at me. "I'm sorry, Mand. Just hang it on my desk chair, will you?"

She frowns and rolls her eyes. "Very well. Now, hurry— get to the meeting."

I thank Mandy and run for the stairs. I have no time to wait for the lift, and the meeting room is just around the corner from the stairwell. Like a galloping horse, I sprint up the staircase. Ugh, what I wouldn't do to ditch this meeting and go back to the coffee shop to talk to Jack more.

I wrench open the stairwell door on the correct floor, but as I step into the corridor, it suddenly dawns on me I haven't got the file I need for the meeting. I run back to my and Mandy's office like a bolt of lighting. Why did I waste so much time being distracted by a hot man? I would probably be at the meeting in time if I had just gotten my sandwich from the coffee shop and left without staring at Jack for so long.

Mandy hasn't gotten back to our office yet, which is probably for the best—I don't need her teasing right now. I grab the file I need and run like a dog chasing a hare through the office corridors, my heart beating faster with every step. At last, I approach the meeting room, with my heart ready to jump out of my chest.

I hesitate before opening the door—I hear voices behind it. Fuck. The meeting has started. I straighten my tie, take a deep breath as if it's my last and open the meeting room door. The voices hush. Corinna stares at me as if I'm something disgusting she trod in with her bargain box shoes from the local market. I look around the table at all of the company directors and feel their eyes piercing me. I want the ground to open and swallow me up on the spot.

Corinna coughs. "So glad you could join us, Mr Willoughby. I presume you have the file I asked you for?" She glances pointedly at her watch.

"Yes, I do have the file." I hold out the sheaf of papers to her, but my fingers become weak, and the contents of the sales reports float to the floor. I bend down to pick the loose papers with hands like jelly. The exertion of my run must be catching up to me.

Corinna stands from her chair, looking like a volcano about to erupt. I stand and hand her the file, successfully this time. "I'm so sorry, everybody," I begin. "I—"

"Just sit down, Mr Willoughby."

I hurry over to the nearest empty chair, apologising in a soft voice to the rest of the board. I sit down to look through the papers arranged in front of my seat. Corinna says, "Now, shall we continue with the rest of the business at hand? First up on the agenda…"

I sit there and listen to God Almighty Corinna Gotobed preach about how we need to boost the company's revenue. I try to concentrate, but Jack sneaks his way back into my mind. My eyes wander around the room, imagining one of the directors as Jack. The things I would love to get up to with him!

I close my eyes to further explore my fantasy, but I am brought back to reality when Corinna slams her hands on the table and says, "What ideas do you have, Mr Willoughby, to boost extra revenue?" I gasp and say, "Sexy pants." The stares from the directors pierce my soul and Corinna looks ready to blow her top. I sink down in the chair. "Um…uh… Corinna , may I be excused? Something has come over me and I feel unwell."

"Very well, Mr Willoughby."

I stand up from my chair and give another round of apologies to the room. As I pick my papers off the table, my hand knocks over the jug of water, and it gushes all over the table. Board members exclaim in shock and leap from their chairs as the water soaks their clothes. I try to mop it up with some tissues from my pocket, but they disintegrate in seconds.

"My files!" a lady screams from where she's backed up against the wall, pointing at a stack of important-looking papers sitting on a currently-dry section of the table. But the water's flowing toward them fast.

I see a spare jacket on the back of one of the empty chairs, and I throw it over the burgeoning water. The lady rushes forward to retrieve her files, safe and dry.

Corinna screams, "No! What do you think you're doing? That's my designer jacket!"

I pick the wet jacket up off the table and walk over to Corinna . She just stares at her jacket without taking it. "Sorry, Corinna ," I mumble. How was I supposed to know it was hers when it wasn't even hanging on her chair?

Best to get out of here before she throws a shoe at me. I drape the jacket over a chair, apologize yet again to the rest of the board who are mopping up the remaining puddles of water, and walk out of the meeting room as fast as I can.

Chapter Two

I take a slow walk back to my desk, my cheeks burning and heart pounding. What I wouldn't give to be having coffee with sexy Jack right now instead of wallowing in embarrassment.

When I arrive, Mandy is there waiting. "So, how did the sales meeting go?" she asks.

I roll my eyes and begin to tell Mandy about the entire fiasco. The second I get to the "sexy pants" part, Mandy bursts into laughter. "Oh, Brayden, I wish I had been there to see Corinna's face!"

I begin to snicker—even though it had been humiliating in the moment, seeing Mandy cracking up is making me realize how hilarious it was. "Yeah, but I haven't even told you the worst part. When I was getting up to leave, my hand knocked over the jug of water, and it gushed all over the meeting room table. I could not find any paper towels—only a jacket on the back of someone's chair. And guess what, Mand? It gets even worse. Guess whose jacket it was."

Mandy frowns. "Whose?"

I start giggling so much I can barely get the name out, my laughter partway between hysterical and terrified. "It was Corinna's!"

Mandy gasps. "Oh, she really is going to have your balls on spear after this!"

I shrug. "Maybe she will forget. She seemed busy enough trying to impress the board. I bet she thinks she'll become the queen of Gallagher & Masons with her new approach to increase revenue."

Mandy laughs. "She thinks she's already the queen."

"Very true. Come on, let's get the hell out of this prison. I think you will agree we have done our time for the day. Do you fancy a little window shopping?"

Mandy smiles. "Window shopping ... this wouldn't happen to be an excuse to visit the coffee shop, would it?"

"Wow! Mandy, you have read my mind. If you ever left Gallagher & Masons, you could easily get a job as a psychic." I laugh. "On second thoughts, I need a drink, but we can still visit the coffee shop on the way."

Mandy says, "Oh, very well. Come on." She stands up and puts her coat.

"Wait, Mand," I say. "Haven't you forgotten something?"

Mandy looks down at her desk, then opens her bag and looks inside. "No, I think I have everything."

I grin. "So you're not going to add more makeup before we leave?"

She smirks at me. "Oh, I already did that before you came back from the meeting. I'm surprised you didn't notice."

I grab my coat. "You apply makeup every minute of the day. I suppose I've gotten so used to it that it's weird when you don't."

Mandy puts her two fingers up at me. "Looks like you are the one who's forgotten something Brayden."

I pat my pockets and squint at Mandy. What is she on about?

Mandy smirks and points behind me. "Look at your desk."

I scan the wooden tabletop, but it looks the same as always—full of boring papers. I bite my lip. "What are you bloody pointing, at Mand?"

She walks over and scoops a pile of envelopes off my desk. "Corinna won't be happy if these don't make the post." She thrusts the stack into my hands.

I gasp. "Oh, shit! Thanks, Mand. I would be served my notice if these don't make the post." I stare wide-eyed at Mandy, but my face soon melts into laughter, which she joins in with. I still feel tense at the memory of my behaviour at the meeting, and the thought of Corinna firing me—but between Mandy's laughter and the promise of seeing hot Jack the barista again sometime, my worry about Corinna dilutes into the promise of future joy. I smile at Mandy and loop my arm around hers, and we both leave the office.

As we walk along the office corridor, we see Enzo, who works in the post room, wheeling his trolley in the opposite direction. Mandy takes the pile of envelopes out of my hands and piles them on top of the trolley. As we both walk onward, we hear Enzo shout, "Oi! You can't just plonk those envelopes on there like this."

We stop walking and turn round to see Enzo glaring at us. Mandy frowns and says, "Leave this to me, Brayden."

As I follow her back up the corridor toward Enzo, I mutter under my breath, "Are we ever going to leave this hellhole today?"

Mandy puts her hands on her hips and stares sternly up at him. "Enzo, what's the problem? We saved you a job and brought the post to you."

"Saved me a job?" Enzo scoffs. "With the amount of extra work you lot make me do, I ought to get paid enough to buy a castle. I could be Count Enzo."

Mandy giggles. "It's all happening today. First we had Queen Corinna, and now we have Count Enzo."

I say, "Yeah, and maybe tomorrow me and you will be the prince and princess, Mand."

Enzo gestures at the letters piled on top of his cart. "I have an alphabetic system. You can't just put envelopes down wherever you like."

Mandy rolls her eyes. "Oh, I am bored now. Come on, Brayden, let's get out of here. Let Count Enzo play with his trolley."

Me and Mandy break into laughter, and we walk back down the corridor, leaving Enzo to carry on collecting the post. We arrive at the lift for the second time today, and it's waiting for us as if it's on our side in helping us get out of here. We enter the lift and Mandy presses the ground floor button. As we descend, she uses the glittering steel panels of the lift door as a mirror to check her lipstick. I giggle, then say, "I hope we haven't missed Jack."

As we walk along the street, though, I realise that all the lights are out in the coffee shop and I have missed my hunk. They must close at five o'clock. Mandy says, "Never mind, Brayden. There's always next time.

I say. "Thanks to you. If you had not chosen to pick an argument with Count whatever-his-name-is, we would have been here ages ago."

Mandy puts her arm around me and kisses me on the cheek. "Come on, let's get pissed."

"Only one for me. I am driving home, and besides, it's a work night."

Mandy grins. "It was you who wanted to go for a drink first."

"Yeah, because of the day I have had. But practically, I can't."

Mandy takes my hand. "Oh, shut up. Come on." She drags me by the arm into O'Ryan's bar and claims two barstools for us. "Wait here. I must be off to powder my nose."

I snicker. "Again?"

She smiles and walks off to the ladies' to powder her nose—and, no doubt, apply more lippie.

The bartender asks, "You ready to order, or you want to wait for your friend to come back?"

Here's my way out of Mandy's teasing about me not drinking. I order Mandy's favourite cocktail, and a mocktail for myself. I tell the bartender to make both drinks look the same. He smiles at me and gets to work.

A few minutes later, Mandy returns, swinging her handbag, and plonks herself down on the stool beside me. The bartender places our drinks down in front of us, and pushes one subtly toward me. I snatch it up and take a sip, and sure enough, it tastes like fruit juice despite looking exactly like Mandy's. Mandy picks her own cocktail up and gulps the whole drink down in one go.

I blink at her as she orders another round of drinks from the same bartender. I point at my drink without Mandy seeing, and give him a sly wink so he knows to serve me the same as before.

When the drinks arrive, Mandy nudges me. "Come on, drink up."

I obey her, sipping my mocktail as my eyes wander the room. The bar is right near the coffee shop, so maybe Jack likes to come here after work. What if he's here right now? But everyone in the room looks unfamiliar except for Mandy.

The bartender brings another round, and I can see Mandy starting to fall asleep. I say, "I think it's time we were going."

She picks up her bag, and we start to walk toward the door. I hope I'll get to see Jack again soon. Perhaps I can stop by the coffee shop before work tomorrow. But if I am late, Corinna will fire me.

As we leave O'Ryan's, Mandy puts an arm around me and starts to ramble about how much she loves me and how I am her best friend. I say, "I love you too, Mand. You're my best friend as well."

"Best friends for life," she slurs her reply to me.

We finally reach the car park, and I open the passenger door of my car for Mandy. I can't let her take the bus home in this state. Because of all the drinks she has had, I think she may have not realised I am stone cold sober.

I help Mandy into the car, place the seatbelt around her, and drive off to her flat. When we arrive, I walk her to her door. "Are you going to be all right from here?"

She says, "Yes, baby. Tell me again how much of a wonderful friend I am." She opens her bag to fish for her keys, but takes out her lipstick and tries to unlock her door with it.

I start to giggle. "I think that's the wrong key."

She snickers, and once again fishes in her bag and takes out her door key this time. She kisses me on the cheek and starts to ramble once again. "I'm so glad we're friends, I really am ..."

I say, "Goodnight, Mand."

She opens the door of her flat and stands in the doorway as I walk back to my car. I start the engine and lean out the window. "See you tomorrow. Don't be late."

She waves and closes her door. Once I see Mandy's living room light turn on and I know she is in safely, I drive home.

I slowly open my front door and creep inside. My mum is reading a book on the sofa. As I take big steps up the stairs, hoping none of my family will hear me, my mum says, "Is that you, Brayden? Where have you been all this time?"

Shit—busted. This is why I hate living with my parents, but I get paid so little at that hellhole that it makes the most sense financially. But not the most sense in terms of how I wanted my life to be. "Evening, Mum!" I say, trying not to sound grumpy.

I hear my mum close her book, and she walks into the hallway. Her gaze scrutinizes me like a detective sizing up a suspect. "Where have you been until this late hour?"

I explain to my mum a sample of my day, leaving out the embarrassing board meeting, and end by telling her that Mandy and I went for a drink after work. I make sure to emphasize that I only had a mocktail.

My mum smiles. "Well, you'd better be off to bed. Work in the morning."

I almost say *that's what I was doing before you called me*, but decide not to. I kiss my mum on the cheek and head off to bed.

Chapter Three

The following morning, I get up early and jump straight in the shower. I'm shaved and dressed and out the door by 8:00. All my family members are already gone to work or still asleep.

As I drive to work, I'm tempted to visit the coffee shop again, but I can't risk getting fired. I'll just wait until lunchtime to see sexy Jack again. With a smile stretched across my face at the thought of him, I park my car and walk up to the office building. It's a lovely sunny day, and I hope Corinna is going to be in happy mood. When the sun is shining, it makes everyone happy.

I arrive at the office steps, and see Miss Motor Mouth herself, Corinna , smoking her cigarette by the door. She's looking away from me, toward the high street. As I dart up the steps, I hear Mandy's voice calling me. "Brayden, wait!"

I pretend not to hear her and dash into the foyer, into the lift, and straight to my office. That was a close one. Corinna almost saw me, and if she remembers I exist, she might decide she's annoyed enough at me to fire me now. I take a deep breath and remove my coat.

The office door flies open, and I shudder, thinking it's Corinna —but it's only Mandy, fresh as daisy. She taps me on my arm and says, "I was calling you. Didn't you hear me?"

I say, "No, sorry."

She shrugs and giggles. "I suppose you had a certain shop assistant on your mind?"

I snicker. "Perhaps. I do fancy a club sandwich for lunch."

She says, "Mmmm, I could just murder one of those now. But seriously, why were you running up the office steps?"

I explain to her that I did not want Corinna to see me.

Mandy laughs. "Oh, yes, her jacket. She not going to let you get away with that so easily. I bet she has something up her sleeve."

I frown. Mandy's right —I might not have escaped punishment as easily as I thought. What I wouldn't give to just hang out with Jack instead of worrying about Corinna so much.

Lunchtime comes around, and Mandy and I arrive at the coffee shop. I take the lead this time as we walk up the counter. My eyes scan the area looking for Jack, but he is nowhere to be seen."

I say to Mandy, "Oh, it must be his day off." I feel deflated like a balloon. Was Jack just in my imagination?

Does he not really exist at all? I suppose such a hot man couldn't possibly be real.

Mandy orders a club sandwich and asks me what I would like. I tell her I will have the same.

The shop assistant hands the club sandwiches to Mandy, and she hands me mine as we leave the coffee shop. I have one final look over my shoulder, but there's still no sign of Jack. The sandwich board I knocked over yesterday stands on the pavement. My mind takes me back to when I first saw a glimpse of Jack's fit body and underwear.

Mandy nudges me. "You okay?"

I nod. "Just reminiscing back to yesterday."

She snickers. Don't tell me, Brayden— you're pining over Jack again."

I giggle, and we step out into the golden rays of the sun beaming down on the street. We eat our lunch on the walk back to the office. As we and continue the with the remainder of the work day, my heart still panics every time footsteps come past our door. I'm just waiting for Storm Corinna to blow through and toss me my long-awaited punishment, but by some miracle, she never arrives.

As the clock ticks close to home time, Mandy looks over at me and smiles. "Come on, then, let's go."

"Go where?" I say.

"Well, I told you yesterday I was in the mood for some window shopping. But first, I think a little lippy is in order."

I snicker. "Not more makeup. Come on—the shops will be closed by time we leave here."

She pouts in her hand mirror. "A girl's got to look her best."

"Come on, Mand."

"What's the big rush?" she says.

"Well, Corinna still hasn't spoken to me about what happened yesterday in the board meeting. I want to leave now so she won't have the opportunity to confront me."

Mandy smiles. "Oh, I bet she is too busy flirting with the board of directors trying to get a promotion."

We both break into laughter as we leave the office.

On our way down the steps, a flock of pigeons swoops over us. I hope they are not going to drop their guts. "Great," I say. "That's all we need—to turn up at the shops covered in pigeon shit."

Mandy laughs. "Brayden, if you were a bird, who would you most like to shit on?"

I giggle. "What sort of conversation is this?"

"Go on, just tell me."

"Ummm … well, Gob Almighty Corinna would be my first choice."

"I knew you were going to say that!" Mandy's grin gets wider. "Oh, I can think of a few people I'd like to shit on."

I say, "Who?"

"Well, Corinna, definitely." She stops walking and her eyes widen. "Oh, look!" She points at the storefront next the coffee shop. "Look at that gold box in the window! Anything that resembles a chocolate sweetie, I am there."

I follow her gaze, but my eyes snag on the coffee shop, where the I catch the back of Jack carrying the last bits of the outdoor furniture inside. Oh no, I have missed him again! I barely have time to process my disappointment when Mandy takes hold of my arm and drags me down the path to the shop, past the coffee house. I strain my eyes to try and catch sight of Jack, but sadly there's no sign of him. Perhaps he went home already.

We arrive at the clothes store, and Mandy pulls me inside. Her eyes grow wider as she zeroes in on a dress on one of the mannequins. All I want to do is go back past the coffee house and see if I can see Jack. That would complete my day, and nearly my week. But no—Mandy insists on dragging me into the store so she can try on what's hot and what's not.

She seems so happy, though, and I can't deny my friend this. I probably wouldn't be able to do anything but stare uselessly at Jack anyway, and that's assuming he hasn't already gone home. If I am not going to see him, I am going to have to settle for some retail therapy to get over my disappointment. As if I could ever ask sexy Jack out on a date.

We walk through the store, and Mandy's eyes light up again when she spots another dress she likes. "Oh, I have to try this!" She drags me to the stand it's hanging from, flings her coat off, and takes the dress down. She throws her coat and bag at me, hitting me in the face."

"Ow!" I fumble with her things, my face stinging from where her handbag strap whacked into me.

Mandy, as bubbly as a bottle of pop, races off to the dressing room. "Sorry, Brayden!" she says over her shoulder.

I follow her at a more sedate pace, still holding her coat and bag. "You really are as mad as a box of frogs."

"Piss off," she murmurs from the entrance to the dressing room.

I park my bum in an old wooden chair next to the dressing room and start reading my messages on my phone. I can hear Mandy humming to herself from the dressing room. The shop assistant smiles at me.

"I say, "It's okay. She is going back to tomorrow."

The sales assistant chuckles and carries on putting new stock out on the clothes rails.

The humming stops, and a grinning Mandy pops her head out from behind the curtain. "What do you think?"

"Well, I can tell you when I see it, Mand."

She giggles and steps out from behind the curtain to do a twirl.

"Bloody hell, you're not on the catwalk," I tease, and then I see she has tucked her knickers into the dress's blue material.

I nearly fall off of my chair in a fit of laughter. Mandy squints at me. "What's so funny?"

I struggle to speak through my laughter, so I point at the dress. She looks the dress up and down, and her eyes go wider.

At last, I get control of my voice. "Nice knickers, Mand."

She gasps and quickly pulls the rolled up dress out of the lining of her knickers.

"Well, I have seen it all this week. Your breasts, and now your knickers. They say it comes in threes—what else are you going to unveil to me?"

Mandy starts to laugh along with me, and then looks down at the dress again with a critical gaze. "I don't think it's me. What do you think, Brayden?"

"Well, it's you who has to wear it, not me."

Mandy decides the dress is not for her. She walks back into the dressing room to change. I say, "Make sure you don't have anything else on show when you come back out!"

"Haha," she says sarcastically. A few moments later, she emerges from the dressing room, and I stand up from the wooden chair. It was so bloody uncomfortable that I feel like my bum has left my body.

Mandy hands the dress back to the shop assistant. As we walk back through the store to the exit, I see through the shop widow that night is starting to draw in. "It was daylight when we first came in here, and now it's dark."

Mandy chuckles and pushes the door open. I'm more than ready to leave the shop behind, but she drags me to the store window. An exact copy of the dress she tried on clings to a mannequin. "I really don't know what to do," she says. "I do like the dress."

"Well go, and buy it. Don't be put off because you tucked your knickers in it. It really did look good."

Mandy frowns. "No, Brayden. I think I will have a browse online. I need to order more makeup, anyway."

"Oh, bloody hell, not more makeup."

She giggles, and as we make our way back to the car park, I hear a clinking sound. I turn around to see my car keys lying on the ground. They must have fallen out of my pocket. I bend down to pick them up, and a pair of shoes appears near my face. A voice says, "Let me help you with those." My hand brushes the stranger's as I glance up. I cannot believe my eyes; it's Jack from the coffee shop!

My knees go weak as Jack picks up my car keys. I slowly stand up and find myself staring into his beautiful blue eyes. *This is it, Brayden. Go in for the kill! Ask him out—you know you want to!* But I can't—my mouth refuses to work. Jack hands me my keys. "Hey, you were in Cappuccino's at lunch time, right?"

"Um … uh …" It's no good. My brain is a useless lump around him.

"Oh yeah, that was us," Mandy butts in, pushing me backward before I can embarrass myself further.

Jack says, "Yeah, I remember you. Two clubs." I hold on to the shop awning's post to stop myself from falling as he smiles at me. "Well, it's nice to meet you outside of work. I'm Jack— dunno if I said that already." When he shakes my hand, I feel like a bolt of electricity has gone through me. He continues speaking. "I'm afraid I have to rush; I have an appointment I have to attend. But before I go, I'd like to ask—how would you like to go for a drink sometime?"

I can't believe it! Did I just hear Jack ask me out for a drink, or was I just imagining things? No—he really did! He actually just asked me out!

But Mandy steps in front of me, pushing her chest forward to make her breasts look bigger. "We would love to!"

Jack smiles and takes a few steps back, away from Mandy and her bosom. He looks down at me. "I mean ... I don't mean to be rude, but ..."

I finally regain my powers of speech and say to Mandy, "I think he means just me and him!"

"Oh, sorry." Mandy sulks and flicks her hair over her shoulders. "Three's a crowd, I suppose. I didn't like your sandwich, anyway. And you're not really my type." She walks off in a huff.

"Mandy ..." I begin to call after her, but Jack touches my arm. I blink at him. "Hey, sorry about Mandy. She hasn't been getting a lot of male attention lately, so I guess when she heard you say go for a drink, she thought her luck was in."

Jack chuckles. "So, about that drink," he says.

"Sure, yeah, I'd love to," I say, staring after Mandy. As hot as Jack is, I can't lose my best friend over him. "Looks like I've got to run." I start speed-walking to try and catch up with her.

Jack shouts, "How about I meet you at O'Ryan's tomorrow night at 8:00 p.m.?"

I glance back at him, happiness bubbling up in my chest. "See you then!" I break into a run to catch up with Mandy, excited as a kid with a new toy at the thought of my date with Jack tomorrow.

Soon, I'm huffing and puffing, and by the time I approach the car park I feel I have run a marathon. My heart beats 100 times to the dozen. In the dim light, I see Mandy sitting on the steps of the car park entrance. She stares into space, her hair moving gently in the breeze.

"You know, if the wind changes, you will stay like that," I say, wrapping my arms around her. She looks like she could use a hug.

She pouts. "I will never find a man."

I give her a kiss on the cheek. "Mr Right is out there somewhere. You will find him someday, hun."

She replies, "How long have you known me now?"

"Um, nearly two years. But what does that have to do with anything, Mand? What's brought all this on?"

"Yeah, nearly two years, Brayden. And I have only been on one date in all that time. You're okay—you have Jack now."

"Don't be silly. I am going for a drink with him, not jumping into bed with him." Even though, deep down, I know that if the opportunity did arise, he would not have to ask me twice.

She pouts. "I'm sorry. It just seems like you have it so easy. And I'm happy for you, but I wish it was easy for me too.

I say, "Well, see, it's not quite as easy as you might think. I have one big dilemma to face if me and Jack do start dating on a regular basis."

Mandy turns her head and looks at me. "What would be the issue?"

"Basically, Mand, my parents and my sister don't know I am gay."

Mandy jumps up from the concrete steps. "Wow, Brayden, you kept that a secret?"

I nod. "I do want to tell them. But I don't want them to be ashamed of me or feel embarrassed. I think they'd be all right with it, but you just never know."

"Oh, you should never be ashamed of who you are," Mandy says. "And I'm sure your parents won't be ashamed either. You need to find a way to tell them. Especially if you and Jack start getting serious."

I nod wistfully. "Yeah. Depending on how things go, I could bring him to meet my family for my mum's birthday in a few weeks."

"And then Christmas!" Mandy says. She seems so happy at the idea that it's like she never even got upset about Jack asking me out.

I give Mandy a hug. "No matter what, you are my best friend. And no one will ever break that bond between us." Now I am Hank Marvin.

"Come on, let's go home." Mandy kisses me back on the cheek and composes herself, and we both head off to our cars.

Driving home, I am buzzing like a bumblebee. My date with sexy Jack is only twenty-four hours away. It's exciting, but also nerve-wracking. What if he doesn't like me once he gets to know me?

Not to mention all the other worries occupying my thoughts. Like being on the receiving end of Corinna's viper tongue. I escaped her clutches today, but I have a feeling that tomorrow I am going summoned by her. And then she'll probably fire me.

And on top of all that, I have to tell my family I am gay. What will they think? How are they going to react? Will they disown me? I wish all these thoughts would find an exit from my mind. Maybe it's best not to think too hard about things I can't control. It'll only make me more nervous.

As put the key in the door, my mum is hoovering the hallway. She says, "Evening, Brayden. Be careful you don't trip over the lead. Love."

I smile. "I won't, Mum." Though she knows I have on a few occasions. I once nearly fell from the top of the landing to the bottom steps by tripping over the hoover cord. I saved myself by managing to grab hold of the rail as I unexpectedly abseiled down the stairs.

"What do you fancy for tea?" she says as I head toward the stairs.

"It's okay, Mum. I will have something later."

My mum looks surprised. "Oh, are you not feeling very well?"

Well, I'm not feeling well with all my worries, but I am still bursting with excitement about my date tomorrow. I want to tell her about it, even though it's just a drink. I reply with a chuckle, "No, it's just that I sort of have a date tomorrow night."

My mum beams at me. "Oh, who is the lucky girl?"

My tongue refuses to work. I stutter for a few seconds before blurting out, "Um … uh … it's a girl from work."

My mum snickers. "It's not that Mandy, is it?"

I burst into a nervous laugh. "No, it's not Mandy. She is my best friend."

My mum says, "Well, you must bring this mystery girl home to meet us."

"It's only a drink."

"I only went for a drink with your father, love. And after just two dates, we were officially together. And after another few months, we were married, and then I got pregnant."

"Yes, Mum, I know." I roll my eyes and dash upstairs to my bedroom. I hear my mum continue with the hoovering, and I close my bedroom door. I have just told the biggest lie to my mum. Well, not much I can do about it now.

I open my wardrobe in search of something to wear for my date tomorrow night. I look through every single article of clothing I own, pulling hanger after hanger off the rack, hoping something will jump out at me. At last, I find a T-shirt I haven't worn in ages. I walk over to my mirror on the back of my door as I pull the shirt on. I am so determined to make it fit me, even if I'll look like the Incredible Hulk in it! All the better for Jack to see my muscle definition.

In the end, the shirt proves to be perfectly flattering. I dance across my bedroom like the cat who got the cream. As I am taking it off, I hear a loud scream, and a stomping like a herd of elephants coming towards my bedroom door. It bursts open, and I am knocked against the wall of my bedroom with one arm out of the T-shirt and the other still in it. My sister, Samantha, runs around my bedroom, screaming bloody murder. "Mum, Brayden, help! There's a large spider in the bathroom!"

My heart thumps from the shock of her intrusion, and I can feel a bruise rising on my shoulder from where I hit the wall. The floor vibrates from my sister's footsteps as she continues her panic. Paper rustles, and a pile of my *Hello Guys* monthly magazines slides from the back of the open wardrobe onto my bedroom floor.

"Fuck, fuck!" I mutter, quickly throwing them back into the wardrobe. I just hope my sister did not see them. "You stupid cow!" I yelp, hoping to draw attention away from the magazines. "You could have broken my arm!"

My mother shouts from the hall. "What in the bloody hell are the pair of you doing up there?"

I pull my T-shirt fully off, and realise it's torn from the force of my sister crashing into my bedroom. *Oh, bollocks, bollocks, it's ruined! Thank you very much, Sis.* I throw the T-shirt down on my bed. "I wanted to wear this for my date tomorrow night."

My sister pauses and gapes at me. "You have a date?"

I can't help smiling a little. "Yes, I have a date. Well, it's just a drink first."

My sister smiles back. "I'm really sorry—You okay?"

"I was until you burst into my room. Can't a man have some privacy in his own room?"

My sister's face turns red again as she seems to remember why she's there. She raises her voice in a panic. "There's a spider bigger then Shirley's cat!" Shirley is our next door neighbour.

I sit down angrily on the mattress and clench the shirt in my hand. My mother steps into the room. "Don't worry, Brayden, I can fix this for you." She takes the crumpled-up T-shirt out of my hand. "I will have it looking brand new in no time. Now, Jo, where is this spider you saw, love? Oh, and did Brayden tell you about his date tomorrow night with one of the girls from work?"

My sister nods. "Yes, but there's an enormous spider, and one of you needs to come squish it!"

I grit my teeth. "Well, I'm busy trying to find something to wear."

My mother and sister leave me in peace, and my frustration ebbs away. Mum really is amazing—I know she'll make my shirt look good as new. If only my mum could wave her magic wand and make the rest of my problems disappear. Now I feel bad, because I snapped at my sister and have to keep secrets from my family. Maybe the pile of magazines sliding out onto the floor was a sign to tell my family that I'm going on a date with a hunk of a guy.

But I'm not ready yet. I walk back over to the wardrobe, add a few extra layers of clothing over the magazines, and push them right against the back wall of the wardrobe before closing the doors

I should shoot Mandy a text to check if she is all right I bite my upper lip as I ponder what to say. I don't need to beat around the bush with her. *Hey, hun, hope you're okay. See you tomorrow. Weekend is nearly here!* I finish the text with two emojis and two kisses. I almost compose another one to tell her about my worries, but she probably isn't in the right mood for it. I don't want to pile my problems on top of hers.

As I climb into bed a few minutes later, I hear a ping from my phone. It's a text from Mandy, telling me she is fine and tucked up in bed with cup of hot chocolate. We exchange a few more emoji-filled messages until I look at the clock. Shit, is that the time? I'd better hit the hay. I have a big day ahead of me tomorrow.

I just wish my family could know about it.

Chapter Four

When the sun wakes me up, I jump out of bed and open my curtains, feeling so excited about the thought of my date with Jack tonight. I check my phone, but there are no more texts from Mandy. I unplug my phone from the charger. Should I have a shower now, or wait until I come home? I decide to wait until I finish work—I'll be perfectly freshened up that way.

I quickly get dressed and whistle as I make my way to the bathroom. I have a quick wash and shave and clean my teeth, and then dance myself down the stairs to the sound of an empty house. Everyone else must have gone to work already. I walk into the kitchen to make a cup of coffee—I am going to need all the caffeine I can take to get me through the day. There's a note on the kitchen table from my mother, telling me she has repaired my T-shirt and placed it on the back of the dining room chair for me.

I can't wait to see what kind of job my mum has done on my T-shirt. If it's salvageable, she'll have fixed it good as new, but I worry that it was too damaged even for her skills. I look at the clock—it's approaching 7:45 a.m. I quickly dilute my hot coffee with some cold water and gulp it down in one go as I walk into the dining room, throwing my tie over my neck. I pluck the T-shirt from the back of the chair and examine where the rip was. I can't believe my eyes—the torn seam really is fixed, good as new. My mum has washed and ironed it, and it smells like a bunch of roses in an orchard.

I am one happy guy as I make my way out the front door. The birds are singing and the sun is shining; nothing will spoil my day. As I turn my key in the lock, I glance over at our neighbour, Shirley, who is cleaning her windows with a bucket of soapy water and a sponge. She looks over and spots me. "Morning, Brayden! What a lovely morning it is."

Any morning is a good one when you have a date with a hot man later. I reply in an elated tone, "It sure is, Shirley!"

I must have sounded too enthusiastic and inviting, because Shirley puts her bucket down, heads over to me and starts talking about her grandchildren, gesticulating so wildly that drops of water fly off her rubber gloves. "So my lovely Hannah, she's turning twelve, and she's always showing me these filter things on her phone that do the most ridiculous things to your face! There was one that turned me into a cat. I'm telling you, technology these days is just…"

I let her ramble on, and my thoughts wander to imagining what my sexy Jack will be wearing for our date. When Shirley appears to have exhausted her supply of grandchildren stories, I start to walk off, but she says "Oh, I hear you have a date tonight with a lovely girl! Your mum was telling me. Anyone I know?"

I roll my eyes. Thanks, Mum—now the whole street will know! I have to think quick. Shirley is the neighbourhood gossip, so it matters what I say to her. "No, it's just one of the girls from work." I take my phone out of my pocket and look at it. "Oh, is that the time? I must be going." I say goodbye to her, and she returns to cleaning her windows.

I'm desperate to see Jack again; I don't know if I can wait for tonight. But maybe I don't have to wait. I get into my car and start the engine. The radio blasts out the song "Tonight Is Going to Be a Good Night." Just as I reverse off my drive, my phone beeps. It's a text from Mandy, asking if I want to meet her for some breakfast at Rosie's Cafe before we go to work.

I text back and tell her I am stuck in traffic. I suppose the short delay with Shirley was technically traffic, as I was not able to move forward while she pumped me for information about my personal life. But still, I am telling my best friend a lie. I really just want to see Jack before work, and I can't meet her too or else I'll be late.

Oh well—I'm sure she would do the same if she had a hot man on her mind.

I arrive at the town centre car park and take my ticket from the pay machine. I look down, and there is a young homeless guy wearing shabby clothes and holding a pot with a few coins inside. I reach into my pocket, find a five-pound note and place it in his tin. "Here you go. Buy yourself some breakfast."

He smiles and grabs his pot to see how much money he has already collected.

I carry on, walking down the car park steps towards the office. But I have a quick stop to make on the way. As the coffee shop comes into view, Jack is just setting up the sandwich board out front. I walk faster so I don't miss him. My heart thuds as I get closer. He looks up, and a radiant smile spreads across his face. I can't help but beam back at him. "Morning," we say at the exact same time, and then chuckle.

"You go first," he says.

"No, you go first," I mimic. Then, more seriously, I continue: "Morning, Jack. How are you today?"

Jack replies, "I am good, thanks for asking. Brayden, isn't it?"

My name coming from his lips makes my brain go all mushy again. I stutter out, "Yeah, and you're Jack." Ugh, that has to be the least intelligent thing I could have said. I try to cover it up by adding, "Are we still on for that drink at O'Ryan's tonight?"

"I am if you are," he says, and his smile makes me tingle all over.

I reply, "Cool, me too."

"Why don't we exchange numbers?" Jack reaches inside his apron, which serves to draw my eyes to his crotch. All I can think about is what's lying hidden beneath his underwear. I force my gaze away from his groin as he brings out his phone. He begins, "My number is—"

"Hold on a minute, I need to get mine. It's in my coat pocket." I grab my phone. There is a text from Mandy, asking where I am. I'll deal with that later—first things first.

"Okay, ready." Jack recites his number, and as he does, I carefully enter it into my phone.

"Let me call you now," I say, pressing the button with the telephone icon. I hear Jack's phone vibrate in his hand.

"Cool," he says. "I have your number. A priceless treasure."

My cheeks flush as my own phone begins to vibrate. I look at the screen; it's Mandy calling. I press the 'deny call' button and shoot her a quick text. *I'm on my way to the office, I promise.* Who cares if I'm late for work? I hate that job anyway.

"You're in high demand this morning," Jack says with a laugh.

A couple of old ladies pass by. "Excuse me, young man," one of them says to Jack, "but are you open?"

Jack replies, "We sure are."

The ladies head into the shop. "I think that's our cue to go to work," I say.

Jack smiles at me. "Yeah, I'd better give these pensioners their daily caffeine."

"Yeah." And I'd better make a move too, since I will be in hot water for being late. Totally worth it, though. "I will see you tonight at 8 p.m. at O'Ryan's."

"See you then!" Jack waves as he goes into the shop to serve the old ladies. I am so happy as I make my way to work. I feel like I am on cloud nine. I punch the air, elated. Nothing will spoil my day! Then I glance at my watch; it's almost 9:30 a.m. "Fuck," I mutter, breaking into a run. I didn't realise just how late I am.

My phone starts to ring again. It's Mandy. I answer, out of breath. "Hello?" The office building looms ahead. Almost there.

"Brayden! You're so major late. Corinna wants you to report to her office the minute you arrive. Where've you been? The traffic can't possibly have been that bad."

I don't want her to know—she got so upset when Jack asked me out yesterday that I think telling her the truth will only make her huffy again. "I have just arrived. See you soon." I hang up before she can say anything else.

I make my way into the office reception, saying a breathless good morning to Vera and Roger—the receptionist and security guard. The lift opens. I run into it and press the button for the tenth floor. It seems to take forever to reach my destination. At last, the doors slide open. I bolt out into the hallway and promptly bump into Judy, the drinks lady who is doing her morning rounds.

"Sorry, Judy!" I say. "I am late."

She pulls a sour face. "You got a train to catch this bloody morning? Hell, what's wrong with you?"

I throw another apology over my shoulder as I run down the corridor. Finally, I arrive at my desk. My angel and best friend, Mandy, stands by the side of my desk with a stern expression across her face.

I quickly remove my coat and hand it to her. I think the frosted expression on her face is starting to thaw—she can never stay angry at me for long. Sure enough, she cracks a smile and says, "I have logged your computer on—its up and ready for you to hit the keys. Why are you so late, Brayden?"

I suppose I was planning on keeping my visit to Jack a secret, but I shouldn't keep secrets from my best friend. She deserves to know. "I had to take a sudden detour on the way to work," I say, smiling at her.

"This sudden detour wouldn't happen to work in a coffee shop, would he?"

I giggle a little. "Maybe." I draw my eyebrows together. "You're not upset at me, are you?"

"Of course not. I'm happy for you." She grins, and I know we're okay again. "Now go on—you'd better go face Cruella de Vil! She is in a foul mood, so tread carefully."

"Carefully is my middle name." I smile and wink at Mandy before making my way to Corinna's office.

After sprinting through the corridors, I arrive at Corinna's office, catching my breath. I knock on the door. Corinna bellows, "Come in!"

Corinna's fingers tap impatiently against the arm of her chair as I enter. "Mr Willoughby, would you explain to me why you are so late for work? And don't think I've forgotten about your outburst at the board meeting the other day. It was extremely embarrassing. My designer jacket is ruined, and so was the majority of the board's papers. What do you have to say for yourself?"

I have to think of something good. I can't say I went to see Jack. As I rack my brains, the image of the shabby young man in the car park flashes into my head. "I am late because I had to help a homeless person," I say. "And as for your designer jacket I'm really sorry, and I will of course pay for a new one." There goes half my next pay cheque.

Corinna stares at me for a few more seconds, then leaps out of her chair, making me jump. "You have just given me a wonderful idea. Yes, a splendid idea. It would be good for public relations if the company appeared more charitable." Her face softens—as much as a wicked witch's face can soften, anyway. "I'll let you off this time, Mr Willoughby. But don't be late again, or I'll have to dock your wages."

I would like to see her try to reduce my pay. I do enough extra hours in this workhouse as it is. After reading me the company policy on lateness—otherwise known as Chapter Sixty-Nine of the Gotobed Bible— Corinna tells me to return to my desk and carry on with my work.

I make my way back to my desk and Mandy raises her eyebrows at me. "Well? How did it go?"

"I am still in shock. When I went into her office, it was almost as if she was ready to explode. I had to make up a reason for why I was late. When she heard it, she totally changed her tune. She said I'd given her a brilliant idea and let me off with a slap on the wrist. She did mention the commotion with the rest of the board members and her designer jacket at first, but after I told her my excuse, it was as if it was erased from her memory. She kept going on about how the company needs to be more charitable."

Mandy laughs. "Brayden, if you fell in shit, you would come out smelling like roses."

I chuckle along with her, but then my phone beeps, and a wave of apprehension cuts off my mirth. I see Mandy's eyes swoop to my phone screen. I walk back to my desk. Who could be texting me at this time of morning? What if it's Jack texting to cancel our date? I knew he was way too hot to be interested in someone like me.

"You won't know until you look," Mandy says, as though she's read my mind.

My fingers are like jelly as I fish my phone out of my pocket.

"Well?" Mandy moves to look over my shoulder. "Is it from Mr Superlative Jack?"

"Hang on." I angle the phone away from her and unlock my screen to find it's not a text at all—it's an email from Corinna, reminding me of what we discussed in my lateness meeting. As the mingled disappointment and relief at not receiving a message from Jack hits me, another email from Corinna pops up in my inbox. This one is addressed to all employees, informing us that she wants us all to bring a tin of food for homeless people in to work within the next few weeks.

Mandy says, "Well, Brayden? Is it from dishy Jack?"

I place my phone down on my desk after reading the messages over again. "No. It's from Corinna."

Mandy joins me at my desk. "Spill the goss! What has she said? Oh, and cheer up, Brayden—remember, beauty is the power within a smile."

I start to snicker, and Mandy says, "Now that's better."

Mandy is truly wonderful—she knows exactly what to say even when I am feeling down. I pick my phone back up off my desk, unlock the screen, and show her the emails from Corinna. "Unexpected, right? Corinna, doing something nice for the community? Next thing we know, she'll be giving us all a pay raise!"

Mandy says, "Do bears shit in the woods?"

I say, "Don't be daft, Mand. Bears do shit in the woods." We both melt into a fit of laughter, and I say, "Don't get your hopes up. Feeding the poor of Kelford may be out of character for her, but pay raises are flat-out ridiculous."

My phone beeps again with a message from Jack. Mandy catches sight of the notification and nudges me. "Looks like you're having all the luck today. Come on, Brayden, open it!"

"Give me a chance, Mandy. Anyway, haven't you got work to be doing?"

"I have, but I want to see what hot Jack has to say first." Mandy stares at my phone screen like a rabbit dazzled by the headlights on a car.

My gut twists—this must be the cancellation text I feared. I open the text. It's practically an essay, beginning with, *Hi, Brayden! Sorry for bothering you, but I just can't stop thinking about you. How is your day going so far?*

My nervousness flips around into joy. He's not breaking it off at all!

"What is it?" Mandy manoeuvres herself to try and snoop at my screen. "Come on, what is it?"

I pull my phone away. "I am still reading it! Hang on." My smile gets wider and wider with every word I devour. Jack finishes his text by saying, *Looking forward to tonight*, with a smile emoji and a kiss to top it all off.

I read the text to Mandy, who starts singing 'Love Is in the Air.' "Don't forget, Brayden Willoughby, I want to be the maid of honour when you and Jack are getting hitched!"

I laugh at her. "Don't get too excitcd. It's just a drink." I'm not sure whether I'm saying it more to her or to myself.

47

At that moment, both our office phones ring. Mandy skips back to her desk, and once again we are back to the grind. As answer the phone and type away, I am counting down the minutes on the office clock, willing it to hurry up and get to 5 p.m. When there's just one hour to go, Mandy leaves her desk and asks if I want a coffee.

"Yes, please. With two sugars and lots of milk!" I give her a wink. It's happy hour now. Just sixty more minutes, and it's action stations to get myself all dolled up for Jack. What better way to celebrate than with a hot drink?

Mandy heads to the staff room to make our final cuppa of the day. I struggle to concentrate on my last account, my head filled with thoughts of Jack. As I save the file, a hand touches my left shoulder, and I almost jump out of my skin. I twist around. It's Enzo, our very own Postman Pat of Gallagher & Masons. "Bloody hell, Enzo, you want to be careful of that!"

He looks confused. "What do you mean?"

"Creeping up on people from behind!"

He laughs and plonks his bum down in Mandy's chair. "Who else did you think it could be?"

"Well, with all the zombies who work in this place, it could have been anyone, I suppose."

Enzo starts to move Mandy's items around on her desk. "I'm no zombie. I'm a bona fide vampire." Enzo holds his index fingers next to his mouth in an impression of fangs.

Mandy returns with two mugs of steaming hot coffee in her hands. She frowns when she see Enzo has taken up residency in her chair. She sets the mugs of coffee firmly down on the desk, as though staking claim to her territory.

"Umm, I think you had better move your sweaty carcass out of my chair now."

Enzo jumps up from Mandy's chair like a jack-in-the-box. "I only called in to ask if I could borrow a pen."

I pass him a blue biro from the pot next to my computer. "There you go."

Enzo takes it and eyes the coffee mugs. "Hey, I could do with a coffee. Where's mine?"

Mandy pulls a face. "It's in the staff room in the kettle, and the mug is on the sink. Now piss off and make it yourself."

Enzo humphs. "You two will think twice about denying me coffee when I come drink your blood later."

Mandy scoffs. "Haven't you got a coffin you should be climbing into?"

He grins, wiggles his 'fangs' next to his mouth again, and sashays off with my pen.

Mandy takes out her can of anti-perspirant and sprays her chair with it. The aroma is so overpowering that it floats to my side of the office, and I start coughing. "Bloody hell, Mand. What are you trying to do? Suffocate me?"

Mandy says, "Well, I don't know what I could catch from Count Enzo."

I chuckle as Mandy finishes exterminating the office. I wonder if she knows anti-perspirant won't disinfect anything. The clock strikes 5 p.m., and I resist the urge to pump my fist in the air. "Come on. Let's get out of here."

She makes a face. "Sorry, I have to stay late today. Got some catching up to do."

I hope Mandy is not feeling left out, with me going on a date and everything. "Are you okay, hun?"

"Yes," she replies with a smile. "Now go on—or else you'll be late for your date. I will meet you in the morning at the car park so you can tell me all about your wonderful night with sexy Jack."

"Deal. See you tomorrow!" I jump up from my chair like a frog leaping from a lily pad. My nerves buzz as I enter the lift full of work colleagues, some of whom apparently don't know what a can of deodorant is. The smell is unbearable. I spot Enzo grinning at me from across the cramped space. It seems my good luck has run out—first the nasty smell, and now seeing Enzo for the second time in a day.

I will the lift to hurry up and let us off already. Suddenly, the lift judders, the lights flicker, and we stop moving.

Chapter Five

Everyone groans. "Oh, for fuck's sake," I mutter.

Everybody reaches inside their coats and bags for their mobiles. I do the same, hoping to alert Mandy, who is still at her desk. But I don't have any reception, and the WiFi doesn't reach through the lift's metal walls. "It's no good, I have no signal," I say to the lady next to me.

"Press the bloody alarm!" someone yells.

If I can't get out of this lift soon, I'll have to kiss my drink with Jack goodbye. My palms begin to sweat. Who knows when I'll get another opportunity to go out with such a hot guy? Maybe I'm doomed to be single forever.

Enzo says, "Shall I tell a joke?"

"No!" we all shout. The temperature in the cramped space rises as all our bodies turn it into a human sauna. I try not to think about how much sweat everyone's producing right now. God, this is disgusting. The time stretches on and on.

The air becomes stifling. I cover my nose and mouth to try and block the smell, but it doesn't work. Someone says that the maintenance crew is working on getting us unstuck, but I wish they'd bloody hurry up.

The minutes turn into an hour, then two hours. Shit, shit, shit. Enzo moves towards me, and I try to move a few steps back. I tread on a man's foot and he yelps at the top of his voice.

I apologise and compose myself before turning to Enzo. "Did you forget something this morning?"

He smirks and pats his pockets. "No."

"I think you have. It's in a can, and it sprays a lovely aroma."

Enzo snickers. I bet he's enjoying stinking up the whole lift.

At last, the lift judders and moves down again. Everybody cheers, and I let out a whoop. I'll have my date after all! But only just—the time on my phone says 7:00 p.m. I only have an hour to get ready!

The lift reaches the ground floor, and everyone races to get through the twin metal doors as if they are entering a January sale. I push my way through my sweaty work colleagues. "Excuse me, please. Excuse me."

Bursting out of the lift and into the cool air of the foyer is the best feeling in the world, but I don't have time to enjoy it. I run like the clappers down the office steps and along the high street, all the way to the car park.

When I reach the car park, I am in two minds—take the lift and catch my breath, or stick with the stairs? The thought of being in another lift makes my chest constrict, so I take a deep breath and begin my task of climbing up to the fifth floor, where my car is parked. I stop several times to rest; I have a stitch in my stomach from all this exertion. At last, I pay my parking charge at the pay station and proceed to my car. The time on my dashboard is showing 7:20 p.m. I need to move.

I quickly reverse out of the parking space and make my way home. I park on the street outside, leap out of the car, and begin to undress as I run up the garden path. I hope none of the neighbours can see me removing my tie and unbuttoning my shirt. As I enter the house, a voice from the kitchen shouts, "Brayden, is that you?"

"No, it's the milkman," I reply.

My mother comes from the kitchen with a cup of coffee and my T-shirt over her arm. "Here you go. I was just making a cuppa and thought you might like one. Help you put your feet up after work. And here's your T-shirt—I don't want it cluttering up the dining room any longer."

"Thanks, Mum." I take the T-shirt off her and accept the steaming mug. I won't have time to finish the entire thing, but it seems rude to refuse outright when she's already made it for me. I take a few sips. The caffeine will do me good.

My mum clasps her hands together. "Now, tell me all about your day at work before Shirley comes for me. We are off to the new community bingo."

"I think you will find it's really called the BCA."

"What do you mean, love?"

I grin at her. "The Boring Cows Association."

"Oh, Brayden!"

"Only joking, Mum. I'm sure it will be fun. But I have to get ready and go—I have a date, remember?"

"Oh yes, with one of those lovely girls from your office. You hardly ever talk about it. I want to know everything!"

"Sorry, but I haven't got time to talk. I am so late." I doubt she wants to hear about how much I hate my job, anyway—and this is definitely not the time to tell her I am going on a date with a man.

As walk towards the stairs, the doorbell goes, and my mum opens it to our neighbour Shirley. "Evening, Brayden!" she says.

I pause on the stairs. "Evening, Shirley."

Shirley grins. Oh yes, you have your date tonight! Your mum and I were talking today about how we're so excited for you. What's the lucky girl's name?"

I start to frown and blush. Here it comes again—another lie. But I can't spout off a fake name, or else they might look into it and find out I'm hiding something. "It's just a girl from work. Would you excuse me, Shirley—I have to get ready."

Like a bat out of hell, I run up the stairs to my bedroom. My phone pings in my trouser pocket. It's a text from Jack, saying he has arrived at the pub and he will be seated near the bar. I text back, *I will leave mine in ten.*

He replies almost immediately with *Okay*, plus a kiss emoji. A rush of happiness goes through me.

After dumping my sweaty clothing in the laundry basket, I throw on a bathrobe and dash to the bathroom. The door refuses to budge. I hear singing from inside. It's my sister. I knock on the door. "Sam? I need to have a wash!"

The singing continues. I knock louder; she shouts from the other side of the door, "What?"

"How long are you going to be in there? I need to use the shower."

"I've only just gotten in the bath."

"Can I come in for a quick wash and shave? I'll only be five minutes. Just put a towel around yourself. Please, Samantha!"

I hear nothing more from her. My request must have fallen on deaf ears, submerged in a bubble bath. My first so-called date with Jack and I will stink like a skunk! I run into my bedroom, strip naked, and pour half a bottle of aftershave over myself from top to toe. I sing the words to the song "Tonight Will Be a Good Night," more for luck than anything else. I don a pair of black boxers, the T-shirt my mother repaired, and a pair of jeans. I splash more aftershave on myself and look in the mirror. Hopefully, Jack likes the mussed-up look. "Let's hit the town!" I say to my reflection.

As I leave the bedroom, I am met on the landing by Samantha, who is clad in a fluffy bathrobe with her hair wrapped in a towel. "The bathroom is free now," she says.

"Too late now; I have to go." I run downstairs and grab my jacket off the coat hook. "I am off now," I shout towards the living room. "See you later!

My mother bustles out of the living room with Shirley, looks me up and down and straightens the collar of my jacket. "Oh, love, could you do me a big favour—could you give me and Shirley a lift to the bingo hall?"

My heart sinks. The bingo hall is on the way to the pub, so it won't take much extra time at all, but I know my mum is trying to play detective and find out who I am going on a date with. I have think quickly. She can't find out about Jack until I've told my family I'm gay, properly, at a good time. I stutter my words out. "Okay, but we have to leave now."

I sprint down the drive to my car. I hear my mum and Shirley whispering behind me. "Come on!" I shout, and they pick up their pace as I reach the car. I fish my phone out of my pocket to see if I have any further text messages from Jack. Nothing.

As I pull out into the road, I see Shirley in my rear-view mirror putting a hanky partly over her nose. She starts to cough. Must be the smell of the aftershave purifying the inside of my car.

A few minutes later, we arrive at the bingo hall. I leap out of my seat and open the back passenger door for my mum and Shirley. Shirley says, "Oh, Rose, you brought him up well. What a gentleman!"

I tap my foot as I wait for my mum and Shirley to hurry up and get out of my car. Finally, they emerge, and Shirley rushes off to buy the bingo book with a quick "Thank you!" over her shoulder.

My mum kisses me on the cheek. "Have a lovely night, Brayden. And don't be too late home."

Either she doesn't notice the overwhelming smell of aftershave, or she's polite enough not to mention it. "Thanks, Mum."

Chapter Six

I arrive at the car park just over the road from O'Ryan's, and as I check my appearance in the wing mirror, my stomach twists with nervousness. What if any of my parents' friends are in O'Ryan's and see me with Jack? But the nervousness disbands into excitement which bubbles up inside me.

I look over at the battered old bus shelter; in the light of the streetlamp, I see a guy and girl making out before their bus arrives. Maybe that's going to be me and Jack in few hours. Although this is just a drink, I want it to be more. I have waited a whole twenty-four hours for this date with Jack, and I don't want to mess it up.

I lock the car doors and take a slow walk across the road. A few drops of rain pat my face. It seems really busy in the bar. I walk around the side of the building and have a look through the window, trying to get a peek at the area where Jack said he would be sitting. I can't see much—a lot of people are blocking my view. Then, someone shifts, and I am able to see the seats near the bar. There is no sign of Jack!

My heart pounds. Where is he? I take my phone out of my pocket to see if he's texted me, but there's nothing. Maybe he had second thoughts and decided to scarper. I know I am no oil painting, but I assumed he would have the decency to tell me if he had second thoughts before I arrived.

I really don't know what to do. Do I go into the bar, or do I go back to my car and sit there, hoping he will send me a text?

My phone rings, and I jab my finger onto the accept call button without checking who it is. "Jack!"

"Guess again," Mandy's voice says.

"Oh. Hi, Mandy." I sag.

"How's your night going? You sound upset."

"I think Jack has gone. I've got no mates. I'm just alone waiting outside the bar, peering in through the window."

"Brayden, of course you've got mates. You've got me, for one—your best friend!" I smile despite myself as Mandy continues. "You should go in. Jack might have gone to the toilet or to the smoking area."

Of course—she's right. That could very well be the explanation. "Thanks, hun. I did not think of that. I just assumed he'd left."

Mandy laughs. "Have a cocktail for me. And if that fit bartender is there, give him my number."

I nervously break into laughter. Mandy and I were only in here the other night, and the bartender who served us is going to see me with Jack. *Lots* of people are going to see me with Jack—maybe even people I know.

Well, I can't live in fear of being seen forever. I say to Mandy, "I will."

She giggles. Whatever would you do without me, honey bee?"

"Not much." I smile. "Thanks. I'll see you at work on Monday."

I hang up, put my phone back into my coat pocket, and enter the bar. A crowd of ladies on a hen night surge past. One of them apologises for nearly bumping into me as she props up the bride, who seems to have had one too many. The bridesmaid blinks at me. "Brayden Willoughby! I haven't seen you in years."

I must look confused, because she continues. "We used to go to school together. I am Leanne Dickinson. Remember? I used to have a braces back then, and all the other kids called me Jaws except you."

I smile in politeness. "Oh, right!"

Leanne smiles back flirtatiously. She's obviously had a few too many herself. I feel her hands wandering up my leg, and my heart sinks even more. I don't want Leanne to know I'm gay, not before even my family knows, and rejecting her might make her suspicious. But I really don't like this. I brush her off, stepping backwards. "Ah … I must be going."

She sulks and walks off in huff with the bride still clinched around her arm. I sigh with relief. Seems like she's more annoyed than suspicious.

When I reach the bar, I have a look around, scanning the crowd for Jack. After a few minutes of fruitless searching, I sink down on a barstool. The barman asks me what I would like to drink. "Pint of lager, please." Might as well drown my disappointment with a drink.

I keep wandering my gaze around, not only looking for Jack but also for the bartender who served me and Mandy the other night. There's no sign of either of them. I suppose neither I nor Mandy are having any luck with men tonight.

Then, someone taps me on the shoulder, and I turn to see Jack's smiling blue eyes. Blood rushes to my face. "I was starting to think you'd left!"

Jack laughs. "I would never leave you. How long have you been here?"

"Few minutes."

"Gosh, I'm sorry about that. I was out in the smoking area, having a cigarette."

I smile. "Well, that's a relief!"

"Do you often get stood up?" His eyes twinkle.

"Usually not." I really want to find out more about this sexy hunk of a man that's standing beside me in the flesh. I glance around the bar for an empty table where we can talk and get to know each other.

"Would you like a drink?" Jack asks.

"I have just ordered one. Can I get you a drink?"

"Yeah, sure. I will have a pint of lager."

"Snap! That's what I ordered!"

"Aha! Looks like we'll get along well." Jack turns his face away and wipes his nose. His eyes appear to be watering a bit. The smell of my aftershave must be quite overpowering. My face flushes even hotter, out of embarrassment this time. Why couldn't Sam have gotten out of the bathroom quicker? I'll be a virgin forever at this rate.

The barman sets down my lager, and I ask for a second one for Jack. A group of guys bump into me, and they apologise. I smile.

One of the guys bends down to pick up some money they dropped, and one of his friends sees Jack gawking at him. The friend shouts, "Matt, watch your ass! Bum boys alert!" The guy places both hands on his backside.

Me and Jack giggle, and Jack draws his eyes away from the guy picking up the money. The group of guys lose interest in teasing us and saunter away. "So, do you come to O'Ryan's often?" Jack asks.

"No—first time in here tonight." In truth, Mandy and I were in here the other night, sipping cocktails and slagging off our boss. If there was a human form of Pinocchio, that's me. "I can't believe how busy it is already."

Jack apologises again for running late, and I say, "Hey, no problem. I was running late, too. You would not believe how my day at work ended."

Jack orders another two pints of lager from the bartender and says, "Hey, Brayden, do you want some nuts?"

I blush and snicker. "Um …"

Jack chuckles as he comprehends what he just said. The bartender sets the two pints down and says, "So who's having the nuts?"

We both melt into laughter, and Jack eventually regains his voice enough to say, "Hc is."

The bartender hands me the peanuts. I split the packaging open and say to Jack, "Help yourself."

Jack tilts his head to one side as he looks at me. "Tell me more about the day you had, Brayden."

I start to tell Jack about my day from hell when I notice a couple getting up from their small table nearby. The two now-empty chairs seem to beckon me. "Want to sit down?" I say to Jack.

Jack follows my gaze to the table, and he slides off his barstool. "Sure." He leads the way in his bum-tight jeans. His form-fitting T-shirt displays his muscles. Have I died and gone to heaven? He's so fit! I can't believe I am on a date with him.

Once we sit down, Jack asks me to carry on talking about my day. I open my mouth to tell him about getting stuck in the lift, but the doors burst open and a huge wave of people—a stag party?—enter the bar. The volume in the room increases, and it is impossible to hear either of us talk.

The group of guys who were at the bar sit two tables away, and I see them whispering to one another. One of them moves his right hand downwards, pulling an offensive gesture at me. Jack catches sight of it and grimaces. I say, "Shall we drink this and head somewhere else?"

Jack nods, and we both down our pints. He yells to me, "I am just going for a ciggy."

"I will wait for you outside."

Jack heads off to the smoking area, while I make my way out of the bar door. One of the guys leaps up from his chair and places both hands on his backside. I shake my head and grin awkwardly at him.

As I am waiting outside for Jack, the group of ladies from the hen party crash through the door. A tad more intoxicated then before, Leanne throws a pink feather boa around my neck and dances in front of me. This will be the second time tonight she has tried to come on to me.

"You're coming home with me!" she purrs, caressing my face.

I think she's so drunk that she doesn't recognize me in the dim light. I mutter under my breath, "Thank God."

When I don't react, Leanne loses interest and makes her way back into the bar. I keep standing still while another one of the ladies shoves an inflatable penis in my face. "Go on, suck on this!" she slurs, tottering on her high heels.

I shrug, and the group apparently decides my reactions aren't fun enough, so they move on into the bar after Leanne.

Fifteen minutes pass, and Jack doesn't make a reappearance. What the hell is taking him so long? I hope he is all right. What if the group of guys picked a fight with him? Or what if he didn't like me and decided to leave?

Finally, the door opens, and Jack appears. "Sorry I took so long! I bumped into someone I hadn't seen in a long time and got chatting."

"No worries at all. I thought the group of guys from before might have been trying to harass you," I say.

He snickers. "The last I saw of those twits, they were being undressed by a gang of women. So, Brayden, what do you fancy doing now that we're out of that noise factory?"

I shrug. "I am easy."

He laughs. "What about a club? Or something to eat? Your choice."

Truth be told, I don't want either of those choices. I want to see the body behind the clothes. I want to skip first base and get to second. I want to explore his hot body and kiss those cherry lips of his. But I suspect he wants to go clubbing.

What do I say? I don't want to make the wrong decision. He might end our date early if I do that. I have to think.

Maybe I don't have to make the choice myself. I say to Jack, "Let's toss a coin. Heads means we go clubbing; tails means we find another pub."

"Okay then," Jack says. I take a coin out of my pocket and throw it up in the air. It lands on tails. "Pub it is," Jack says.

Is he disappointed? I can't tell. But at least I'll be able to talk to him and get to know him more easily in a pub. I smile. "Shall we go to the Cock and Fox?"

"Lead the way." He sounds happy enough, so hopefully he doesn't mind not going to a club.

"I need to bring the car over."

"Leave it there. The Cock and Fox is just up the road."

We walk off to the pub, discussing our jobs as we go. When we arrive, we find it closed.

"Oh, shit, " I say.

"Never mind," Jack says.

I feel like a boat with the wind blown out of its sails. I want to spend as much time with Jack as possible, but I suppose that isn't happening tonight. Then, he smiles at me and takes my hand. "I know a place."

Maybe the night isn't ruined after all. A big smile stretches across my face. I feel like a kid seeing Santa Claus for the first time. "Really?"

"Yep," Jack says. "Come on—it's within walking distance."

As we get closer to our mystery destination, I hear music and see a cascade of colours shining bright from a building's facade. It's the Over The Rainbow Kelfords gay club. From this distance, I see two well-built doormen watching a group of people enter the club. My stomach sinks—it's the ladies from the hen party. They must have taken a car to beat us here.

As I look further down the queue, I see Leanne with two of the guys from O'Ryan's bar. I can't face these people again. And if Leanne sees me here with Jack, she might put two and two together, and suddenly my secret will be out.

I have to think of a good excuse not to enter the club. I say to Jack, "Hey, actually, do you mind if I call it a night? It's getting late, and I promised my mum I would help her with a few chores starting early tomorrow morning. They could take most of the day, actually."

That's the worst bullshit I've ever spouted off. Jack looks confused and disappointed. That's it—I have blown ever going on a date with him again. But he just replies, "That's a shame. I was going to ask you if you wanted to go for a bite to eat tomorrow night."

My stomach does a somersault. On the outside, I try to play it cool. "Sounds great! I'm sure I can find the time." I really don't want to miss another date with Jack, especially after this disastrous first outing.

As we walk back to my car, Jack tells me how much he would like to know more about me. I blush and say the same to him. "I could give you a lift home, if you like," I say hopefully.

"It's all good. I only live up the road, and it's a nice night for a walk." He smiles and inches a little closer. I close my eyes, willing him to kiss me. His lips brush against my cheek, and when I open my eyes, he is already walking away. "See you tomorrow night at Luigi's Bistro!" he calls.

Disappointment and electric excitement mingle in my chest. My cheek practically burns where he kissed it, but I so wanted him to snog my face off. "See you tomorrow," I murmur, turning to open my car door. Then, I spin back in Jack's direction and shout as loud as my voice can handle, "Hey, what time are we having dinner?"

"Eight p.m.!" Jack yells back.

I watch his reflection in my wing mirror until it fades. Then, I get back into my car and drive home. On the way, my thoughts swirl with excitement about Jack and worry about bumping into Leanne from school. I just hope she was too drunk to notice that I was obviously on a date with a man. I'll have to tell Jack that I am not out yet, and for the time being discretion is a must.

I park my car on the driveway and make my way up to the front door. As I do, a black cat zooms out of the bushes and darts in front of me. I stop in mid-step and gasp. I don't want any bad luck, especially since I have another date with Jack tomorrow.

I open the front door and close it as softly as I can so as not to wake any of my family. I creep up the stairs like a mouse, tiptoe across the landing, and sneak past my parents' bedroom to mine. I hear my father snoring, and I smirk. I suppose he is keeping the monsters away, as he used to tell me and Samantha when we were little. Poor Mum.

I reach my bedroom and close the door. After my ninja adventure, I undress myself for bed, put my phone on the charger and get under the covers. Jack's face floats in my mind's eye.

After a few minutes of lying there, I turn on my front and switch the bedside lamp back on. I sit up and look at the ceiling. All I can do is think about Jack. What is he doing right now? Is he asleep, dreaming of me? I desperately want to text him to make sure he got home okay. I reach over and grab my phone to send Jack a goodnight message, being sure to include a kiss emoji.

I lay the phone down on my duvet, hoping that I'll receive a reply from Jack soon, but nothing comes. Just as I put my phone back on my charger, it vibrates and pings. I rush to see if it is from Jack, but I end up dropping my phone down the side of my bed. Oh, fuck!

I reach down to retrieve it, but as I am leaning over the side of the mattress, I hit my hand on the back of the bedside table. The jolt of pain makes me yelp, but at least I have the phone in my hand.

I open the screen to find a text from my mobile phone provider, telling me how I can save on a promotion they are running. I feel so disappointed. The time on my phone says 2:00 a.m. I decide to text Mandy—she should be awake at this time on the weekend, because she loves watching all those American talk shows.

Hey, are you awake? I send her.

There's no reply, so I assume she's skipped the shows today and is already asleep. I reach over to turn off the lamp and begin to drift off to dreamland. My phone vibrates again, startling me from my half-doze. Maybe Mandy was just engrossed in a show and now she wants to talk. I have so much to tell her!

But the text is not from Mandy—it's from Jack!

Hey, thanks for a good night. See you tomorrow!

He ended the text with two kisses. I don't think it was much of a good night. The bar was so loud, and a group of guys wanted to pick a fight with us, and we walked to the other side of town to a pub which turned out to be closed— and on top of all that, I ditched Jack with a bad excuse right when he was trying to save our date. At least Jack's being nice about it. And he invited me out on another date!

I text Jack back with, *See you tomorrow*, with two kisses and a smiley face. I am now excited like a box of Smarties! How in the world am I going to fall asleep now? I try to count sheep, but I give up when I reach one hundred. I put my hands on the back of my head and lie there. It seems like I've only just drifted off when golden light streams through my bedroom window.

It can't be morning already! As the sun's rays pour through my curtains, I reach over and look at my phone. Panic floods my body. It is 6 p.m.! I have slept through most of the day! I suppose the excitement of last night required a lot of recovery for my body. Perhaps my other stresses are also catching up to me—all the late nights trying to get projects ready for Corinna, and being scared of what people will think of me if they know I'm gay. Not to mention the hell of a week I've had.

At least the only important thing I have to do today is go on my date with Jack, and I still have two hours to get there. I place my phone back on the table and pull my duvet over my head. As I relax, there is a knock at my bedroom door. I don't say anything. Then, I hear my mum say, "Brayden, love, how did your date go last night? And do you have any clothes you need washed?"

"Ugh," I mutter. I am so tired I can barely process what she's saying.

She knocks a little louder and cracks the door open. I drag myself up to a sitting position. "Yes Mum, I have clothes for you. I will bring them down in a minute."

"Okay, love," she replies. Her footsteps shuffle away down the hall. I throw the duvet off and sit on the side of the bed. I pick my phone up and read the text I received from Jack last night, with the two kisses at the end. I can't believe he likes spending time with me!

My mother's voice shouts up the stairs, "Brayden, the clothes, love! I am waiting to put the machine on!"

"Coming, Mum!" I quickly throw on the clothes I wore last night and gather my dirty laundry from my basket. It occurs to me that I also need a shirt to wear tonight for my second date with Jack. I place my dirty clothes down on my bed and explore my wardrobe to find something nice. A white shirt, still in its packaging, is stuffed in the back. This will do nicely!

I pull the shirt out of the plastic wrapping and throw it over my arm to try on in a second as I pick my dirty clothing up off the bed. I head downstairs, where my mother is still loading the washing machine. "Here you go, Mum. My clothes."

"Thank you! Now tell me about your date last night with that girl from work." She takes the pile out of my hands and dumps it in the washing machine—including the shirt I want to wear for my date with Jack tonight!

Here I go—more BS. I feel terrible making up lies to my mum. I have to find a way to tell her I wasn't on date with a girl, but with a man. And it's her birthday soon; she deserves the truth. Why am I such a coward? "Mum, wait! That's the shirt I'm wearing tonight." I snatch the shirt out of the washing machine.

"That was lucky, love. I was about to press the start button. What are you doing tonight?"

"Oh, um … I have another date with that girl."

She claps her hands together. "How wonderful! Sounds like it went well last night, then. Tell me everything!"

I give her the run-down, keeping some of the details true for realism, but largely spinning a tale of a girl who doesn't exist. Just as I'm explaining that the Cock and Fox was closed, my father enters the kitchen. "It was probably closed because Harry, the baker, has been popping in and out of their house frequently," he says. "Sounds like he's been playing with her baps. You know, the woman who…"

My mother interrupts him. "Oh, I know, the hussy with the oversized breasts. The one whose chest arrives on time and she's fifteen minutes late!"

My dad lets out a laugh, and my mother grins at him as she continues with the washing. I couldn't care less about the baker's shenanigans—I'm just relieved that my shirt won't be still in the wash when I need it tonight. The white fabric is wrinkled to hell and back, though, so I set the ironing board up and plug the iron in. I smooth the shirt out and begin with the sleeve. A burning smell worms up my nose. I pull the iron away and a brown mark sits on the white fabric.

"For fuck's sake, what's this?" I mutter. I peer at the bottom of the iron. Something brown has melted on its metal plate. "Mum!" I shout.

She rushes over from the other side of the kitchen to see what the matter is. I show her the stain on my shirt and the matching spot on the bottom of the iron.

"Oh, love, this must be Samantha. The iron was fine when I used it this morning, but she used it in the afternoon. She must have gotten something stuck on it."

"Oh well, that's just great. That makes two items of clothing Samantha has ruined for me."

"Calm down, Brayden. I will pop next door to see Shirley and ask if she has anything that might help. She bought a new book last week about old wives' remedies for removing stains."

I snicker. That makes a change from Shirley buying shedloads of scratch cards.

My mother goes next door to see our neighbour, taking my shirt with her. I sit down at the kitchen table and rest my head in my hands. First Mum almost washed my shirt, and now Samantha has ruined the sleeve. Things happen in threes! Two down, one to go.

My phone vibrates and pings in my trouser pocket. It's a text from Mandy. *Hey, how did your date with sexy Jack go? I want to know all the gory details! Sorry I didn't text back last night.*

She ends her message with a kiss emoji, as she always does. I give her the run-down, which makes my fingers ache from all the typing. Just as I send the text, the back door opens. It's my mother with my shirt. "There you go, love, all sorted for you."

She hands me the garment, and I check the sleeve. It's snow-white once again. "Oh, wow! Thanks!" Looks like the old wives in Shirley's book had the right idea with their stain remedies. The fabric is still horribly wrinkled, but I don't trust myself to iron it again after what happened last time. "Mum, can you do me another favour?"

"What do you need, love?"

"Would you iron my shirt for me?"

"Yes, of course." She takes my no-longer-stained shirt out of my hand.

I feel a bit guilty about her doing all my chores for me, so I'd better lend a hand. "Hang on, I'll clean the bottom of the iron for you." I take the iron over to the kitchen sink and use a cloth and some soap to remove the tacky brown lump. What in the world did Sam stick on there? It looks like some kind of chocolate.

As my mum irons, she says, "Now, you never finished telling me about your date!"

Here I go again—more BS. God, I feel so bad, As I tell her about our walk back to the car from the Cock and Fox pub, my phone vibrates and pings.

I dash into my trouser pocket to retrieve it. It's a text from Jack. My mum manoeuvres around the other side of me to see who the text is from. I step back, holding my phone tightly in my hand. I glance at the screen to see the first few words from Jack's text. *Hey, hope you had a good day! Looking forward to tonight.*

He ends his message with a kiss! My hands shake as I reply, *Same here.* Oh God, that sounded way too bland. At least I don't think my mum saw the screen.

My mum admits defeat and walks back over to the ironing board to continue her task. "Mandy again, love?"

"Yes, Mum." Something about Jack's texts makes me want to keep them all to myself.

Finally, she says, "There you go, love. All ironed for you! You must have made a good impression last night if you're going out with her again so soon."

"You know me, Mum. I always make a big impression." I giggle, and so does my mum. She hands me the crisp, clean shirt "Thanks!" I kiss her on the cheek. She smiles as she proceeds to put the iron and ironing board away for me.

I dash upstairs to the bathroom, hoping no one is in there so I can get ready for tonight. Mercifully, the door is unlocked. At last, I can have a shower in peace.

I get undressed and jump into the shower. "Owww!" The water is freezing! I forgot to turn the shower on by the cord which heats the water. I leap out to fix my mistake and jump back in with a flash. The water becomes lovely and warm as it gushes over me. I imagine Jack pouring shower gel over my back. It slithers down me, and I become lost in the moment.

My fantasy ends with me wrapped in the shower curtain, water and shower gel dripping everywhere. I hear my sister's voice bellowing from landing, telling me to hurry up so she can go to the toilet.

I play her at her own game and don't reply. I smile to myself. I could stay in this shower all day and night, but I only allow myself another fifteen minutes. I don't want to be late for my dinner date with Jack. Besides, I couldn't let Samantha suffer for too long.

After I brush my teeth, I rub the condensation off the mirror with a towel and spread shaving cream over my face. I take each stroke with the razor carefully. I don't want to cut my face. What would Jack think if I turn up at the restaurant looking like something out of a horror movie?

I dry myself off with the fluffy bath towel my mum had put on the warm radiator and wrap myself in it. I open the bathroom door, and my sister barges past me saying, "I got to pee! I got to pee!"

"Well, bloody pee, then." I dash to my bedroom, take out a fresh pair of black boxer shorts and spray deodorant on them so they smell like a summer orchard. I pull them up and walk over to the mirror, doing a little dance. I take my time buttoning my shirt up. I don't want to put the buttons in the wrong holes and end up with a lopsided front. After donning my socks and jeans, I walk over to my wall unit and throw a few drops from the bottle of aftershave on my face. Not too much this time! I don't want to make Jack feel like it's allergy season again.

As I am about to leave my bedroom, my mother calls up the hallway. "Brayden, would you like a cuppa?"

I reply, "No, Mum, I am going out now!" I meet her at the stairs and she immediately does what all mothers do—plucks at my clothes to make sure I look smart. I roll my eyes and chuckle. "Mum, I am not a child. I can dress myself!"

"You'll always be my little boy. But you're growing up fast, with your new girlfriend and all! When are we going to meet this young lady?" She stands on her tiptoes and reaches up to pat my head.

I blush and let out a nervous laugh. "It's only been one date." I kiss her on the cheek, and out the door I go to meet Jack.

Chapter Seven

As I get to my car, my phone vibrates with a text from Jack, telling me he has arrived at the restaurant. I jump into the driver's seat and zoom off down the road. Unfortunately, the petrol light flashes. Can I make it to the restaurant without filling up first? Maybe, but I don't want to risk it. And if Jack gets in my car later for whatever reason, it could be a bit embarrassing if he sees I'm running low on fuel.

I find the nearest petrol station on the way and fill up the tank. As I am lining up for the counter, I see some boxes of party hats sitting on a shelf behind the counter. Condoms, that is—party hats are my personal slang for them. Shall I buy a pack? What if Jack and I sleep together tonight?

The queue builds up behind me as my head whirls with indecision. I don't want to lose my place in the line—I'm verging on being late as it is—but keeping my position means I'd have to ask the sixty-something-year-old sales lady for a box of party hats in front of everyone. I decide to step out of the queue, and I wander around the shop, praying for the other customers to disperse quickly so I can pay for my petrol and get the party hats without anyone hearing.

The sales assistant catches sight of me loitering by the magazine stand and bellows out as loud as her voice can go, "Who used pump number seven?"

I freeze on the spot. Nobody else answers. I raise my hand in the air and say, "That's me."

The sales assistant rolls her eyes at me and beckons me forward to the counter. The other people in the queue look daggers at me for getting to cut in. As I approach the counter, my hands grow clammy.

"That's ten pounds for the petrol," the lady says.

I blurt out, "Can I have a box of party hats, too?"

She looks at me strangely. "We don't sell party hats. This is a petrol station, not a party shop."

"Oh … okay. Just the petrol, then." I'm not sure whether I'm relieved or dismayed that she didn't know what I meant by party hats. As I hand the cash to the sales assistant, my face must be redder than a baboon's bum. I make a quick getaway, and I can feel the sales assistant's eyes on my back as I approach the door. The customers in the queue shuffle and mutter behind me.

I reach the car and open the door, but pause before I get in. Should I go back in and buy the party hats, making sure I actually call them condoms this time? If I do get the chance to sleep with Jack tonight, what will he think of me if I don't have protection? But I don't think I could face going back and asking again for a box of party hats from someone who is old enough to be my nan. I decide not to, and I drive off.

As I pull up to the restaurant, the clock on my dashboard flicks over to 8 p.m. Right on time! I close my car door and look at the menu board on the wall next to the entrance. Wow—these prices are expensive. The outside of the restaurant looks posh, but luckily I don't think I look too out-of-place with my newly ironed shirt.

The waiter opens the door for me, and Jack waves at me as another waiter leads me to the table my date is sitting at. I have trouble controlling my jaw as I sit down. Jack looks hotter than a piece of chicken cooking on a barbeque, with his top three shirt buttons undone so I can just see the top of his chest, his hair styled to perfection. "Hey, you found this place! Not a lot of people do at first." He smiles at me with his perfect teeth.

"Have you been here before, then?"

"No, this is my first time."

"Oh." How does he know that people have trouble finding it if he's never been here before? I'm about to question him, but we are interrupted by the waiter bringing our menus and asking us what we would like to drink. I order a pint of lager, and Jack does the same. Once the waiter leaves, Jack studies the menu with his eyebrows drawn slightly together and his lips pursed in concentration. I just can't take my eyes off him. He looks up, his blue eyes piercing mine. "Brayden, what do you fancy?"

"You," I say.

He laughs. "I think I will order garlic mushrooms and spaghetti carbonara. There's plenty of time to order dessert later."

"Oh, I hope so," I mutter. I force myself to look at the menu, but all I really want is to get Jack into bed. I want to get lost between the sheets of lovemaking with him.

The waiter returns with our drinks, placing Jack's down first and then mine. "Are we ready to order?"

Jack smiles. "Yes. Brayden, you go first."

"No, you first." I tear my eyes away from Jack and try to spear the words on the menu with my gaze. I need a little more time to actually figure out what options there are. Why does Jack have to distract me so much?

"I'll have the garlic mushrooms and spaghetti … actually, no, on second thoughts, I'll have the steak." Jack nods and hands his menu back to the waiter.

"And for you, sir?" the waiter says, turning to me.

"Uh … I'll have the same." I mentally kick myself as the waiter takes my menu. That steak is bloody expensive.

Jack starts the conversation by saying, "So you're a red meat kind of guy, eh?"

"I love any kind of meat."

He bows his head and starts to giggle. "Oh, you do, do you?"

Is Jack flirting with me? My mind freezes. I have no idea what to say.

Jack says, "What's that aftershave you're wearing? It smells good."

Okay. Aftershave. Focus, Brayden. "Oh, it's The One by that famous footballer ... aww, I can't remember his name."

"Cool," Jack says.

Well, that line of conversation went nowhere. I search my brain for some more interesting topics, but then my phone vibrates. I put my hand in my pocket out of habit, but I lift it out immediately afterwards, leaving my phone inside. It would be rude to text on a date.

A riff of music blasts from Jack's pocket and he pulls his own phone out to look at the screen. "Would you excuse me, Brayden? I am just off for a ciggy." He stands up and walks off with his still-ringing phone in one hand and his cigarettes in other.

I'm momentarily taken aback—he ditched me to answer his phone!—but I decide to give him the benefit of the doubt. It must be an important call. I take advantage of his absence by reading the text I just received. It's from Mandy, asking how my night is going.

It's going well, I write back. *Now piss off.* I add a kiss and laughing emoji.

The waiter brings our starters to the table, but Jack has not returned. "He'll be back soon," I say to the waiter. The waiter nods and sets Jack's food down at the vacant place.

Twenty minutes later, I find myself wondering if Jack is okay. I would have thought he'd take care of his business as quickly as possible if he's on a date and there's delicious food to be eaten. I begin to nibble at my starter, but my worry quenches my appetite. Each swallow feels like a thorn in my throat. I'd better see if he is okay. Or worse—if he's gotten tired of me and gone home.

I put my fork down, but just as I am about to head off to look for Jack, he appears from the direction of the toilet. He sits back in his chair with no apology or explanation of what took him so long. "Is the food good?"

I say, "Yeah, it's delicious."

He takes a mouthful of his. "Mmm, you're right! This is really good."

The main courses arrive in short order. Jack takes a bite and accidentally smears some sauce on the side of his mouth. "How's your steak?" he asks after swallowing.

I can't help laughing. The mess on Jack's face reminds me of when Mandy had mayonnaise on her blouse.

Jack smiles. "What's so funny?"

"You have a little sauce on the side of your face."

He tries to dab it away, but he just ends up spreading it around. I dip a serviette in my water and lend him a hand. His lips are so good-looking—I want to kiss him so badly.

"There you go, it's gone," I say, a tad breathlessly. We finish our main meal, and the waiter returns with the dessert menus. He lingers by the table as we look at the choices, but truth be told, I'm not focusing on food with the delicious hunk of a man sitting across from me. "Could we have a bit more time?" I ask.

The waiter says, "Sure," and leaves. Despite how nervous Jack makes me, I can't resist any longer. I remove my shoe and move my leg up to where Jack is sitting. I slowly glide my foot over Jack's leg and move it down to his groin area, rubbing my foot over his penis—which I am pleased to find fully erected in his trousers.

He grins at me. "Boy, it's starting to get hot in here."

I move my foot closer to his zipper, gaining confidence. He likes me! My own crotch is getting quite hot and bothered too.

Jack giggles. "Stop. You're turning me on."

"You're the one turning me on."

"Oh, really?"

"Oh, yes."

"Shall we have dessert elsewhere?"

Finally! "I thought you were never going to ask." I laugh, rubbing my foot over his penis again. Just then, the waiter returns. Jack quickly removes my foot from his groin area, and I end up banging my leg on the table. Pain rips through my shin. "Fuck," I say through clenched teeth.

"Are you all right, sir?" the waiter asks.

"Yes," I say weakly.

Jack tells the waiter we are going to skip dessert, which is music to my ears, and asks for the bill. I am so turned on, and I know Jack is too. Jack excuses himself from the table. A smile stretches across my face. Maybe he is off to buy the party hats!

The waiter returns with the bill, and my heart sinks as I take in the cost. I root around in my wallet, but my card is absent. I panic for a second before I remember that I removed my card a couple of days ago in order to put my details into an online shopping app. It's probably still sitting on my unit in my bedroom. But I only have thirty pounds in cash, and the steak I ate costs far more than that. What am I going to do now? I can't expect Jack to pay for my meal!

A few moments after Jack returns, he looks at the bill and says, "Hey Brayden, this is my treat."

"No, let me pay for mine," I say, though I don't know how I'll do it. I suppose I could call my mum and ask her to bring my card to the restaurant. How embarrassing. Not to mention that she would probably use it as an excuse to meet my date, and that would not be ideal right now.

"Don't worry about it. You only live once." Jack pays the bill against my protests, though I'm secretly relieved.

We leave the restaurant, and excitement builds up inside me. It's happening! Jack asks, "What do you want to do now?"

"You know exactly what I want," I say.

We find an empty doorway a few buildings down from the restaurant, and we can't resist one another anymore. We start kissing, and my hand slides down his body to the erection in his underwear. I rub him as our tongues dance together. He whispers in my ear, "I want you so bad."

"I want you too," I breathe.

"Can I come back to your place?" Jack says, and kisses my neck.

"Uh … no. No, we can't go there. There's, um, decorators at work." It's such an unconvincing excuse, but there's no way we can do what we want to do with my parents and sister around. Although maybe if they just see Jack in my bed, it would be an easier way to come out to them instead of me having to tell them face to face. "Can we go to your place?"

"No," he mumbles into my neck, "but I do know where we can go. I have my keys with me, if you don't mind going to the coffee house."

"I will go anywhere with you. I want you so bad."

We quickly dash to the car. After we're seated, he says, "Go down on me. Right here and now."

I giggle. "No! Someone could see us."

He looks over his shoulder. "Well, I don't see anyone around." He reaches over, grabs hold of my head, and thrusts his penis into my face. I can feel he is as solid as an iceberg in the Atlantic Ocean.

After it's done, I pull out of the parking space. I drive with one hand on the steering wheel and the other on Jack's groin. When we arrive at the coffee house, he opens the front door and the alarm goes off. He quickly disables it and grabs my hand. "Come on!"

He takes us to the back of the coffee house and moves two tables and some chairs aside. I begin to unbutton my shirt as he comes back to me. Our bodies align as one. I start to undress him. "Have you got any party hats … I mean, rubbers?" I stutter.

He pulls one out of his wallet. "Party hats aplenty."

"I'm a virgin," I blurt.

This seems to excite him even more. Half-naked, we cannot keep our hands off of each other. I glide my hands down his abdomen and passionately kiss his neck. I undo his belt as he unfastens my button and zipper. His erection bulges as I caress it through his underwear, and a rush goes through my body.

I slowly pull away from him, dropping to my knees. I stare up at him as I pull the zip down on his trousers. He practically leaps out of them. I stand back up and start to kiss down his body as he pulls my own trousers down. His nipples become solid as a rock under my mouth. His manhood is now bursting to be released in his white boxer shorts. He takes his boxers off. "Lie down on the sofa."

I obey. His commands turn me on. He lies on top of me and kisses me passionately. "I want you so much," I moan into his ear.

With that, he sits up and grabs the condom. He removes it from its wrapper and wets the end. "It might hurt. But I'll try to be gentle."

I just lie there and let him take control. He makes love to me, and it feels so amazing. Afterwards, we kiss for what must be thirty minutes. I giggle as the absurdity of the situation hits me. I just lost my virginity to a gorgeous man on the sofa in a coffee shop. "Thank you," I say, and immediately cringe. Jack just made love to me, not processed a sale.

He smiles. "How was I?"

"It was perfect."

He kisses me one more time, taps my leg and says, "We better move."

I wish I could lie there for the rest of the night with him, but he jumps off the sofa and gets dressed in the subdued lighting. I have the most beautiful view of his fit body and his manhood. Did that really happen, or was I just dreaming?

"Get dressed. I'm going to go for a ciggy. You better get rid of the evidence." He grins at me.

I jump off the sofa to get dressed. Even after we are both clothed, we can't seem to keep our hands off one another. As he pulls up his trousers, I push them down while kissing him passionately. I touch his boxer shorts to pull them down and he shifts away. "Easy, tiger!"

I take the hint and back off. "Where's the toilet?" I ask as I button my shirt. He points me in the right direction.

When I get into the cubicle, I take my phone out of my trouser pocket. Thank God I didn't crack the screen during that hot steamy lovemaking. Still on cloud nine, I text Mandy. *Guess what's just happened!*

A minute later, my phone rings. Mandy says, "You'd better tell me everything right this second."

"I just had sex with Jack in the coffee shop!" My voice squeaks with glee. Somehow, saying it out loud makes it even more real.

She gasps. "No way! You're kidding me!"

"No, honestly!" I hear Jack coming towards the door, so I hang up on Mandy. It would be so embarrassing if he caught me discussing what just happened with my best friend.

The door cracks open. "You okay?" Jack asks. I open the door all the way and throw myself at him, and we are kissing again. After a few minutes, Jack pulls away. "We better get out of here, just in case someone sees us. And I need a fag."

As we leave, I look over at the sofa where we just made love. All the tables and chairs are back in place, as if nothing ever happened. But the memory of Jack making hot, passionate love to me, taking my virginity away from me in the heat of desire, remains imprinted in my mind. Or was that all just a dream?

Jack asks me to wait outside while he sets the alarms. I watch him through the glass window of the door. Instead of setting the alarms, he fiddles with his phone. I wish he'd hurry up—it's freezing out here. A few moments later, Jack goes to the alarm box and does his thing, then joins me and locks the coffee shop door. As we walk away, Jack lights up a ciggy and says, "I need this."

We pass a war memorial bench, where I sit while he finishes his cigarette. Once he stubs it out and tosses it in a nearby bin, we start to talk about life in general. After a couple of minutes of conversation, we start to kiss again. I don't care who sees us. I just want to snog his face off.

Suddenly, I hear footsteps coming toward us, accompanied by the sound of male voices. Jack pushes me away quickly and whips his phone out of his pocket to stare intently at the screen. I do the same. My heart pounds. I feel like a secret agent in one of those action films.

One of the men in the group pauses next to us. "Oi," he says. "Got a light?"

My heart pounds. It's one of the guys from the bar who harassed us.

"Yes." Jack hands his lighter to the guy. Does Jack recognize him? I'm not sure. But I don't think the guy has recognized us.

The man grunts and lights a ciggy. "So what are you two up to, then?"

I shrug. "Sitting on a bench."

"Hey, Si!" one of the man's friends calls. "Stop yakking and let's go!"

"Thanks for the light," the man says, and walks off to join the rest of his mates.

Jack smiles. "That was a close one. I thought we were going to get caught." He lets out a little giggle.

I say, "Yeah. We're just lucky he didn't recognise us from O'Ryan's."

Jack says, "What do you mean?"

"He was with that group of guys who were taking the piss out of us."

Jack says, "Really?" He dissolves into laughter. "If you ask me, I think he is in the closet."

I don't reply. I'm in the closet, too, and I'm nothing like that rude man. Thankfully, we're alone again. I move closer to Jack and wrap my arms around him. We kiss again; my hand is on his knee and I am heading towards his groin, when we hear a noise behind us. Jack stops and pushes me away again. We wait a few moments and the noise is gone. Jack says, "We better make a move."

"Just one more kiss?"

He says, "Yeah, sure, but let's start walking." He plants one on me quickly.

We take a shortcut through the park to get back to my car, just in case we see the group of guys again. As we speed-walk past the trees and flowerbeds, Jack asks me about my family. He tells me that he is an only child.

"What is your family name?" I ask. It's so odd that I've had sex with him and I don't even know his surname.

"It's Holiday. What's yours?"

"Willoughby," I reply.

"That's a pretty cool name. I live with my father. My mother ran off with the local baker." He shudders, as if reliving a bad memory.

I remember Dad telling me and Mum about the landlady running off with a man from the Cock and Fox. Could that be where Jack lives? I shouldn't push it further, though—I might upset him. I change the subject and say, "I have something to confess to you."

Jack stops and looks at me. "What is it?"

I take a deep breath. "Well, I am not out. Um … I am out, to some people, but my family don't know I am gay."

Jack smiles. "Hey, I never told my parents either. They kind of guessed, I suppose, when I was more interested in the footballers than the game."

I giggle. Jack continues, "Now it's starting to make sense why you didn't want to go into Over the Rainbow the other night."

I say, "Kind of. Yes. I was scared that some family friends might see me." I take a deep breath. "But I would love to go with you. At some point I'll need to stop being so scared all the time."

Jack smiles. "Come on, then!"

He takes my hand, and we sprint out of the park. The familiar club comes into view with its neon lights. The song "It's Raining Men" pumps from inside. As we walk over to the entrance, I start to become edgy. I don't know what to expect. This will be my first time inside a gay venue—the only club I have been inside before is the Kelford Social club for my dad's birthday, and soon I'll visit again for my mum's birthday.

As the doorman opens the first set of doors to the venue, Jack says, "Don't be offended by women who are between six and seven feet tall, and don a pair of breasts, and shout insults at you. It's just men dressed up as women, but in the gay community, we refer to them as drag queens."

My eyes grow wider. I remember watching a TV show with my mum which was hosted by a drag queen, but I've never seen one in real life. I giggle, and we walk through the last set of doors, into my first ever encounter with the gay scene.

Chapter Eight

A wave of sights and sounds envelops me, and I gasp. "Wow!" I say over the music, loud enough that Jack can just about hear me. I am lost for further words. The cascade of colours dances with the music, and the venue is packed to the rafters with people.

Jack tells me to wait by the door just inside the club while he nips off for quick ciggy. After what seems to be a long time, he returns and grabs my hand. I feel at ease every time he touches me. He says, "Let's get a drink!"

As we walk toward the bar, one of those tall women in heels—taller then Corinna, my boss—approaches us and says, "Oh, here she is! Looks like you picked up a little trade, love, on your way here."

Jack leans towards me. "Oh yeah, that's another thing I forgot to tell you—they will call you her instead of him."

I smile, perplexed. My eyes are drawn to a poster stuck on one of the pillars of the club, informing people that tonight is Fanny Trix's going away party.

The drag queen says to Jack, "Are you going to introduce me to your bit of trade?"

Jack snickers. "Brayden, this is Fanny Trix. Fanny, this is Brayden."

Fanny walks over to me and goes to feel my crotch. I place my hands over it, and Fanny is taken aback by my ninja movement. She takes a couple of steps away in her high heels and says, "Oh, love, you're not shy, are you? No need to be shy with Aunty Fanny."

I blush and giggle. "No, I'm not shy."

Fanny pats Jack. "Oh, this is nice of you to come your Aunty Fanny's leaving party."

Jack snickers and looks at me, making me giggle even more. Fanny catches sight of our mirth and slaps Jack on the arm. "Yes, this time tomorrow, I will be sipping cocktails on the Costa Blanca beaches, rather then walking the floors of this old dump."

Jack smiles. "I'm sure you will. Where's Polly tonight?"

Fanny rolls her eyes. "Oh, that slut is probably up a lane somewhere, with her knickers and tights around her ankles."

Jack melts into laughter. Fanny walks off, tossing one last comment over her shoulder at Jack. "I prefer the other one, love. This one got a lot of meat on her."

Jack laughs harder, and Fanny cackles as she walks off to insult her next victim. I nudge Jack. "Who is Polly?"

"It's the other drag queen who works here."

We walk over to the bar. Other guys wink and call Jack by his name. I am amazed at the amount of people who know Jack here. And he knows them, too. I mutter to myself, "Seems like Jack is one popular guy."

Jack orders two pints of lager for us. "I am just off for a slash and ciggy. I will be right back." He kisses me on the lips. It feels so good—I don't want those lips to separate from mine. He walks off to do his business. A few minutes later, he returns and says, "Come on. Let's head down to the dance floor area."

We walk down to what seems to be a raised balcony off the dance floor, with a few padded stools scattered across the carpet. We pick a stool each, and Jack leans forward to take a sip of his drink. "Are you enjoying yourself?" he yells over the music.

I smile back and nod. The truth is, I am worried that one or another of my family's friends could be in the club. It is the weekend, after all. But I don't have much time to worry before Jack asks me, "Do you want to dance with me?"

I stand up and head to the dance floor with him. A crowd of people stand on the stage, with the drag queen Fanny Trix rolling her eyes at the large group that has invaded her territory. The music reminds me of a film I once saw, with a catchy chorus about working nine to five. It suddenly hits me—this song is just like my life! I follow Jack as he demonstrates how the dance goes.

After several minutes of laughing over my attempts to dance, we walk back up to our drinks. Jack fishes inside his pocket, takes out his phone, and then places it back. He says, "Hey, you ready to make a move?"

I say, "Sure," and I finish my drink. As we walk back through the club, we spot Fanny trying to scrounge drinks from guys at the bar. She is all over them like a rash. I see her poke her tongue out at Jack, and he does not react.

We reach the club exit, the music fading to a soft serenade in the background. Jack smiles. "Well, there's two things you can tick off your bucket list tonight."

I smile back. "Go on. What do you mean?"

"Well, you're not a virgin anymore, and you survived your first gay club."

I snicker. As we reach the shortcut through the park, I kiss Jack, and he does not refuse me. I just can't resist the temptation. I push Jack up against a tree, and our kiss deepens. I can see and feel Jack getting turned on. "We should go behind the bushes," he groans.

"It's dark, and I can't see," I stammer.

"Then we'll use the light on my phone."

Before I know it, we are in the wooded part of the park. I start to undo his shirt, but he stops me, moving my hand down to his trousers. He puts his hand on my bum and squeezes it firmly. My skin blazes all over. Despite the cold air, I might as well be walking through fire. He undoes the button on my trousers and pulls them down along with my boxer shorts. "Bend over against the tree," he commands as he opens his wallet to take out another condom.

He makes love to me until he climaxes for the second time in a night. It doesn't seem to last as long as the first time. I feel his lips on my neck. "You have a great ass," he whispers.

I turn around and start kissing him again until he pulls away. "We have to start going home before it gets too late. I need a shower," he says.

"I need a shower too," I say.

We both get dressed, and he lights up a cigarette as we head back through the bushes and trees to the park's main path. I grab his hand. "Wow, I can't believe I had sex twice in one night on the first go."

Jack giggles. "How was it for you?"

"It was amazing, and I feel horny again." As we are about to reach the park exit, I swallow. I need to tell him I am falling in love with him. I just need the right moment. No— fuck it. There's no time like the present.

I stop Jack and move in front of him as he finishes his ciggy. I take both of his hands in mine. "I need to tell you something."

His deep blue eyes are like twin lakes. "What, Brayden?"

I take a deep breath. "I am falling in love with you."

There's silence. Jack releases my hands from his. My stomach sinks down to my feet. Why did I say that? He must think I'm so clingy and naïve.

Finally, Jack opens his mouth to reply, but a guy passes and looks at us. After several more moments of silence, Jack says, "Well, I guess this is where we say goodnight."

"Can I give you a lift?" Maybe if we spend more time together on the drive home, he'll say whatever he was planning on saying.

"No, that's okay. I'll walk."

We kiss, but there's no tongue, and I wrap my arms around Jack. As I release him, I can see the shadow of a figure a few yards up the path. "Can I see you again?" I ask.

"Sure. I will send you a text."

Well, I suppose it's a good sign that he's not breaking up with me right now. I walk out of the park alone, but I take a sneaky look back to see Jack running up the path, heading away from me. Odd.

The night is lovely, so I think I'll walk home and come back for my car in the morning. Some exercise will help me process all the emotions inside me. I open my car door to fish my house key out of the door panel. By the time I close the door and look back into the park again, there's no sign of Jack. The birds are breaking into their early morning song.

I check that all the car's doors are locked before starting the long hike home. I can't help smiling. If my face was a light, it would illuminate the whole dawn sky. I reach inside my pocket and grab my phone to text Mandy. *I'm in love. Tell you all about it later.*

My phone rings. "I want to know everything!" Mandy says in my ear.

"Meet me at Rosie's Cafe in the morning," I say.

On the way home, my phone vibrates. It could just be Mandy whining about being kept in suspense, but it could also be the promised text from the man I just confessed love to. My breath hitches as I see Jack's name on the screen. I open the message, my heart hammering.

I'm falling in love with you, too. Can I see you tomorrow night?

He ends his text message with four kisses. All my apprehension evaporates into one huge explosion of joy. Christmas has come early this year! And my present is true love!

I finally arrive home. As I fall onto my bed, all I can think about is Jack's message. My happiness dampens a little. Now, with me and Jack becoming a couple, I have to tell my family I am gay. I just have to find the right time, and not chicken out of telling them. I turn over onto my side and drift off to what little sleep time I have.

The next day, my mother knocks at my bedroom door as per usual. "Brayden, love, do you have any dirty clothes? I am putting the machine on in five!"

I get dressed in my jumper and jeans, grab my dirty clothes and open the door to face my mum. Jack's aftershave still lingers on the shirt I wore last night, which sits at the top of the pile in my hands. The smell begins to turn me on, and it's only 9 a.m. "There you go, Mum!" I hand the clothes to her.

She looks at the shirt. "What's this, Brayden? You seem to have a green stain on it."

An image of Jack making love to me in the park flashes into my mind. "Do I?" I say, trying to sound nonchalant.

She looks at me with a puzzled face. I step past her before my face can give anything away, and I make my way down the stairs. As I reach the bottom, I grab my phone from my jacket and text Mandy to tell her I am on my way to Rosie's Café. But first, I have to go and get my car from last night.

My mother's voice drifts down from the top of the stairs as she talks to my dad. "You know, dear, I just don't understand it. The shirt was squeaky clean yesterday, and now there's a green stain right there. It's like he's been rolling around on the lawn or something."

It seems the mystery of the green stain is the topic of the hour this Sunday morning. But there's no time to think of an excuse—I have to get to the café. "Bye, Mum and Dad. Bye, Sis!" I shout.

My mother calls, "Brayden, where are you off to now? You hardly spend any time at home these days."

"Busy life, Mum!" I reply, shutting the front door behind me. I start my walk back to the park to pick up my car. The sun is beaming down on me, and its golden rays light the stony path as I walk past the coffee shop. It looks dormant with its lights off. I stop and stare at it. As if by magic, I am catapulted back to last night. How I lost my virginity, how wonderful it was—even more wonderful now that Jack has told me he loves me.

My thoughts are interrupted by a group of boys passing me by. One shouts, "Out of the way!" as if I'm causing an obstacle to him. I roll my eyes. This is a public footpath, not a skating park.

When I reach my car, I can't help glancing over at the secluded spot in the park where Jack made love to me for a second time. I smile to myself as I open the car door. My phone vibrates; it's a message from Mandy, telling me she is running late.

I shoot her a quick message back. *You will be late for your own funeral, lol!* I add a laughing emoji and a kiss.

I arrive at the café and find a table next to the window so that Mandy will see me when she arrives. Before I can even sit my bum down on the seat, the waitress pounces on me like a jaguar. "And what can I get you today?"

"I have just arrived. Give me five minutes."

"Very well." She bustles away to serve the next table. I take my phone out of my jacket to have a look at Facebook, just as I receive another text from Mandy saying she has arrived and is trying to find a parking space.

I text back, *It's a Sunday, there are plenty of parking spaces, lol.*

Found one, she replies a few moments later. *Just touching up my makeup.*

It's not London fashion week, it's just a backstreet café. I add a smile and a kiss.

The waitress returns to take my order, and I ask for two milky coffees. "Do you mean lattes?" she says.

"That's the one, yes."

"D'you want to order any food?"

"No, just the coffees for now."

She leaves just as Mandy walks in through the door. My friend's face glows with the amount of cosmetics she's wearing. "You got more makeup on you than Coco the clown!" I say with a grin.

She laughs. "At least I look fabulous." She hits me gently with her bag, places her coat on the back of her chair and sits down. "So, come on. Tell me all about it!"

The waitress arrives with our coffee. I say to Mandy, "I ordered you a milky coffee. I mean … a latte."

"With skimmed milk?" Mandy asks.

"Um … I just asked for two milky coffees." I turn to the waitress. "Do you know if the milk is skimmed?"

She laughs. "Hang on, I will just ask the farmer now." She rolls her eyes, and the sarcastic tone in her voice becomes more apparent. "How would I know? Milk is milk is milk!"

She walks off. Mandy stares at her retreating figure. "How rude!" She takes a sip of her drink. "Hmm, it's quite creamy. Probably whole milk."

"I'm sorry, Mandy. I should've waited to order till you arrived."

She flaps a hand. "Never mind. Thank you, Brayden." She sits forward in her chair. "Now, spill!"

I grab Mandy's hand. "I am in love with the most gorgeous man on the planet. He is FAF!"

Mandy's eyes go wide, but she still looks a bit confused at my acronym. I say, "You don't know what I mean by FAF, do you?"

She replies, "No."

"You know, Mand—fit as fuck!" We both dissolve into laughter, and I whisper to her so no one else can hear, "The sex was amazing. He made love to me twice!"

Mandy's eyes grow round. "Wow, twice in one night! Where did you do it?" She takes a sip of coffee.

"The first time was on the sofa at the back of the coffee shop." I could swear I already told Mandy about that, but maybe she didn't believe me and wanted to see if she could catch me out by asking me again. Well, you can't trip me up that easily, Mandy! Doubt me all you want—my magical first time was as real as can be.

Mandy splutters coffee out of her mouth, and she bursts into laughter. "You had sex on the sofas in the coffee shop?"

"Well, not all the sofas. Just the one by the table and chairs."

Mandy giggles. "Next time we go there, be sure to point it out to me so I know not to sit there." She dabs at the spilled coffee with a napkin. "You said that was the first time. What about the second?"

I pause for suspense. I haven't had any good romantic gossip to spill in ages, and I intend to milk this for all it's worth. "In the park. Well, in the park's woodland, behind the bushes."

Mandy covers her mouth. "No way!"

"Yes way!" I grin.

"Did you use protection?"

"Of course, Mum."

"No, Brayden, you have to be so careful in this day and age. Some guys don't care. They just want to have sex with no protection."

"Well, Jack is not like other men. He had condoms ready in his wallet. Oh, speaking of condoms …" I tell her the story of my party hat mishap at the petrol station. I then proceed to give her all the details of the night, including how Jack ended up paying for my steak dinner.

Mandy laughs. "You did well. A meal and two shags in one night!"

I puff out my chest. "You know me. I always come up smelling of roses!"

"You're not wrong! When are you seeing Jack again?"

"Tonight!" A buzz of excitement goes through me just thinking about it.

"When do I get to meet him?"

"Soon!" I explain to Mandy how I confessed my love to Jack, and he reciprocated. I'm crazy about him. I can't eat, and I can't sleep. I just want to be with him night and day.

"I am so happy for you, Brayden. I can't even get a man. God knows I have tried many. Even those that are married or living with their parents!" She pulls a face.

I giggle. "Don't worry, hun. Mr Right is out there for us all."

"You're only saying that because you have fallen in love with your Mr Loverman Jack." She grins slyly. "What's he like under his clothes?"

"Oh, he's bloody amazing!" I melt like an ice-cream on a summer's day as I explain how fit he is.

"Does he have a big one?"

"Oh, yes, there are no problems. When he was born, he was truly blessed."

We both burst out in a giggle fit. Mandy wants to know more about Jack's body parts, but we are interrupted by the waitress, who tells us they are closed with a sour expression on her face. I glance at the clock—Rosie's does close early on Sundays, but you'd have thought they'd be a bit nicer about it.

When we exit the café, I say, "Does that waitress remind you of someone?"

"Hmm." Mandy taps her chin. "I think I need a clue."

"She has the loudest gob in Kelford, she wears bargain box shoes, and we will be seeing her tomorrow!"

"Could it be … the Wicked Witch Corinna?" Mandy wiggles her fingers in an impression of witchy talons.

"That's the one." I snicker. "Come on, I will walk you back to your car."

Chapter Nine

As we head towards Mandy's car, my phone vibrates. I don't answer it—it's not going to be from my Jack. Mandy says, "Are you going to read your text?"

"No point. It will probably be one of those competition companies. You know, they sent me a text the other day informing me I had won a prize. I don't think so! I don't even reply to their messages."

"But you never know. It might be from someone important."

I love Mandy to bits, but she is getting on my nerves today! She probably thinks the text is from Jack and wants to get the gossip first-hand. I open the screen on my phone, and it's a text from my mother, asking if I can pop into Mr Petal's convenience store to pick up a bag of potatoes, a box of OXOs, and a bar of chocolate with bubbles and mint in it.

Mandy peers over my shoulder. "I shall give you a lift."

"Oh hun, it's out of your way. You live on the other end of town."

Mandy does not take no for an answer, and before I know it, I am in the passenger seat of her car. Oh well—might as well make the best of it. "What kind of sounds do you have?" I ask.

"Oh, the usual. Show stopper music." She laughs, and just as she goes to turn on the CD player, my phone rings. My stomach flips as I read the name displayed on the screen. Jack is calling me.

I accept the call and speak in a soft voice. "Hello, you sexy beast."

Mandy lets out a quiet squeal. On the phone, Jack giggles. "Why are you whispering?"

"Is that Loverman Jack?" Mandy says at the top of her voice. I feel like I could die on the spot. I give Mandy a nudge, hoping she gets the message to shut up. "Oh, sorry," she giggles.

"I'm sorry, Jack," I say. "Don't worry. She is going back into her box after this call."

Jack chuckles. "She seems fun."

I begin to tell Jack how wonderful last night was, but Mandy keeps glancing at me, trying to earwig in on my conversation.

"Jack, hold on one moment." I put the phone down and turn to Mandy. "Keep your eyes on the road and concentrate, hun. You nearly knocked one of those traffic cones over!"

"They shouldn't be on the road!" she says, trying to defend herself.

"Of course they should. That's what they are used for!" I exclaim. Jack's laughter crackles from the phone speaker. I lift it back to my ear. "Again, sorry about Mandy. But yes, last night was amazing."

"Was I really that good?" he says.

"Well, you have a tool and you know how to use it. Honestly, I am horny right now just thinking about it."

"You flatter me," Jack says. "Anyway, the reason I'm calling you is that I would like to introduce you to two of my friends. Well, they are the owners of the Over the Rainbow club, and it's the closing party this evening. Do you fancy it? Bring Meline with you, too."

"Her name is Mandy. And are you sure? You can probably tell she's as mad as a box of frogs!"

Mandy slams on the brakes, and I almost hit the dashboard. "Hey, what'd you do that for?" I laugh.

Jack says, "What happened?"

"Oh, Mandy just decided to pull a James Bond driver stunt," I say. Mandy shoots me a snide look.

"Sounds fun. So, are you up for tonight?" Jack presses.

"Yes, but I won't be able to stay out too late, because Mandy and I have to work early in the morning."

Jack chuckles. "Don't worry—it won't be a late one."

Before I can reply, Mandy leans towards the phone and shouts, "Don't worry, Jack! I will be there!"

I push Mandy away from the phone. Jack says, "Make sure you do bring her. I think she could be interesting company."

"You can say that again!" I wink at Mandy.

"I shall meet you both there, then," Jack says.

"Sounds good. I love you."

"I love you too," he says.

My heart floats like a balloon. "Jack, I want you so bad."

"You will have me tonight," he reassures me.

"See you tonight, then." I smile to myself. We say "I love you" to each other one last time, and I blow a kiss into the phone before hanging up. "Why have we stopped, Mandy?" I say.

"Um ..." She gestures out the window. It appears we have arrived at Petal's and I didn't even notice.

"Are you coming in?" I ask her.

"No, I am busy getting ready for my threesome." She grins wryly.

"You really are crazier than a box of frogs!" I giggle. Mandy gives me a light tap on my face. I get out of the car and say, "Thanks for the lift! I shall see you tonight."

As I walk into Petal's, Mandy rolls down the passenger window and shouts, "You've never given me a kiss like the one you gave to Jack on the phone!"

I run back and give Mandy a kiss on the cheek. "There you go!" she says. "Now, what do you think I should wear tonight?"

"Something that stands out!" Though she'll have a hard time standing out among all the fabulous flamboyant people who frequent Over the Rainbow. I've only visited the place once, but it was so glorious that I can't help feeling sad that it's closing down.

"We can go into the club together. I will meet you by the clock tower," she says as she pulls off.

I wave after her, then turn and enter the shop. Mr Petal sits behind his counter, talking to someone on his phone, just like he is every time I come here. He smiles at me and angles the phone's mouthpiece away from his face. "Do you need any help?"

"No, thank you, Mr Petal." Under my breath, I add, "Stay on your phone."

As I make my way to the vegetable section, I pass the magazine stand. A cover with a fit guy on it catches my gaze. I close my eyes for a second, thinking of my Jack showing off his six-pack body with his matching huge package. He could give that cover model a run for his money. Luckily, it won't be long before I see Jack again.

I grab all of the items my mum needs and pay Mr Petal, who manages to complete the transaction while still talking on the phone. I arrive home and place the groceries on the kitchen table.

"Thanks, love," my mum says, kissing me on the cheek. "Can I settle up with you when I get paid?"

"Yes, of course." With my mum on her own in the house, maybe I should tell her I am gay now. Just get it over with. I take a deep breath and say, "Mum, there's something I want to tell you …"

Just then, my dad bursts through the door, happy as a pig in shit. "I won on the horses!" he crows, showing his phone to my mum. "Look at that. Two hundred pounds!"

My mum beams with delight, and she gives my dad a celebratory hug. When they've finished doing a victory dance around the kitchen, she turns back to me. "So what did you want to say, Brayden, love?"

I smile and shrug. "It's okay, Mum." It will keep for another day, even though the more I prolong it, the harder it's going to be. The clock is ticking. Jack and I are in love with one another, and I need to tell my family about him soon.

I help her put the potatoes away. I add, "Oh, Mum, I forgot to tell you that I am going out again tonight." This will make three days in a row—the whole weekend—that I've spent the night out.

Her mouth tightens a little bit, but all she says is, "Don't forget you've got work tomorrow. You must be really in love with this girl. You are seeing her a lot more than me and your father have seen each other lately!"

I chuckle, and the biggest of smiles stretches across my face. Even if it's not with a girl, she's right about me being in love. "Yes, Mum."

I leave the kitchen and walk upstairs to my bedroom to start selecting my outfit for tonight. A few hours later, my mum calls from the bottom of the stairs: "Brayden, your dinner is ready!"

I throw on the clothes I picked out. Once I spray on some aftershave, I am ready to hit the town. I dance my way down the stairs, singing some random pop song which comes into my head. Mum's Sunday roast dinner is delicious, but I down it as fast as I can and dart out the door like a bolt of lightning.

As I reach the end of the driveway, I realise I forgot to kiss my mother on the cheek like I usually do when I leave the house. Oh well. Car or bus? Bus it is!

As I walk to the bus stop, I buzz with excitement at the thought of seeing Jack for the third night in a row. My weekend has been an amazing one, and I don't want it to end—but Monday is just around the corner, and then it's back to five days in prison.

It's not long before the bus arrives. I buy a single ticket to take me to the stop next to the clock tower. Nestling down in a red-carpeted seat, I text Mandy to tell her that I am on my way. It seems to take forever for the rattling vehicle to get from one end of the town to the other. The bus heaves with people. Next to me, a young man whines into his phone, grumbling about how shit his life is. A few rows down, a man with a cardboard sign yells, "Judgment day is upon us! Repent before it is too late!" Another passenger bops along to the music on his headphones, singing a very out-of-tune version of a popular Top 40 song.

A smelly guy sits beside me, and the memory of that time I was stuck in the office lift surrounded by BO flashes into my head. I press my nose into my sleeve to dilute the walking odour sitting next to me. I wish the bus would hurry up and get to the clock tower so I can be free.

At last, the bus arrives at my stop, and I leap out of my seat like a frog jumping from one lily pad to another to be the first at the doors. I step off the bus and run straight into Mandy, who is dolled up to the nines with red lipstick and a lovely dress that suits her perfectly. I nod approvingly. "Did you just get off of the red carpet?"

She giggles. "I just wanted to look my best for our threesome with Jack."

"Uh … threesome?"

"Yeah, that's what all you men want, isn't it?" She laughs again. "Don't worry, I'm only joking."

I laugh and lead her to the Over the Rainbow club. As we arrive, beams of colours light the sky. Mandy says, "Brayden, I have finally reached the end of the rainbow, but I don't see the pot of gold."

I chuckle and shake my head. "You are mad as a brush."

She slaps me on the hand and drags me nearer to the entrance. Jack loiters outside, smoking a ciggy and talking to two other guys. Mandy taps me on the shoulder. "There's your Prince Charming! Who are his friends?"

"I'll tell you when I meet them in about two seconds." I stride towards Jack with a huge smile stretching across my face, Mandy at my side.

Jack stubs out his ciggy and beams at me. "Ah, there you are! Tyler and Aaron, this is Brayden. Brayden, meet Tyler and Aaron."

My happiness falters a little bit. I would have thought that, after confessing our love for each other, Jack might introduce me as his boyfriend or partner instead of just 'Brayden'. Mandy and I exchange a glance. Judging by her drawn-together eyebrows, she's probably thinking the same thing.

I brush off my misgivings. Maybe Jack already explained our relationship status to them. "Hi, I'm Brayden," I say, shaking Tyler's and Aaron's hands.

"Yes, Jack just said your name," Tyler says.

"Oh, right." My face grows warm. I smooth things over by introducing Mandy to the other three. She grins at them and twirls a strand of perfectly styled hair around her finger.

I whisper to her, "You got no chance. They are on my bus."

"Well, anyone can change buses. Especially if it gets crowded, if you know what I mean." She winks at me.

I shake my head and chuckle to myself. As we stand and talk, a passing lesbian winks at Mandy, making her turn bright red. "Hey, Mandy, you have pulled!" I say.

She nudges me and mutters, "I don't drink from the furry cup, Brayden." I have to work hard to stop myself from dissolving into a fit of hilarity. Mandy continues, "As you know, I like cock, and lots of it."

"Yeah, when you can get it, that is," I chuckle.

Jack says, "It's getting cold. Shall we head on in?"

Oh, Jack, you won't be cold later on! I think to myself. As we walk through the doors, I pinch Jack's bum. Tyler and Aaron are talking to Mandy—no doubt she is asking them one hundred and one questions. I chuckle. It gives me the perfect opportunity to whisper to Jack, "Come on, give me a kiss."

He raises an eyebrow and obliges.

Tyler and Aaron lead us over to the VIP area of the club, which has been reserved for our group. I have to work hard to prevent my jaw from dangling open. During my last visit here with Jack, I did not see this area—it must have been hidden away by the sea of people. "Is this really for us?"

"It's not what you know, babe, it's who you know," Jack whispers in my ear.

OMG, did Jack really just call me his babe? I could get used to that.

We sit at the table, and Mandy pushes me closer to Jack. I push her the other way, and she knocks into a passing bartender, who was bringing us glasses of champagne. Mandy ends up in a perfumed heap on the floor. No one can control their laughter, including her. We pull her back up off the floor onto the seat, and I apologise for making her take a tumble.

"That was lucky," Tyler says as the bartender straightens up and passes out our drinks. "None of the glasses fell off the tray."

I say, "Aw, don't worry. Even if they did spill, we could have gotten down on our hands and knees with straws to suck it up."

Jack and Mandy giggle, but Tyler and Aaron just sip their champagne and look at each other with impassive faces.

I say to Jack, "It's a shame that this place is closing. It has a cool atmosphere."

"Oh, it's not really closing down," Tyler says. "Aaron and I have bought the lease. We are going to be closing for a week, changing the name, and springing back open like a jack-in-the-box."

My eyes widen. Tyler and Aaron seem to be living the dream. What could be cooler than owning your own nightclub? Well, owning a toy shop, maybe.

"Cor!" Mandy says. "So what will the new name be?"

Before Aaron can reply, the resident drag princess, Polly Easylay, sashays up to our table. "Here she is," Tyler says.

Polly says, "Excuse me! I'm a dame, darling." She runs a long pink fingernail over Jack's cheek. "Mmm, looks like my supper has arrived."

Tyler, Aaron and Jack giggle, and I join in a tad awkwardly. Mandy folds her arms and presses her mouth into a thin line. Her cheeks are already flushed, a telltale sign that she's had a drop too much.

"Does he have a well-packed lunch box?" Polly asks me, putting her hand on Jack's crotch.

"Uh …" I open and shut my mouth a few times. I don't know whether to laugh, or to tell her off for touching my boyfriend's penis. What is it with these drag queens thinking they can touch every guy's penis?

Jack laughs. "You can rub it all you like, but it's not going to stand to attention for you."

Polly replies, "Oh, I think that means you need Viagra, love."

Jack giggles a little and shoots back, "Where is your sister tonight? Fanny?" Even though Jack knows Fanny Trix has retreated to the Spanish waters.

Polly snickers. "Oh, love, don't talk about the dead."

Tyler and Aaron laugh, and I chuckle quietly to myself. I know just how amazing Jack's penis is, and Polly never will.

Mandy stands up and shoves Polly away from Jack. "What do you think you're doing?"

Tyler says, "Let's calm down, ladies. This is a respectable establishment."

Mandy pulls a face at Polly, and the princess snorts. "Back off. Drag is my armour, darling, no matter how you look at it. Once I become Bambi, nobody can hurt me. Not you in your mother-handed-down clothes, nor any of the other drunk assholes in this club."

Fuming at Polly's viper tongue, Mandy glares at the drag queen. Her fingers twitch. I can practically see the plan formulating in her head, and I start to reach for her. "Mandy, don't—"

But before I can stop her, Mandy leaps from her seat and throws her glass of bubbly into Polly's face.

Chapter Ten

The two stand there frozen for a few moments, as if they're hypnotised. The bubbly trickles down Polly's face, and her beautiful makeup starts to run, like if an artist accidentally tipped their water over onto a painting.

When the first drop of liquid slides off her chin and onto her chest, Polly begins to shout. "You bitch!" she screams. "Look what you have done! This dress cost over five hundred pounds—that's a damn sight more than your mother's hand-me-downs, you old troll!"

Fear flits across Mandy's face. But then she begins to giggle, a high-pitched sound full of hysteria and victory. I join in, the laughter releasing the tension from my chest. Jack, Tyler and Aaron follow suit a few seconds later.

Polly snarls and raises her fist to hit Mandy across the face. Mandy ducks out of the way, and Polly punches one of the drink hosts in the jaw. Mandy shoves her hands into Polly's torso. The drag queen loses her balance and trips into the nearby table, her wig falling off her head and floating down to land in a neat pile on the floor. A roar of laughter erupts from the nearby crowd, and I have to hold my sides to stop myself from splitting in two with hilarity.

A wigless Polly stands up, composes herself and goes to take another swipe at Mandy, but Tyler and Aaron grab her arms. "All right," Aaron says, "that's quite enough."

Mandy sniffs, wipes her nose and lunges at Polly again without warning. Jack and I stop Mandy by pushing her back down in her seat. Mandy doesn't seem fazed, though her makeup is smudged under her eyes. "Enjoy your fall, Polly," she says with a snigger.

I keep my grip firmly on her shoulder in case she tries to make a break for it again. "Enough, Mandy. You're going to get us thrown out." I take a deep breath and bite my lip to avoid laughing again—I don't want to encourage Mandy, no matter how funny the scene was.

Aaron says, "Polly, love, go and dry yourself off and fix your makeup. You're on in five."

"But my dress is ruined!" Polly stares down at the discoloured trail the bubbly left all down her chest.

"Well, change into something different. How about the sparkly sequin one? But be quick!"

As Polly begins to head toward the dressing room, Jack says, "I need a ciggy after that warm-up act. You coming, Tyler?"

Polly throws a scoff over her shoulder as they leave. "Oh, off for a shag, are we? I shall see you out there." She walks behind them, giving Mandy an evil look and a grin.

Mandy puts her two fingers up at the retreating Polly. "I don't like her. What sort of name is Bambi, anyway?"

I try to explain that Polly is a man dressed up as a woman. Mandy widens her eyes in shock. "I thought he might be a drag queen at first, but then I wasn't sure. Where's his ... you know?"

I say, "I know what?"

Mandy blurts, "Where's his man bits?"

I go to explain, but Aaron speaks first. "Oh, darling, it's tucked away like a present underneath a Christmas tree."

Mandy still looks bewildered. I start to explain, but I give up halfway through. She's too tipsy to process much information right now. To his credit, Aaron clears his throat and steers the conversation in a less embarrassing direction by explaining some of their plans for the club. Mandy takes some audible deep breaths and asks what they are renaming the club.

At that moment, Jack and Tyler return to the table with cocktails for us all. Tyler says, "Let's raise a toast to our new club, BillyJeans!"

"To BillyJeans!" we all chorus, clinking our glasses. Mandy takes a sip of her cocktail just as a new song comes on over the speakers. "Oh, this is my favourite!" She leaps to her feet and grabs hold of my hand. I decline, so she lets go and runs to the dance floor alone.

Tyler and Aaron are kissing one another. I move around to Jack, running my hand up his leg and kissing him slowly.

I'm just starting to undo his shirt when Mandy comes back to the table. "That's my weeks' worth of exercise! Looks like you lot have been having a little tounge exercise."

I pull back from Jack and snicker. I'm just about to make a joke about my own version of exercise when a familiar figure catches my eye. Enzo, the post guy from work, is perched on a stool at the corner of the bar.

I gently kick Mandy, who seems to be doing her own research on her phone about how drag queens tuck their penises away. I roll my eyes. "Mandy, is that Enzo from work?"

She looks up and squints in the direction I point. "Oh, fuck, it is," she says.

"I thought it was. I never knew he was gay."

"Neither did I." She sucks on the straw of her cocktail.

"Well, we don't know for sure that he doesn't like women. This might be your chance to get some cock tonight. You know what they say—good things come to those who wait, and tonight is your turn, hun."

"Piss off, Brayden," she mumbles into her drink. Jack, Tyler, Aaron and I burst into laughter, and Mandy puts her middle finger up at us.

"Who is Enzo?" Jack asks. I explain it to him, and at that moment, Enzo slides off his stool and walks past our table.

Mandy shouts, "Hi Enzo!"

I groan inwardly. You gobycow, Mandy! Now we are going to be stuck with Enzo all night!

Enzo pauses. "Oh, hi, Mandy. Brayden."

"I never knew you were gay!" Mandy blurts.

I glance at Mandy and pull a face. Enzo snickers. "That's because I'm not. You look so different out of your work clothes."

Mandy says, "If you're not gay, then why are you in here?"

I poke her. "You don't have to be gay to visit a gay club. Obviously. I mean, you're here. Although, let's not forget, you nearly pulled when we arrived."

Mandy says, "Piss off," and takes a sip of her drink.

Jack and Enzo laugh. Enzo tells us he just likes to come here because of all the hen parties.

"Now you know why he is not gay," I say.

"Oh, shut your face." Mandy slaps my hand and turns to Enzo. "Come on, I'm bored of third-wheeling. Let's dance." Before Enzo can say anything, Mandy whisks him off to the dance floor.

I say to Jack, "Alone at last."

He sips his cocktail, leans over and kisses me. I feel as if I am melting like those ice cubes in our drinks. Time seems to stop as I lose myself in him.

Jack pulls back and looks over my shoulder. "Well, the privacy was good while it lasted."

"Huh?" I turn to see Mandy and Enzo coming back to the table together, hand-in-hand. I smirk at Mandy. "Oh, yeah? What's going on here?"

Mandy blushes. "Um …" She glances at Enzo, who is all smiles.

Jack looks at his phone. "Hey, did you know it's almost 12:30 a.m.?"

My eyes go wide. "12:30 a.m.! Shit, we'd better go, Mand. We have work in the morning. You too, Enzo." I shake my head. "Christ, I'm sounding like my mother."

"Ugh, you're right." Mandy rolls her eyes.

"Okay," I say. "We will finish our drinks and make a move."

"What about me?" Jack pouts. "I feel neglected."

"Come here," I say, launching myself onto Jack's lap. I feel a sudden bump, and he smiles at me and kisses me more. I am so horny, and I know he is too, because I can feel it.

"Follow me to the bathroom in two minutes," he whispers, biting my ear. "I want you now."

"I want you." I lift myself off Jack's knee and sit back down on the seat.

Jack says, "I am just off for a ciggy," as he gives me a sly wink. I turn around to check whether Mandy saw our little exchange, but she's too busy with her tongue down Enzo's throat.

I rub my eyes to make sure I'm seeing this correctly. Someone Mandy has always been rude to is now her conquest of the night. I glance at my watch, waiting uncomfortably until the two minutes is up. "I am just going to kiss Jack goodnight," I say to Mandy as I stand up.

She doesn't even pause in her making out, but she lifts a hand to wave goodbye to me. Well, I'm glad Mandy is getting some action, even if it's not from someone I would have picked.

I make my way to the bathroom, where Jack is waiting with his hand down his trousers. Several other couples are making out in the area. Jack says, "Come on, follow me," and leads me to a fire exit door.

We step outside into a secluded alleyway, with the light from the doorway scattering over the ground. Jack closes the door, plunging us into pitch darkness, and takes my hand. "Keep following me."

As I do, sounds of moaning and sighing surround us. "What's that noise?" I ask.

He just laughs, and my face grows hot as I realise there must be a lot of people having sex out here in the blackness.

"I can't see a thing," I tell him.

"Shhhh. We are nearly there."

We keep walking. I knock over a bottle, and the sound rings out all around. Voices shout in the darkness to be quiet. We both snicker, and Jack continues to lead me to the back of the alleyway.

"Where are we going?" I ask.

Suddenly, he stops and pushes me down on a hard, slightly curved surface. The bonnet of a car, maybe? "Go down on your knees," he says.

I obey, my heart thumping. I hear the sound of him undoing the zipper on his trousers. "Pull my boxer shorts down," he says.

I feel my way to his waistband and slide my fingers inside, looking up towards his voice, although I can't see his face because of the dark. I can sense he is enjoying himself. Before I know it, we are kissing and touching one another all over our hot bodies. I undo my trousers and pull them off.

Jack's hand creeps inside my boxer shorts and eases them down.

Our tongues dance inside each other's mouths. Jack makes love to me on what I think is a bonnet of a car. He is so gentle with me, and I feel like I am in paradise. He finishes with a grunt. I sigh. Fuck, that was amazing.

Jack gets his breath back, and a cigarette flares in the dark, illuminating his face as he takes a drag. "Did you use protection?" I ask Jack.

"No," he says. "But don't worry—I am clean as a whistle. Besides, we are a couple now, and I am only going to be making love to you, babe."

I sort of already suspected we were a couple, but I did have my doubts tonight when Jack did not introduce me to Tyler and Aaron—who I suspect are out here somewhere too. But hearing Jack say it out loud sends my heart racing all over again. I don't think I've been this happy in … well, maybe forever.

Jack's phone screen lights up as he checks it, sending blue light onto his face. "Fuck, Brayden, it's 1:30 a.m."

Reality crashes back in as I imagine Corinna shouting at me for being late again. "OMG, I better go, Jack."

We get dressed and make our way back to the club, only to find that the door is closed and secured. No music comes from inside. "Well, I guess we'll just go around the side," Jack says.

A shadowy feminine figure approaches, tottering on high heels. I hope that it's Mandy, but Polly Easylay's voice comes out of the dark. "Oh, that's better. I just had my weekend shag, and now I am ready for the long drive home."

"Why is the club door all locked up?" I ask.

"It's closed, darlings," Polly says. "You know it is 2 a.m., right?"

"Yeah, we know," we both say at the same time.

"Well, off you pop, then." Polly stumbles down the path in her huge shoes, trying to pull up her tights as she walks. "Goodnight, darlings!" she calls over her shoulder.

"I better go," I say.

"Okay, babe," Jack says, and we kiss each other.

"Hey, what are you to up to?" Tyler's voice floats out of the dark. He and another man—Aaron, presumably—walk up to us.

Jack says, "Just about to get a taxi for Brayden. What about you?"

"We were just heading back inside the club," Tyler says.

"I thought the club was closed," I say.

Aaron says, "It is, but we are the owners and we can do what we like."

"Oh. Of course." I feel a bit stupid now. I'll just chalk it up to my tiredness, the drinks and the amazing sex I just had.

As Jack leads me around the building to the taxi rank, a guy approaches us, asking if we have a condom. Jack fishes in his pocket and hands the guy one. The stranger grins and runs off to the dark lane where Jack just made hot passionate love to me. I frown. If Jack had a party hat all along, how come he didn't use it with me?

But all other thoughts flee from my brain when I catch sight of Mandy snogging the face off Enzo, illuminated by the street lamps. His hands are exploring all parts of Mandy's body. I say to Jack, "Look at the new love birds. Shall we go say hi?"

"Nah. Leave them alone," Jack says.

Once we reach the line of taxis, I kiss Jack goodnight. "Love you," he mumbles against my mouth.

I try to feel his hot body, but he pushes me away and says, "I will call you tomorrow."

I say, "No, text me later tonight."

As I sink into the back seat of the taxi, a wave of exhaustion hits me. My legs seem to float away from my body. A soft bed and sleep sounds like a great idea right now.

Finally, the taxi stops at my address, and the driver opens my door to help me out. "That'll be ten pounds," he says.

"What?" I say. "Even though it's just a few yards from town?"

"Them's the rules."

I grab a £10 note and hand it to the taxi driver. "There." I stomp off up the driveway. I just want to sleep forever.

I greet my father at the door—he's holding what seems to be a plate of curry. The smell is overpowering.

My dad says, "I asked for an extra hot curry, and Curry Shack can't even get that right. Here, have a taste." My dad spoons up the curry and holds it out to me.

I start to heave—the aroma of curry does not mix well with the alcohol boiling in my gut. I barge past my dad, and he marches down the drive with the plate of curry to take back to the Curry Shack.

I creep up the stairs and slope into my bedroom, crash onto my bed and stare up at the ceiling. The room seems to spin around me. I close my eyes, and sleep hits almost instantly.

*

My phone alarm beeping from inside my jacket pocket wakes me up. I grab it and look at the screen. It's 8:00 a.m.

"Oh, shit," I mumble. I am going to be late to work again. Even so, I just don't seem to have the energy to move. My limbs feel like they're made of lead. But I know have to get my arse to work. I force myself out of bed, strip and run to the shower. After a quick shave, I dress in my work clothes and tiptoe down the stairs.

There's no way I can drive a car in this state, so I run for the bus stop, my head pounding. I imagine Jack's naked body to take my mind off the pain. The bus is packed, and I find myself having to stand. I take my phone out to text Jack and make sure he got home safe. Then, I text Mandy to tell her I survived the night, that I'm on my way and that I want to hear all about her and Enzo.

The bus arrives outside the office block. I run up the steps and through the reception, not bothering to say good morning to anyone in the lift. I reach my floor and walk slowly to my desk. Each step I take makes me regret showing up even more. Quitting my job and starting a toy shop sounds like an even better idea than ever right now. And now I have Jack in my life to give me purpose.

Speaking of Jack, life is too short to wait around. I have to tell my family today that I am gay, and that I am in love with Jack.

Mandy appears next to me, grinning despite the bags under her eyes. "Morning, Brayden. My head is spinning."

I set my things down on my desk. "Join the club, hun. Now, what happened to you last night with that Enzo?"

"You rang?" The post guy himself steps out from behind the door.

Mandy giggles, puts her arms around Enzo and kisses him. "I guess you could say a lot happened last night."

My eyebrows shoot up into my hairline. "So this romance survived the night, did it?"

"Yes, Brayden," Mandy says.

"Well, I never. You and Enzo." I shake my head. "You'll have to give me all the details!"

"So will you!" Mandy says. "Where did you and Jack go off to last night?"

I waggle my eyebrows. "He took me somewhere dark."

"Oh, he did, did he?" Mandy grins. "Well, you weren't the only one who got lucky this time."

"No way!" I clap my hands over my mouth in exaggerated astonishment.

Mandy giggles and tightens her grip on Enzo.

"Enzo, you'd better have used a party hat," I say.

Enzo looks confused. "Party hat? What?"

Mandy rolls her eyes. "Don't worry, Brayden. He did."

"Well …" Enzo glances at his watch. "I'd better get on with my work."

"No, don't leave me!" Mandy whines. She grins and stands on her tiptoes, and they proceed to snog each other's faces off.

I pretend to gag. "Jeepers, Mandy! You suck the air out of him."

They finally break apart, and Enzo says, "I will see you later, my little snow leopard."

"Okay, my little stud," Mandy says.

Enzo lights up like a Christmas tree. He blows her a kiss as he leaves, and she returns the gesture.

"OMG, Mandy!" I say. "Well, you and Enzo!"

"Oh, he's so good in bed, Brayden. So dreamy!" Mandy fans herself. "So, how's your Jack this morning?"

"I haven't heard from him yet."

Mandy frowns. "That's a bit funny, don't you think?"

"It's too early to panic. He's probably still recovering from last night. I don't blame him—I have the biggest hangover going! All I remember is the sex, Jack putting me in a taxi, arriving home and meeting my dad at the front door—he was carrying a plate of curry for some reason. Oh, and of course I saw you and Enzo the office clown eating one another's faces."

Mandy play-punches me. "He is not the office clown! And his real name is Eric. He just prefers Enzo," She sighs. "Brayden! When you get to know him, he is a lovely person deep down."

"Oh, I gather that you have already been deep down." I giggle. "Do me a favour—keep an eye out for the Wicked

Witch. I just want to phone Jack and see how he is this morning."

Mandy opens the office door a crack so she can see if Ice Queen Corinna is about. I phone Jack's number, but it goes straight to voicemail. "That's strange. Maybe he's speaking to someone else," I say. "Oh, well."

"Ugh." Mandy presses a hand to her forehead. "I wish Eric—I mean Enzo, I can't seem to get his name right—stuck around to keep me company. I feel like crap."

"From the drinks, or from your spat with Polly Easylay? I don't think I have seen anyone challenge a drag queen like that before last night. Shame about the champers. But Polly's face when you threw the drink at her was priceless!"

She sighs. "Don't remind me. If she was chocolate, she would eat herself . There's only one word I have to describe her: vile. And what sort of a name is Bambi?"

I just giggle at her as she mutters "vile" under her breath a few more times.

Mandy continues, "I still don't get where Bambi puts her man bits, too. The cocktails were nice, though."

"Not this again—you going on about where drag queens hide their cock and balls. It's far too early in the morning to be on about balls. And yeah, the cocktails were great. But I am definitely feeling them this morning."

"Yeah, me too."

I start to log onto my computer when my phone pings with a text from Jack. *Morning, babe! How about you meet me for lunch at the coffee house?* He ends the text with four kisses and a smiley emoji.

"Aw," I say to Mandy. "He wants to meet for lunch."

"Mm-hmm." Mandy nods slowly. I would have expected her to be a bit more enthusiastic, like she usually is, but I just chalk it up to her hangover.

I text Jack back. *Great! See you at 1 p.m.*

Mandy and I finish our last file before lunchtime, and just before our break Enzo enters our office with a bunch of flowers for Mandy. She squeals and kisses him.

"Are you ready for lunch, Mandy?" I say.

"I brought my own today, and I am going to eat it in the post room with Enzo."

I say under my breath, "That's not all you're going to be eating!"

She doesn't hear me—she's too busy snogging Enzo again.

I proceed to say bye to Mandy and escape the prison of an office building. Jack is serving a table when I arrive at the coffee house. I stand at the counter and pretend to study the menu so I don't seem like I'm waiting around for Jack on purpose—I don't want to get him into trouble with his boss for having a social visit at work.

I glance at him as he finishes setting the plates down in front of the customers, and he beckons to me slightly. He whispers to me as he passes, "Meet me upstairs in the staffroom past the toilets."

I say, "Okay," and Jack goes back behind the counter.

I make my way up the stairs and find the staffroom he mentioned. I knock on the door in case someone is in there, but there's no reply. I open the door and walk in, thrumming with excited energy.

A few minutes later, the door bursts open and Jack enters, fully naked and with a beautiful erection. I shed my clothes faster than a snake can shed its skin, and before long, we are at it like rabbits all over the staffroom area.

"Oh Jack," I say, "I don't want you to stop."

"Me neither," he sighs. Sweat pours off his body like he's in the Sahara Desert.

My phone alarm goes off in my coat, signalling that I need to get back to work. Jack finishes and kisses me. "Thank you for lunch." He pulls his clothes back on and heads out the door. I quickly get dressed and make my way to the bathroom to wash my hands.

On my way out of the coffee house, I catch sight of Jack innocently serving another table. He winks as I walk past. Jack's skill has done wonders for my hangover and my mood in general. Today might not be so bad after all.

But when I arrive back at the office, Miss Bargain Boxed Shoes Gotobed stands at my desk, her face like thunder.

Chapter Eleven

I gulp as my stomach sinks down to my toes. Corinna pierces me with her steely gaze. "Mr Willoughby, not only are you late returning from your break again, but you have managed to incorrectly format the sales reports you just handed in."

"Um … sorry?" I have no idea what she's talking about. I formatted them just like I usually do.

"I like them double-spaced and indented. I had to spend fifteen minutes fixing all your mistakes. In all the years I have worked for Gallagher & Masons, I have never seen poorer quality of work than yours!"

I don't know if it's the hangover, or if all these months of office misery are catching up to me, but my blood begins to boil. I clench my hands into fists. "I'm sorry my work isn't up to your standards, Corinna. And for the record, you never told me exactly how you wanted those reports formatted."

"If you'd been paying attention, you'd know! It's like you don't even want to be here."

I laugh hysterically. My reckless anger rises, and my mouth runs off on its own, saying everything I've wanted to fire at Corinna for so long. "You're absolutely right! I hate this place with a flaming passion. I always have. I'm sick of being bullied by you all the time. And you know what? You can shove the heel of your bargain boxed shoes right up your ass!"

Corinna's face pinches with fury. "Mr Willoughby, you're fired!"

"No, I quit! I needed an excuse to leave this dump anyway."

"Well, your wish has come true!" She thrusts a finger toward the door. "Now, get out right this second!"

I pick up a pile of files from my desk and shove them at Corinna. She fumbles, and all the papers scatter on the floor. I grab my coat. "Enjoy picking those up." I stomp out, slamming the office door behind me.

On my way to the lift, I pass Mandy. Her eyes widen. "What's wrong, Brayden? You look like you're about to punch a wall!"

I shove my hands in my pockets, just in case I do get the overwhelming urge to punch a wall. "The Wicked Witch Gotobed just fired me."

Mandy gasps, her face turning pale. "Oh no, Brayden! No!"

"I will text you later," I tell her. "I have to get out of here right now."

The faint sound of Corinna's heels clips along the corridor, and Mandy scurries away. The lift arrives, and I quickly run inside before Corinna can show up. A hot tear falls down my face, followed by another. I press the button for the ground floor and keep my hand on it until the lift stops. I've either done a really stupid thing, or a really great thing, and I'm not sure which.

I take a deep breath to compose myself and walk calmly from the lift, past Vera the receptionist, who smiles at me. I make my way down the office steps for the last time. My sentence in that prison has truly been served.

I pause at the bottom of the steps, thoughts flying through my mind. I rock back on my heels for a moment, scarcely able to believe it. Did I make the right decision? Was quitting my job a mistake? Maybe I should go back in and apologise to Corinna, grovel at her feet to redeem myself to her. But she'd probably just laugh in my face, and I'd have made a fool of myself for nothing. Besides, even if she did let me come back, she'd only make my life even more of a misery than she did before.

I wipe the tears from my eyes as I make my way around the corner. I take my phone out of my coat pocket to call Jack.

He picks up almost immediately. "Hi, Brayden!"

"Hey, Jack." I sniffle.

"Brayden, are you okay?"

Between sobs, I tell him everything that just happened. He's quiet for a second before he says, "Meet me on the bench in the park."

As I hang up, I receive a text from Mandy. *Are you okay? Do you want to talk about it?* She adds a kiss.

I text back, *I'm fine. Just upset about what that evil bitch said to me.* I know I wasn't exactly a model employee, but couldn't she have kindly offered to show me the way she wanted me to do things instead of yelling at me the second my work fell below her strict standards?

As I make my way to the park to meet Jack, I see a colourful poster on the side of a bus stop. It proclaims: "Start Your Future Now, and Make Your Dreams Tomorrow's Reality."

I pause for a second. Maybe I should take those words as a sign. Now that I'm out of the office, my life is full of possibilities. A ray of sun breaks through the clouds overhead as I resume my pace. Perhaps this isn't a disaster, but an opportunity.

Jack is already waiting on the bench when I arrive. He stands up and pulls me into a hug. "It will be okay, babe."

I sigh into his jacket. "I know. It's just … all the years I worked in that place, and I still never got any respect from that woman. She hated me right from the start. Never even gave me a chance."

Jack comforts me as we both sit down on the park bench. "Onwards and upwards, babe. Now you can find another job—a better one. One that brings you joy. You could start your own business, even. The world is your oyster!"

I say, "Well, I have always wanted to own my own toy shop."

"That's funny. So have I!"

A huge smile stretches across my face. Suddenly, being fired seems like the best thing that's ever happened to me. "Let's do it!"

"Yes, let's do it!" He touches my face and kisses me. When we pull apart, he says, "Hey, there's something I need to tell you. You know a few days ago, when we went for a drink at O'Ryan's and walked to the Cock and Fox?"

"Yeah."

"Well, the Cock and Fox was my parents' pub. My mother had an affair with the nearby baker and left my dad and me." He smiles bitterly. "I just felt like I should be honest with you. Seeing as we're going to be business partners and all."

I run my hands through Jack's hair and look into his eyes. "I had feeling it was your parents' pub. I'm sorry." I kiss him again.

"Yeah, well, it's in the past now," Jack says. "But the future is still to come. Come on, no time to waste. Let's go find ourselves a shop!"

"What, right now?"

"Yes!" Jack takes my hand and lifts me off the bench.

Excitement fills my chest. I say, "Oh, one more thing."

His eyes widen. "What is it?"

"I still haven't told my family about us. But I am going tell them today."

Jack smiles and kisses me one more time. "Sounds perfect."

As we walk along the park path, I catch sight of the spot where we made love in the woodland. I nudge Jack, and the smile on his face shows that he remembers. "Come on," he says, and he drags me behind the bushes.

Our mouths collide, and the bulge in his trousers presses against my leg, waiting to explode. He places my hand on his trapped penis and guides it up and down. Then, he pushes me onto my knees and undoes his zipper. His penis emerges, and he places it in my mouth, pushing back and forth— slowly to begin with. As I suck, he groans and moves faster, and my body fizzes with the excitement of pleasing him so much. Before long, he pulls out and ejaculates on my face. He looks down at me and smiles.

I find an old piece of tissue in my coat and I wipe my face clean. He does his trousers back up and pulls me to my feet. We kiss again, long and slow, before we head off into the town centre to look for empty shops.

Jack says, "Have you got any money to put a deposit down for a lease?"

"I have a few months of savings I could use. And I am sure my parents would help." Oh God, my parents doesn't know I am gay or that I've been fired yet. I'll have to tell them tonight. I don't know which piece of news will shock them more.

Jack says, "Speaking of your parents, when do I get to meet them?"

"Very soon?"

Jack grins.

"When can I meet your dad?" I ask.

"Soon, Brayden. He is not in a good place at the moment. Mum leaving took a toll on him. Even getting out of bed every day is a chore for him."

"Oh, Jack." I hug him.

"Look!" he says suddenly.

"What?" I turn around to stare in the direction he's pointing. A boarded-up building sits between a bank and a men's clothes shop. I walk up and peer into the windows. It's small, but kind of cute, and looks to be in good repair. A sign on the front says 'To Let'.

"Go on, Brayden. Call the letting agent's number on the board," Jack urges.

The next few hours pass in a blur. The letting agent takes my details on the phone and arrives a short while later to show us around the inside of the shop. I can almost see the shelves and racks of toys filling up the space already. It's perfect.

The letting agent lets me and Jack explore the shop on our own while she makes a call. We walk to the back of the shop and admire the place—the large windows, the slope of the roof. Jack glances at me. "What do you think?"

I say, "I think it's perfect. What about you?"

He replies, "Yeah, it's perfect. But I think we need to look around a bit more." He grins and pulls me into a hidden corner behind an angle in the wall, and elation fills my body as he pushes me against the plasterboard and starts to kiss me. Our tongues lock together, and Jack moves my hand down to his waistband, pulling his neatly-ironed shirt out from his trousers. My hand finds his penis, which starts to get excited … but not for long, as we hear footsteps coming toward us.

I snatch my hand away from Jack's crotch just as the letting agent says, "So, what do you both think?"

Jack sniggers. I say, "Could you give us a few more moments? We want to have one final look."

After one last circuit of the shop, this time without any kissing, Jack and I tell the letting agent that we want the shop. She hands me a card with the landlord's contact details so I can pay the deposit.

I'll have to talk to my parents about lending me the money right away. I can't lose this beautiful building when I've only just found it. What started out as a bad day has become a good one, and I hope it will continue. Especially with the bombshells I have to drop on my family later.

Jack tells me he has to head off home to prepare his dad's tea and check that the old man has taken his medicine. He hugs me and gives me a sly bite on my cold earlobe. I grin. He lights up a fag and walks off.

I take one last look at the shop—what could be a new chapter in my life—and take a slow walk home. I fish my phone out of my pocket, and in a moment of madness, I call the landlord's number on the business card the agent gave to me.

The landlord answers and informs me that he requires a deposit and a month's rent. Once he has those, the shop is ours.

I tell the landlord that is fine—Jack and I will contact him in a few days to sort out the transfer of that money. I text Jack to tell him, and just as I am about to the reach the corner of my street, the clouds build a fortress. It's going to rain very soon.

My phone pings with a text from Jack. *Cool*, followed by a smiling emoji and two kisses. I suck in a breath. Today could stay great, or it could quickly go downhill, given the news I am about to tell my mum and dad.

Chapter Twelve

As I arrive home, my heart sinks, and crazy thoughts flow into my brain. What if my parents disown me and they throw me out? I turn the key to open the door. Get a grip, Brayden. You can do this.

I open the door, and joyful voices and laughter come from the dining room. I don't think my family heard me open the door. I take off my coat, hang it up and walk in to join them.

My mum is writing out her last-minute invitations for her birthday party, and my sister is laughing at old photographs of us. My dad is making everyone a cuppa—he must have just finished work.

My mum looks up at me. "Brayden, love, you're home early."

My tongue freezes. Just a few minutes ago, I had my whole speech planned out—now, everything I was going to say has disbanded from my mind.

I stand in the middle of the room, staring at my dad in the kitchen. My mum says, "Are you all right, Brayden?"

I stammer for a few seconds before I regain control of my speech. "Yes, we were allowed to finish early." I sigh. Judging by the look on her face, my mum does not believe me.

I turn and look at the photographs Samatha is thumbing through. I give her a watery grin. "Remember that one where you were dancing and your trousers fell down?"

Samantha roars with laughter. I try to join her, but I only manage a weak chuckle.

My dad comes in with three mugs of tea, the hot steam evaporating into the room. "Brayden, if I knew you were coming home, I would have made you a cuppa."

I smile. "It's all right, Dad. I am not thirsty."

My mum laughs at another photograph my sister's holding up. "Oh, that brings back memories."

With all my family present, I have to find the voice within me to tell them my two huge pieces of news. Which one should I say first? How can I be tactful about this? A brief silence hangs in the air between my family's fits of laughter, and before I can stop myself, the words "I have lost my job" roll off my tongue.

Everyone goes quiet. My mum puts her pen down, leaps from her chair and throws her arms around me. It reminds me of how she used to hold me when I was little and had fallen over. Those childhood treasures start flowing back into my mind. I hope I get to keep them after tonight.

Mum says, "Oh, love, what happened?"

My sister and dad stare at me. I take a deep breath and explain what happened, each word lessening the weight on my chest. When I'm done, my mum hugs me and kisses me on the cheek. "Things happen for a reason," she says. "You'll be on to bigger and better things soon!"

"Yeah, Mum." I grin. "And speaking of bigger and better things ... I have some exciting news."

"Well, tell us!" my dad says.

After a long pause for suspense, I drop my bombshell. "Jack and I are opening our very own toy shop!"

They blink at me. "Who's Jack?" Samantha says.

For a moment, I consider taking the easy way out. I could tell them Jack is just a friend, just a business partner. But all this time, I have had to lie, and I'm done with it. I have to tell my family who I am at long last.

I pull the spare chair out from under the table and sit down. I clasp both my hands together and push my thumb into the other hand. Come on, I just have to spit it out. "So ... I am gay, and Jack is my boyfriend."

Silence. My family sits like frozen statues.

Sweat breaks out on my forehead. Words come tumbling out, desperate to fill in this empty space. "There was no girl I was dating from work. It was a guy—I met him in the new coffee house, and we went out for drinks, and it just grew from there. I am so head over heels in love with him. And I know this seems like a really sudden thing, but it's not. It's the way I've been my whole life. While other boys in high school were looking at the girls' netball team, I was too busy looking at the boys in the football and rugby teams. I'm still the same old Brayden I've always been, I promise I am."

My parents and sister stay quiet for several tense moments. I rub my hands on my trousers and lick my dry lips. "Well, say something!"

My mum picks up her birthday invitations. "I am just going to pop over to Shirley's with these." Her voice sounds strained. She hurries out of the dining room.

I still need the money for the toy shop lease as soon as possible. Maybe if I talk to her about that, the gay thing will seem like less of a shock. I stand up and dash after her. "Mum, mum, I need to ask you something!"

She shuts the door behind her before I can catch up to her. Okay, that's disappointing. Even though I feel like a big weight has been lifted off my shoulders by coming out to my family, it seems that I have a big hurdle to cross with my mum.

My dad smiles at me as I come back into the living room. "I forgot to check the lottery numbers last night." He fishes in his pockets, takes out the receipt and walks off.

My sister says, "I had a feeling you liked men. My friend saw you and another man holding hands a few nights ago. What a great birthday present to give Mum, eh? I need a sleep after all this." She heads up the stairs to her bedroom.

I take my phone out of my pocket and text Jack. *Well, I have told my family I am gay and that we are a couple.* I hear my sister close her bedroom door. It takes a few seconds before the emotion hits.

I dart up the stairs and run into my bedroom. I slam the door and fall face down on my bed, tears leaking out of my eyes and into the pillow. I don't know if these are tears of joy, or tears of grief. This padlock I have had around me for so long has finally been opened, but at what cost?

A few moments, later my phone pings. It's a text from Jack, asking if I am okay. He finishes his text with a smile emoji and two kisses.

I text him back. *I am not sure*, with two kisses and a sweating emoji.

I lie back down on my bed and stare up at the ceiling. I should text Mandy. She deserves to know about this. And I have to tell someone else, or I'll burst.

I sit up and look at the sun going to hide between the clouds. At least I'm not living behind my own clouds anymore. I text Mandy. *Well, I told my family about me and Jack.* I place my phone back down and lie on my side, just as a knock comes at my bedroom door I hear my mum softly calling, "Brayden, can I come in?"

I sit up. "Come in, Mum."

My mum enters my bedroom with two mugs in her hands. "I made you a coffee, love."

A peace offering, perhaps? I take sip of coffee and set the mug down on my bedside table.

My mum sits down on the bed, taking a sip of her own coffee, and stares out my bedroom window. "So, what is this Jack guy like? Do you have a picture of him?"

I smile and press the unlock button on my phone. A text from Mandy is waiting for me. Strange—I didn't hear my phone ping. I show my mum a picture of Jack. She smiles and says, "He's got piercing blue eyes."

"Oh yes he has." I shuffle my feet on the carpet. "I am sorry. For lying to you about going on a date with a girl from work. I just thought that if I told you it was a man, you and Dad would have disowned me or thrown me out. Or something. I don't know—I was just scared."

My mum puts her mug down on the floor and throws her arms around me. She squeezes me tight and kisses my forehead. I feel my eyes fill up with tears, ready to stream out onto my cheeks, but I hold them back.

My mum says, "So when are we going to meet this Jack?"

I smile as she releases me from her hug. "I can ask him to come round tonight, if you and Dad don't mind."

My mum breaks a smile and nods. A sigh of relief overcomes me. It took her a few moments, but my mum is accepting me as being gay. Maybe she'll be generous enough to do something else for me. "So Mum, about the idea me and Jack had for opening a toy shop. We need some money for the deposit and some for buying some stock. I can pay for some of it, but we really can't do it without some extra investors. Would you be willing to help, please?" My mum says, "I will speak to your father about it. Now come on, Brayden. Let's join the others." She picks up her mug of coffee and heads out.

I wipe some misty tears from my eyes and follow her downstairs. We meet my sister on the landing, and she comes with us to the living room, where my dad is sitting in his favourite chair.

Samantha picks up her magazine and starts to flick through the pages. My mum says, "Right, you two. Brayden is inviting Jack around tonight. And Clive, I need to have a chat with you."

My dad sighs and walks out to the kitchen. My sister pauses on a magazine page as she finds a juicy story to get engrossed in. I walk by the door to the kitchen and try to listen to what my mum and dad are saying, when it suddenly dawns on me that I haven't texted Jack to invite him round to meet my family tonight.

I head up to my bedroom. My parents' muffled voices float up from the kitchen as I ascend the stairs, but I can't tell what they're saying. With excitement, I text Jack.

A few seconds later, my phone pings with a reply from Jack. *Are you sure?* He adds an awkward emoji and two kisses.

I text back, *Yes, my mum can't wait to meet you*

Okay! and two kisses.

My mum calls my name up the stairs. I hurry down to the kitchen, my stomach churning. My parents stand by the cooker with poker faces. My mum glances at my dad, then looks back at me. "We'll do it. We'll help lend you some money."

"But spend it wisely," my dad says. "Owning a shop is a big challenge."

"I will, Dad! Thank you so much!" I hug them both, jumping up and down with pure delight. "Oh! And I have invited Jack around to meet you. He is definitely coming."

My mum smiles. "I guess I need to get cooking. But first, I must sort out the list of songs I want played at my party."

My dad shakes his head, snickers and walks back into the living room. Samantha enters the kitchen. "What's all going on in here?"

Mum tells her she is going to meet my Jack tonight. Samantha smiles and walks back into the living room. As my mum ponders what she is going to cook, I walk back into the hallway, feeling thankful that everything has turned out of good. I fish my phone out and I read the text Mandy sent to me earlier. *How are you? Is everything okay?* She ends it with a kiss.

I text back, *Everything is fine, and Jack is coming to meet my family tonight!*

She writes back with just a smiley face emoji and a kiss.

A few hours later, the doorbell rings. I open the door, and there he is, looking hot as usual. I get a sneaky kiss in, which turns into an impromptu make-out session. Between kisses, I tell him my parents are lending us the money for our toy shop. He hugs me and trails his lips down my throat, but the moment is interrupted by my mother calling from the dining room, "Brayden, what are you doing?"

We both giggle. I say, "Just hanging Jack's coat up on the hook!"

Jack meets my family, and they take to him like a duck takes to water. He praises my mum's delicious cooking and she practically glows from his compliments. Time flies by, and before I know it, it's time for Jack to go home. He says his goodbyes to my family, and my mum insists that he come to her 60th birthday party.

A big smile stretches across his face. "I would love to, thank you."

I beam with delight, and announce that I'm going to give him a lift back to his place. As we leave the house, Jack says, "I know it's early days, but I really like your family."

"I think they like you too. Am I taking you to your place at the Cock and Fox?"

"Yeah, that would be great."

During the drive, Jack's phone pings. It's a text from Tyler and Aaron, inviting us to the grand opening of BillyJeans.

"Why not?" I say. "A night of clubbing sounds like a perfect way to celebrate my coming out and our shop!"

"I tell you what," Jack says, "let's go and see the shop again right now."

I smile and put my hand on Jack's knee. He giggles. "Keep both hands on the wheel."

My hand wanders down to his groin, and I can feel him getting turned on. "On second thoughts," he says, "one hand on the wheel might suffice."

We soon arrive at our shop-to-be, and we stand on the opposite side of the road to look at the signage. "Have you thought of any names for our shop?" Jack asks.

"How about BJ Toys?" I say.

Jack kisses me. "I love that name. Come here." He takes both of my hands, looks into my eyes and says, "I love you, Brayden Willoughby. More than anyone in the world."

My heart leaps. "I love you too, Jack Holiday."

We kiss again, not even caring who sees us at this point. I tingle all over. Jack suddenly says, "I want to share the rest of my life with you, and wake up every morning next to you."

"Jack, do you mean you want us to live together?"

"Yeah, that's what I want us to do."

We kiss a little more. "How are we going to afford it all?" I say. "The shop, and now a place to live? My parents' loan can't cover everything."

"We will get a small place, maybe a flat. I will pick up extra shifts at the Coffee House."

"You have it all worked out, don't you?"

"Not just a pretty face, am I?" He grins.

"Oh, I know." I kiss him.

Suddenly, Jack's phone pings. His face falls when he glances at it. "I have to go. It's my dad."

I ask him, "Shall I give you a lift?"

He insists on walking. As he is about to leave me, he says, "Ring the landlord in the morning and tell him we have the money for him. I will sort out a place for us to live." He lights up a ciggy and strolls off.

As I am walking back to my car, I phone Mandy. It's only fair to tell her my news over the phone rather than via text messages. She picks up after two rings. "Hi, Brayden! What's up?"

I talk for ages, telling her everything that happened after I left the office—coming out to my family, starting a toyshop, getting a loan from my parents and moving in with Jack.

When I finish, Mandy remains quiet on the other end. My brows knit together. It's not like Mandy at all to be tongue-tied—she has something to say about everything. I clear my throat. "Hello? You there, Mandy?"

"I'm here," she replies. "It's just … it's a bit much, you know?"

"I know it's a lot, but I know it's right. I can feel it."

"Brayden, listen. I'm your friend, and I want to support you, but … don't you think this could be a bad idea?"

"What do you mean?" My excitement falters. I thought Mandy was going to be happy for me.

"Not the coming out part, I mean. I'm so proud of you for that. But the rest of it … Brayden, you've known Jack for such a short time, and now you're starting a business with him and moving in? That's … I'm sorry, but that's kind of stupid."

The words pierce my heart, and I feel like crying. "Are you jealous of our relationship?"

Mandy replies, "I have no need to be jealous. All I'm saying is, I think you're making a big mistake. Jack might not be the person you think he is. You just don't know—he could be hiding behind a mask. Or maybe you just won't work well together long-term. There isn't any way to know beforehand, and if you don't take it slowly, you could get hurt."

My throat constricts. "How can you be bursting my bubble like this? I thought you were my friend. I thought you'd be excited for me. Now you're insulting my boyfriend and telling me I'm stupid!"

"I'm not saying that. I'm just saying you're doing something that a stupid person would do."

"Look, this is my choice and you have no right to tell me it's the wrong one. If you're going to be like that, then I think

..." I take a deep breath. "I think it's best if we end our friendship."

There's a beep. Mandy has hung up on me.

Oh, shit, what have I done? I call her back, but she does not answer. I drive home with tears welling up in my eyes. It's okay. I don't need people like her in my new life. I have Jack, and that's enough.

The next day, I leap out of bed. The sun is shining excitedly, although my call with Mandy last night hangs over my mind. She was so bitter about me and Jack. Oh well—who cares about her opinion anyway? I throw on my clothes, have a quick wash and shave, and dart down the stairs.

I meet my mother in the hallway. She is in an elated mood. "Brayden, I have the laptop all powered up and ready. I just need your bank details to pay the money into your account."

I hug my mum, give her a kiss on the cheek and thank her. A few moments later, she makes the transfer from her account to mine. I call the landlord. I can hardly keep myself from bursting with joy as I say, "We have the money for you to rent the shop. How fast would we be able to have the keys?"

The landlord replies, "I can meet you there later today."

I hang up the phone with immense satisfaction. I am going to have a wonderful new life, and not even Mandy can stand in my way.

Later that afternoon, I meet Jack at the shop with the landlord. I fish my phone out of my pocket and make the payment for the deposit and the one months' rent. The landlord checks his phone to see if the transaction went through. He smiles and hands the keys to me, and congratulates us before he leaves.

We survey the shop, which finally belongs to us. Aside from the shelves, the room is completely bare. "There's one thing we haven't done." My voice echoes around the space.

Jack says, "What?"

I throw myself at him. It doesn't take long before we are half-naked and he is making love to me on the shop counter. He puts his hand over my mouth to muffle my sighs and groans so we aren't heard by the neighbours. I grab onto his arm muscles as he takes control. All of a sudden, there is a knock on the shop door.

"Fuck," Jack says, jumping off me. "Who is that?"

"I don't know." The delivery we scheduled for our first lot of stock isn't due to show up for another few days.

We rush to get dressed. There's another knock, and Jack tells me to go to the back of the shop to fix my clothes. As I pull my trousers up, out of sight of the front door, I hear Jack say, "Hello, there. Can I help you?"

"I am Harry from the men's clothes shop next door," says an unfamiliar voice. "Just thought I'd come say hello to our new neighbours. Seeing as we'll be near each other whether we like it or not."

Jack introduces himself, and he calls to me to come meet Harry. I button my trousers and come to the front door. "Hi, I'm Brayden."

Harry looks me up and down. "Working up a sweat there in the back, I see."

I flush and Jack grins. "Yep, we're hard at work getting everything ready," he says.

"So, when will you be opening?" Harry asks.

"Saturday," Jack says.

Harry says, "Oh, you have got a fair bit to do to be ready for Saturday . I'll leave you to it." He walks away, muttering under his breath. I frown. I'm not quite sure what to make of that Harry.

We spend the rest of the day putting up shelves and cleaning the windows of the shop. Around seven, Jack says, "I am shattered. Shall we call it a day and carry on tomorrow?"

"Yeah, absolutely."

"And we got something nice to look forward tomorrow night. The grand opening of BillyJeans."

I suck in a breath. "Oh, shit, Jack, I forgot about Billyjeans. But I can't go. It's my mum's party tomorrow night."

Jack smiles. "Hey, that's fine—we will kill two birds with one stone. We can go to your mum's party and then go to BillyJeans." He chuckles. "You can't let your coming out celebration just pass you by."

I throw my arms around him, and we kiss, our tongues dancing with one another. He pulls away and taps my bum. "Right, you grab the coats, and I will take care of the lights."

THE MASKED LOVER

Chapter Thirteen

It's the day of my mum's birthday party and the reopening of BillyJeans. The sunlight pierces its rays through my curtains. I text Jack to tell him I am awake and will meet him at the shop at 8:30.

I sit up in my bed and stretch my arms out as far as I can without pulling a muscle. I walk over to my window and pull back the curtains, and I am blinded for a few seconds by the sun.

My phone pings, and I rush over to my bedside cabinet. It's a text from Jack. *Morning, babe, I am just leaving mine now. Meet you at the shop.* He finishes his text with two kisses.

After a quick shower and shave, I dash down the stairs, grabbing my coat from the coat hook halfway down. As I settle into my car, I see Jack walking up the path. I stop and say, "Hey, sexy, do you want a lift?"

He chuckles and stubs the cigarette he was smoking on an old fizzy drink can lying on the side of the footpath. He steps into my car, has a look over his shoulder, and plants a kiss on my lips.

I say, "Wow, I was not expecting that."

He snickers. "I am full of surprises."

"Oh, I know." I reach over and fondle his groin area. I feel his penis becoming excited.

He pushes me away. "Later. Everyone is going to see I have hard-on now."

I laugh. "You know what they say—if you got it, flaunt it. And you sure have got it."

I park the car just a few doors down from our shop. As we walk up the façade, a large lorry pulls up. The toy delivery, coming right on time.

Jack and I spend the whole morning into lunchtime putting everything on the shelves. I chuckle to myself as I place the ten boxes of train sets in the boys' section, while Jack arranges a few toys around the counter area. Finally, in the late afternoon, the workmen arrive to hang our BJ Toys sign above the door. It's red and blue lettering on a white background, and it looks spectacular.

"All right," Jack says, looking with satisfaction at the sign. "Everything's ready. Now let's go celebrate!"

I say, "Whatever you want. Your wish is my command!"

We switch off the shop lights and lock up. I drop Jack back at the Cock and Fox pub. We have a quick kiss before he ejects himself from the passenger seat. "See you later.

And bring a spare T-shirt with you—things could get a little steamy, if you know what I mean." He winks at me.

I say, "Now that sounds like a plan. I shall pick you up near the park entrance."

He says goodbye and darts up the road. I beep my horn as I drive off home. I glance in the rear view mirror and don't see Jack—he must have run inside faster than a bolt of lighting.

As I arrive home, I call out a greeting, but nobody answers. I suppose everyone's preparing for Mum's birthday party. I dash up the stairs, abandon my clothes on the landing, and run into the bathroom. In a matter of minutes, I am shaved, showered, and dressed.

I text Jack to tell him I am leaving mine in five. A few seconds later, he texts back. *I am here waiting for you. Don't forget your T-shirt.* He ends his message with a smiley emoji and two kisses.

I grab a spare T-shirt, catching a glimpse of my gay mags buried at the bottom of the wardrobe. I need to throw them away—I don't need them anymore.

I gallop down the stairs into the kitchen, just to check that my family hasn't left any electrical appliances on—my sister has a habit of leaving the iron plugged in. But everything is fine. I am about to leave the kitchen when my eyes are drawn to a note on the table from my mum, asking me if I can give our neighbour Shirley a lift to the party.

I ponder what to do. Should I obey the note? It would mean Jack and I would not be able to have a fondle in the car on the way. Well, damn it—I have seen the note now, and after all, it's my mum's party. I can hardly say no to her.

I lock the house up with my T-shirt in one hand and car keys in the other. I dash across to Shirley's. As I walk up her front path, she opens the door, all dolled up and ready. She smiles and says, "Oh, Brayden, there you are. I thought you might have forgotten me."

I smile back. "No, just running a bit late, that's all."

Shirley starts a conversation about her grandchildren. I roll my eyes—not this conversation again. There seem to be only two things in Shirley's vocabulary: bingo and her grandchildren.

As we walk to the car, I text Jack to tell him I am on my way, and that we have an extra guest with us.

He texts back, *Who?* with a confused emoji and two kisses.

I reply to tell him it's Shirley. It dawns on me after I send the text that Jack won't have a clue who Shirley is.

As we set off to meet Jack, Shirley changes her conversation topic from her grandchildren to bingo. She rambles about how she nearly won twenty thousand pounds, only to find she had marked the wrong bingo ticket. She then starts asking about how many people mum invited, and who did the catering, and who the DJ is. I answer most of her questions with an absent shrug—all my thoughts are focused on seeing Jack.

As we turn the corner near the park, Shirley says, "Oh, Brayden, I think you have taken a wrong turn. This is not the way to the social club."

I smirk. "No, I have to pick Jack up." In the interior mirror of my car, I can practically see Shirley's brain going faster than a hare around a race track to try and work out who Jack is.

As I drive up the road, Jack comes into view. He looks so hot—I am already undressing him in my mind. I stop the car, and he opens the door with a grin.

I say, "Evening, sexy."

He winks and jumps in, and the smell of his aftershave replaces my car's air freshener. He takes out a card for my mum from his jacket pocket. "Where can I put this? I don't want to bend it."

I say, "Place it in the glove box."

As he obeys, I can tell Shirley is waiting impatiently for me to introduce Jack to her. Might as well oblige. "Jack, this is Shirley, the local goss—I mean, our neighbour."

Shirley draws her eyebrows together, but her expression quickly changes to a smile when I say, "Shirley, this is Jack, my boyfriend."

Shirley gasps and put her hand out. Jack shakes her hand and says, "Pleased to meet you, Shirley."

"And you as well," Shirley murmurs.

I say, "Well, now that all the meets and greets are over with, let's go and party!" I switch the radio on, and a song plays. Jack and I start to sing along. Shirley seems to be trying to ask questions about Jack, but her words are lost in the music.

When we arrive at the social club, Shirley opens the back passenger door and gets out of my car with all the enthusiasm of an eager bee. Jack leans over and says, "Quick, give me a kiss."

I kiss him, and although it's quick, it still feels good. The taste of mint from his tongue lingers on mine.

As I go to lock the car, Jack realises he forgot my mum's card. I open the door and Jack reaches into the glove box for it. At this point, Shirley is having kittens—she just wants to get into the club to see who is there.

I lock the car up, and the three of us walk to entrance of the social club. Just inside the door, there's a colourful rainbow sign made out of flags saying "The party is this way!"

Jack says, "They knew we were coming. They put the flags out for us."

I chuckle. We reach the door to the function room, which is decorated with balloons and a birthday banner. Down the side, there is a collage of pictures of my mum when she was growing up. Shirley looks closely at every picture, as if she's a detective working on a case.

I chuckle and lean over to Jack. "I bet my mum nearly died on the spot when she saw some of these. I know she sorted them herself, but my dad probably snuck some embarrassing ones in."

We both laugh. After Shirley has finished her on-the-spot investigation, we enter the room. My mum comes over to greet us. "Oh, love, you're very late arriving. But never mind—you're here now. Hello, Jack, nice to see you again!"

"Sorry Mum." I say. "Big day tomorrow—we wanted to make sure everything was all ready for the grand opening of our shop."

Jack says, "Happy Birthday, Mrs Willoughby."

"Oh, you can call me Rose."

Jack hands my mum her birthday card. She smiles like a Cheshire cat and gives him a kiss on the cheek. "Now, you boys go and get yourselves a drink. We are all going be sat near the stage."

Shirley butts in to ask my mother if there is any bingo tonight. I say to Jack, " Come on, that's our cue to disappear."

He laughs, and we walk up to the bar to get our drinks—a pint of coke for me, and a pint of lager for Jack.

Jack says, "What's wrong? You not drinking tonight?"

Just then, the DJ starts with first song of the evening. The lights turn on, and beams of colour fill the room. I tell Jack over the music, "I need to keep a clear head for our big day tomorrow."

He says, "What? I can't hear you."

I raise my voice a little more, and there's a sudden silence as the DJ speaks over the microphone to welcome everyone to my mum's 60th birthday party.

Jack and I giggle as we make our way over to the reserved seating area. My mum is circling the room, saying hello to friends and family she has not seen in while and accepting gifts and cards from them.

We sit down between Samantha and my dad. Shirley walks over to our table, sipping her G&T. I whisper to Jack, "I gave her a lift, and she could not even show the courtesy of buying us a drink? Tight cow—I bet her knickers are welded to her thighs, too."

Jack chuckles as he sips on his drink.

An hour or so later, we finish having some food from the buffet table, and my mum asks me and Jack if we've had enough to eat. I say, "Yes, lovely food. We are both full now."

I glance at Jack, who is scrolling through his phone. He leans over to me and says, "I think we'd better start making a move to BillyJeans. You need to celebrate your coming out party, too."

I chuckle. "Sure. Drink up, then."

Jack drinks his pint down in one go. We walk over to my mum to say goodnight to her and my dad, who are sitting at another table reminiscing about the old days. I'm just about to open my mouth to say goodbye when the DJ plays an old family tradition song, and before I know, it I am whisked up to the dance floor to perform the actions to the song.

Jack stares from the table and smiles tightly. I think he is not pleased. He looks at his phone again and seems to be texting someone. I am guessing it's Tyler and Aaron.

As the song goes into the instrumental portion, I kick my leg up into the air, and all of sudden my trousers become loose. Everyone is clapping along to the rhythm, so I try to fix my fly before anyone can notice, but my trousers slide down my legs.

Everyone bursts into fits of laughter and starts pointing at me. I quickly stop dancing and pull my trousers up. I must not have fastened the button properly in my rush to get ready earlier. I glance over at Jack, who is still texting on his phone.

The song finishes, and the DJ points out the added entertainment, turning me redder than beetroot. I leave the stage and walk back over to Jack and my mum, who is in fits of laughter with Shirley.

Jack and I say our goodbyes to my family. Strange—Jack looked unhappy a few moments ago, and now that we are leaving, he is all smiles again.

I kiss my mum on the cheek. She says, "You can't be going already, love?"

"Yes, mum, big day tomorrow. Me and Jack have to be up early in the morning." I don't like lying to my mother, but I can't tell her I'm off to another party—after all, this is her 60th birthday.

Jack kisses my mum on the cheek and shakes my dad's hand, and as we exit the function room, I catch sight of Shirley starting to walk towards us.

"Jack, come on—follow me!" We run like a naughty pair of schoolboys out of the club door, over to the car park. We reach my car, out of breath and panting like dogs, and I unlock the doors and jump in.

As I pull out of the parking space, I say, "That was a close one." Jack looks at me confused, and I clarify, "Shirley was trying scab a lift home off us."

"Oh." Jack giggles.

"I can't believe my trousers fell down when I was dancing. One minute, everyone was clapping, and then they were in fits of laughter. Didn't you see?"

Jack replies, "No, I did not see that."

I roll my eyes. "Well, there's one thing you should know—there is never a dull moment in the Willoughby family."

As I ease the car to a stop at a traffic light, Jack laughs and leans towards me. We kiss, our tongues twisting together. My hand brushes over Jack's groin, and he pushes my hand further down until I feel his penis starting to erupt. He then eases away and says, "Come on—BillyJeans."

I smile and move the car forward again. Jack takes his phone out of his jacket pocket and texts Tyler and Aaron to tell them we are on our way.

A minute later, I pull up across the road from the club. The signage is spectacular, with neon pink and blue colours flowing through light tubes. The queue stretches around the corner. I say to Jack, "I am glad we are not queuing in that."

"Babe, we are VIPs tonight," he says. "Come on, let's go."

I say, "Can I have a kiss?"

Jack snickers. "You just had one." In a flash, he kisses me and says, "Come on."

As we both go to get out of the car, I say, "Wait, what about my T-shirt?"

He says, "It doesn't matter—we will wear what we've got on. Open the boot for me. I want to put my jacket in there."

Once that's done, I lock the car and we walk over to the club. I can't help looking up at the sky. It's a clear night, and there's only one star out. I mutter a wish under my breath.

Jack says, "What did you say?"

I giggle. "Oh, I made a wish. There is only one star in the sky."

"What did you wish for?"

I smile at him as I look into his eyes. "If I tell you, my wish might not come true."

He laughs. As we arrive outside BillyJeans, formerly known as Over the Rainbow, Tyler and Aaron are there to meet us at the club door. Tyler says, "Oh there you are! Aaron and I were just going to send out a search party to find you. You know we will be closing in two hours."

Jack says, "Sorry. Brayden's mum was celebrating her 60th birthday, and we kind of got lost with the time."

I catch a flash of a pink dress in the crowd. "I see Polly is still here."

"Yes, darling, by the skin of her teeth," Aaron says.

I say, "Looks like she is on a mission to ogle every man who enters the establishment."

Tyler says, "That's Polly for you."

Polly looks at us and licks her lips. "Aha, there you are. Now, where did I put my knife and fork?"

Jack and I start to giggle. I slip my arm around his waist. "Sorry, Polly, he's mine."

Polly sniffs. "So, where's the vermin with the red lipstick got to? Has she been caught and put in her trap? She owes me five hundred pounds for my dress she ruined!"

Tyler says, "Polly, dear, not the dress story again."

Aaron says, "Yes, darling, it's our big night and we don't want to hear no more about your dress. I don't think our ears can take it. It's in the past where it belongs—let's leave it at that."

Polly leans forward and whispers in my ear. "When I see her again, she'll be smiling on the other side of her face. Tell her from me, sweetie—she's an old washed-out bag with no dress sense!"

That's if I ever see her again to tell her that. My heart aches as I remember my so-called best friend Mandy. I wish she could have just been supportive of me. Polly looks like she's about to insult Mandy further, but then she sees someone she knows and walks off to have a ciggy with them.

Jack says, "Hey, Brayden, you okay?"

I take a deep breath to calm myself. "Yes, babe. Just Polly reminding me of Mandy, that's all." I told Jack about Mandy earlier at the birthday party.

"Hey, look at me. You don't need Mandy or anyone else to tell you what to do. You got me, and you always will." He gives me a quick kiss. "I'm just going for a ciggy with Tyler. You go on into the club. I will be right there."

I smile at Jack, and I hold his hand for a few moments before he walks off with Tyler. Jack and Tyler head off down the dark lane around the corner from the club, and Aaron and I head inside.

It strikes me as odd that Jack and Tyler went down the alleyway when there was a smoking area right outside the club, but I decide I'm just being paranoid. They probably just wanted to avoid Polly Easylay—I sure do. In fact, I'd like to avoid most people at this club right now. It's our big day tomorrow with the grand opening of BJ Toys. Should I be home in bed to rest up? It will be a long day tomorrow, but I guess you only live once. I only wish Mandy could have joined in the celebration.

I gaze around at the new changes Tyler and Aaron have made. They've switched out the hard wooden chairs for plush comfy ones, and the lights are a softer purple colour. Aaron tells me about how they want to buy a second venue in the not too distant future. "Here we are," Aaron says as we reach an area decorated in fluorescent pink. "Welcome to the Candy Lounge!"

My mouth drops open. "Wow! I think I need my sunglasses."

"Do you like it, love? It was my own design. Well Tyler, helped a little when he could get off his phone. Take a seat here. I will just go to the bar and get a bottle of champs." Aaron smiles and heads off.

I lower myself into a comfy pink chair. I hope Jack and Tyler are okay. They're taking an awfully long time to have their ciggy. An empty beer bottle sits on the next table, and I absently reach over and pick it up. I start to peel the label on the bottle when Aaron arrives back at the table with a bottle of champagne and four empty glasses. "Oh, love, you're not sexually frustrated, are you?" he says.

"No." I smirk.

"Peeling labels is a sign, you know."

"Well, trust me, I'm perfectly fine with the amount of sex Jack and I are having."

Aaron replies, " Seems you have a great sex life, love. With me and Tyler, either he's knackered or I got a headache. I am not sure which one it'll be tonight."

I chuckle. "No, I think I can say Jack and I have a an active sex life. Speaking of, Jack and Tyler have been gone a long time."

Aaron shakes his head. "Tyler's over there, talking to the DJ about his music set tonight."

I follow Aaron's gaze, and sure enough, there's Tyler with no Jack in sight. Now I start to panic. Is Jack okay? What should I do? I'm sure he would have come straight back inside after his cigarette. Did he get lost somehow?

Just then, Tyler shows up at our table. "We're all set," he says to Aaron. "The music tonight is going to be smashing."

"Have you seen Jack?" I ask him.

"No," Tyler says. "Last I saw him, he finished his ciggy and said he had to take a slash."

"Okay." But even if Jack had to go to the loo, surely he'd be back by now?

Tyler whispers something in Aaron's ear, and they both grin and giggle. I can't take it anymore. I need to see if Jack is okay. I make my way through the packed club and head to the toilet area. Male and female couples canoodle all around. I take my phone out of my pocket just in case I might have missed a message or call from Jack, but there's nothing from him.

Where the hell is he? I head into the men's toilets. The first door is unlocked, but when I push it open, I find a couple sitting on the toilet seat about to have sex. "Oh, sorry." I quickly shut the door, my face heating up. The other cubicles are all locked, and there's no sign of Jack in the urinal area.

"Jack?" I call, but there's no answer.

I head out of the toilets and make my way out the back door into the pitch-black lane where Jack and I had sex a few nights ago. I don't wander too far. In the darkness of the night, I can hear groaning. I walk back through the door and head back across the dance floor to the Candy Lounge.

Tyler and Aaron are sipping their champagne, and Tyler waves for me to come and sit down. Before I do, I take my phone out of my pocket and open the screen to text Jack. *You okay? Where are you?* I add three kisses.

Just as I sit down next to Tyler, Jack appears and says, "Hey, how's everyone doing?"

Tyler and Aaron raise a glass to him. A few minutes later, a guy walks past our table and stares at me with a smirk as he passes. Why the hell is he looking at me like that? Maybe he's mistaken me for someone he knows, and he's too shy to say hello or shocked to see me in here.

Aaron says, "We were just going to send a search party out for you, love. Well, I wasn't, but I think your husband was."

Normally, I would be thrilled at hearing someone refer to me as Jack's husband, but my remnants of worry make it hard to enjoy myself. "Where did you go?" I ask Jack. Why am I being so paranoid?

Jack shrugs. "Well, I got to talking and lost track of time."

"I thought something bad might have happened to you."

Tyler coughs and smirks at Aaron.

"What?" I say.

"Nothing," Tyler says, and kisses Aaron. "So, how is your shop is coming along?"

"We are all set to open tomorrow," Jack says.

"This calls for a triple celebration!" Tyler says. "What is the name of your shop?"

"BJ Toys," I say.

"Splendid! Let's drink to BillyJeans and BJ Toys."

Jack says, "Don't forget Brayden coming out to his family."

Tyler looks at Aaron. "Of course! Celebration all around. Bottoms up!"

We all down our champagne. Tyler burps. "Oh, sorry!"

Aaron says, "Oh, I think it's show time."

The lights dim, and Polly Easylay takes to the stage for her show. Jack takes advantage of the distraction to kiss me. Thanks to his caresses, I end up missing Polly's entire routine.

When Polly finishes her show, Tyler and Aaron rush up to the stage to congratulate her on her first show in BillyJeans. Jack looks at his phone. "We better make a move soon. Big day tomorrow for us." He takes my hand and kisses it. "I am just going for a quick ciggy. Meet me outside. I will be quick, I promise you."

"Okay." I leave the club to wait for Jack outside.

The door security asks me to move to other side of the entrance, which is just around the corner to the pitch-black lane. The guy who was gloating at me earlier in the evening passes me. He does not speak; he just lights up a cigarette and heads over to the taxi rank. Again, I try to remember if I know the guy, but it's no good—I can't put a name to the face.

After a minute, a pair of arms wraps around me, and Jack's voice says, "What are you thinking about?"

I reply, "I was just wondering how my mum's party went after we left. I bet Shirley conned a lift with the DJ."

Jack smiles and pulls my hand. "Come on, babe."

We move to the back of the club and kiss in the dark. "Make love to me, Jack," I say.

"We have to go, babe. But I will make it up to you tomorrow."

I smile. "Yeah?"

"Yeah. We'll need to celebrate the big surprise I have for you tomorrow."

"A surprise? What is it?"

He chuckles. "Gotta wait till tomorrow, Brayden."

"Give me a clue!"

"Nope. Otherwise, it won't be a surprise."

We say good night to each other with a passionate kiss. I assume he's going to leave, but instead he pulls me back behind the club. My heart lurches—we're back in the place people call Shag Alley. He places my hand on his raging hard-on, and in a flash, he thrusts me up against what feels like a brick wall and undoes the zipper on his trousers. He pushes my head down towards the floor and feeds me his penis, and I do my best to please him. He groans and grunts, then ejaculates in my face, spreading warmth over my previously-cold skin.

After that quick moment of passion, Jack pulls his trousers up as I stand panting on the pavement, wondering if all that was just a dream. It happened so quickly that I almost don't know whether it was real or not. I ask Jack if he would like a lift home, but he tells me he wants to walk and wind down after the night we both had. He disappears into the night.

Tomorrow can't come fast enough. As I arrive home, I am greeted with a trail of birthday banners and balloons lining the drive. I open the front door as quietly as I can. Using the light from my phone, I walk into the kitchen and pour myself a glass of water. I stand with my back to the sink, and as I sip my drink, my eyes are drawn to the mountain of cards and presents my mum received. I smile, wash the now-empty glass, and leave it to dry on the drainer.

I complete my silent ninja course to my bedroom and close the door, pushing the handle down as far it will go to make sure it's secure. I undress and fall onto my bed, and within minutes, I am asleep.

Ready for whatever tomorrow will bring.

Chapter Fourteen

On the morning of our toy shop's grand opening, I float out of bed at the crack of dawn. There are still a few things we need to do before we cut the ribbon. I text Jack, *Meet you outside the shop in 30 minutes.*

I don't receive a text back straight away, so I stretch, place my phone on my bed, and tiptoe to the bathroom for a shower and shave. By the time I walk back into my bedroom, towel around me, my hair dripping like a drowned rat, Jack has texted back with *See you there.* He ends his message with two kisses.

I am so excited I could burst! I get dressed, and I am out the door. Dawn is breaking, and the sun is coming up to shine. I glance at my reflection in the rear view mirror. Brayden Willoughby, business owner.

Before I drive off, I take care to fix my tie; the image of myself all dressed up like a businessman makes elation rise in my chest all over again. I open the glove box, take out my spare bottle of aftershave, and splash a little on for some extra flair. I start the engine and drive to our new shop. A slight panic enters my mind as I draw closer—will Jack and I have enough money to survive on? As my father said a few days ago, owning a shop is a big challenge . But I know that, together, Jack and I will succeed.

*

I arrive at the shop and park outside. As I get out of the car, I see Jack walking from the other end of the street in his grey joggers, with his full package swaying. We have a morning kiss, and I only just manage to stop myself putting my hand down the front of his joggers.

Jack asks, "Did you enjoy yourself last night?"

"Of course. Did you?"

"Definitely. Even with the pit stop at your mum's birthday party."

We chuckle. He hands me the keys to the shop, and I see there is an extra key on the bunch. "Hey, what's this for?" I ask.

He grins. "It's the key to the new flat I sorted yesterday for us. Surprise!"

"No way!" I throw my arms around him. Intertwined, we hug and kiss, and we don't care who sees us.

"Come on," Jack says. "Let's open up the shutters. Helen has given me the day off, but she still wants me to turn on the coffee machines for her, so I will have to run and do that soon."

I am as excited as a jack-in-the-box, and I can't stop looking at the extra key on the bunch. Am I dreaming? I have a hot boyfriend, our own business, and even a flat.

Jack taps me on my shoulder, and we open up the shutters and add the last few pieces of stock to the shelves. Now, the shop is ready to open.

We stand at the counter and admire all the hard work we have done. "Let's get a picture of us together outside the shop before people start coming," Jack says.

We head outside, just as my mum walks up the pavement. She looks fresh as a daisy even after her party last night, and she carries two large bags. When she reaches the door of the shop, she says, "Morning, both! Take these love, they weigh a ton. I think I may have had one too many of those cocktails last night. Still, I am not going to complain—it was a good night, even though your father fell on top of Shirley while they were jiving."

I am unable to control my laughter as I take the bags from my mum's cold, soft hands. "Mum, what are you doing here this early?" I ask.

"Well, after all the excitement of last night, and with you and Jack opening your shop today, I could not sleep." She beams. "Morning, Jack! Oh, I think I already said morning to you both, didn't I? Still think I am a little tipsy. Anyway, what happened to you both last night?"

I stutter, "Oh … oh, Jack and I wanted to be up early, ready for today."

Jack looks at me and smiles. My mum then says, "I brought you some bacon rolls."

"Aw, Mum, you're a star," I say. "I think we are almost ready to open. Jack and I are just going to take a picture of ourselves outside the shop. You're welcome to be in it if you like."

"Oh, that's all right, love. You're the owners. Besides, I haven't put enough makeup on at this time of the morning. Is it all right if I go inside to have a look at the shop?"

"Of course."

She bustles inside. With the town starting to come to life with shoppers, Jack gives me a quick peck on the lips and holds his phone up, positioning it to take the picture. "Make sure you get the sign in," I say.

He angles the camera up to capture the blue and red lettering. "Ready? Say cheese."

I say, "Sex!" as he takes the picture. He breaks out into a giggle as he shows me the photo. I feel proud as punch—the picture is perfect.

He says, "I am going to turn on the coffee machines. I will be back for the grand opening." He lights up a cigarette and walks off in the direction of the coffee shop.

I stand outside for a minute or two. I can't stop thinking about my amazing luck. Today has been so wonderful—a new shop and a new flat—and the morning isn't even over!

I head back inside the shop full of smiles. My mother looks up from where she is arranging the change in the till. "Oh, Brayden, love! We are all so proud of you! I never thought my little boy would grow up to be so successful."

"Aw, Mum, I have never been so happy. And I can't tell you how how sorry I am for keeping my secret about me being gay from you and Dad. I have the best boyfriend anyone could hope to have. And guess what? He got a flat for us to move into!"

Mum frowns a little. "Oh, are you sure? You have only known Jack for a short time. Having a business together is a big step as it is, but moving in together is a whole new level, love."

I say, "I know it's fast, but Jack is my world." I take my mother's hand. She has to understand. She'll always support me—not like that stuck-up Mandy.

She sighs. "Just be happy."

"Oh, I am, Mum. Believe me, I am." I hug my mother and kiss her on the cheek.

She smiles and says, "Oh, I'm parched. Time for a cuppa."

At that moment, there is a knock on the door. It's Jack, back from the coffee shop. My mother goes to the kitchen part of the shop while I let Jack in. "Everything okay?" he says.

"Yes, babe," I reply. "Everything is perfect, with a capital P."

"Only twenty minutes to go!"

"See, we have got time for a quick one."

He raises an eyebrow. "With your mother here?"

I giggle. "If only. Oh, I just told her about the flat."

"How did she take it?"

"Better than I thought she would." Better than Mandy did, anyway. "When can I see the flat?"

"As soon as we close the shop."

I go to kiss him when my mother comes running from the kitchen, holding the red ribbon. "Boys, it's time to open!"

We step outside to greet the gathering crowd of customers. My mum hands us the big pair of scissors and holds up the ribbon.

"You ready?" I say to Jack. We have another kiss. "Here we go!" We both take hold of the scissors and lead the crowd in a countdown from ten to one. "Three … two … one …" The jaws of the scissors split the ribbon in two. "We are open!" I shout.

The first lot of customers stroll in through the door, and Jack and I stand outside to savour the moment. Harry from the men's clothes shop says, "Well done, boys, the shop looks great. I can see you are going to be very successful here. If a horrible disaster doesn't happen, that is."

"Um … thank you?" I shake his hand, a little bemused. He grunts and heads back inside his own store.

"I am just going for a ciggy," Jack says.

"Okay, babe." I head inside to man the till, where customers are already queuing up to pay for the items they have selected. Children hop up and down with excitement as their parents hand them their new toys. An old lady smiles at me as I ring up an action hero figure. "My grandson will love this."

The shop is buzzing, and the till is ringing with sales. Jack comes back from his ciggy and gets straight to serving people, helping them find things on the shelves.

"Brayden, love, I am off," my mum says.

"Okay, thank you for your help!" I say.

Jack comes over and gives my mum a kiss on the cheek. She smiles at him with a hint of sadness in her eyes. "Look after him, won't you?"

Jack replies, "Oh, don't worry, Rose. I will!"

My mum gives me one last kiss before leaving the shop.

"With how well BJ Toys is doing, you will soon be able to give up your job at the coffee shop!" I say.

Jack replies, "Soon. One day, babe."

The local press arrives to take a picture of our new shop— we are the first toy shop to open its doors in the town centre, and they want to run an article about us. Jack and I pose for the photographer, and a reporter writes down my excited ramblings about how I've always wanted to own a toy shop, and how we came to open one.

Our first day of opening soon draws to a close. The last few customers pay for their items and leave with smiles stretched across their faces. I lock the door after the last one, and we cash the till up. "We have had a very productive first day," I say to Jack as I tease him with my finger around his mouth. "Are we going to have a productive night?"

Jack giggles. "You've made me lose count now."

As we tally up the takings of the till, we chat about how successful today was. After the final wad of money is bagged, he tells me to put the till drawer in the safe. He goes and has a ciggy while I finish up.

After turning the lights off, Jack says, "Where have you parked the car?"

"Around the corner, near the park."

"I will go and get it." He takes my car keys out of my hand. "What's yours is mine, and what's mine is yours."

"Oh Jack, that's so romantic. And how very true. I am so excited to see our new flat, and I'm excited for you to …"

"Pull the shutter down," he tells me.

"Oh flip, yeah, forgot about that."

Jack heads off to get the car. As I close the shutter and go out to stand on the pavement, my mind whirls with thoughts of how lucky I am to have a gorgeous guy, and hopefully a great business and a flat. They say good things come in threes, and boy, haven't they just?

I fish my phone out of my pocket and text my mum to thank her for her help today. A few moments later, Jack arrives to pick me up. I get into the car as my phone pings. "Come on, then. Take me to our new home."

"Who is the text from?" he asks.

I unlock my screen. It's a message from my mum, telling me how proud she is, and saying that Jack is a lovely man. I show the text to Jack, but he seems uninterested—just a crack of a smile breaks through. "Buckle up," he says.

A few streets away from the flat, Jack stops the car on the side of the road. "Babe, put this on." He hands me a piece of black fabric.

"What, a blindfold?" I say.

"Yeah. I want it to be a surprise for you."

I tie the blindfold around my head, covering my eyes, as he pulls off. "Can you see anything?" he asks.

"No. But Jack?"

"Yeah?"

"Can I have a kiss?"

The car's movement falters, and his soft lips touch mine. As the car picks up speed again, I ask, "Babe, how far is it now?"

"We are nearly there."

Anticipation builds up in my stomach—this feels like a ride on a ghost train, but with something wonderful at the end of it. Suddenly, the car stops, and Jack announces we have arrived with a happy tone in his voice. My excitement is building up so fast that I think I will burst like a balloon. He opens the door, and I hear him say, "Get out."

"Can I remove the blindfold now?"

There is a pause. "No, not yet. Put one foot out of the car."

I follow his direction.

"Now the other. Watch your head," he adds as I raise myself off the seat. I step onto the pavement, and the door slams shut. Jack's fingers wrap around my arm. "You're going to love this flat. I know you will."

"Can't wait. But please, can I remove the blindfold?"

He starts leading me forward. "No, not yet. Nearly there." He stops.

"What about now?"

"Yes. Take it off."

I slowly remove the blindfold and gaze at the entrance to our very own flat. The door is even painted my favourite colour—red. "What do you think?" Jack says.

"Oh, Jack. It's lovely. Is this really our place?"

"Yes, babe. Who else's would it be?"

We both giggle. "I am lost for words," I say.

"Come on. Let me show you the inside." He reaches into my pocket and grabs the bunch of keys. Jack puts the key to the flat in the door and turns the lock. The hinges creak as he opens it. "Don't worry about that noise. It just needs some oiling."

"I could use some oiling right now," I murmur.

"What was that?" Jack says.

"I love the wallpaper," I say.

"I got another surprise for you. Close your eyes."

I do, and he leads me forward a few steps. "Now open them."

My eyelids flutter open. To my amazement, Jack shows me a room full of all the equipment we need to decorate our new flat. Jack has thought of everything, down to the colour of the paint for the rooms and the perfect size of the paintbrushes. I am feeling so elated. "When can we move in?" I ask.

"Whenever you like, babe."

"Tonight!"

Jack frowns apologetically. "I can't tonight. My dad needs help with his meds."

"Okay. How about tomorrow?"

"Yeah, sure. Let's move in tomorrow. But for now, let me show you the rest of the flat."

He leads to me to the huge kitchen area, which is already fitted with furniture and appliances. "I can't believe we have landed so well on our feet!" I say.

"Yeah. The guy who was here before told me he didn't want to take any of his stuff with him, since his new place had everything he wanted. He would only end up throwing this stuff out, and would have to pay a removal company to help him. So I told him we would have it. I just thought you would like to decorate it first with a fresh splash of paint." Jack shows me around a few more rooms. "What do you think?"

"I hope we are going to get to christen all the rooms, if you know what I mean." I pinch his bum and lead him upstairs to the bedroom. "Wow, we even have a bed!"

"Looks like we do."

"Well, we could start by christening our first room tonight."

Then, we're kissing against the wall. Not long after, we're getting undressed, and we fall onto the bed, our lips locked in a deep, passionate kiss. My hand moves up and down his body. When he pulls down my boxers, I do the same to him, and we're fully naked on the bed with our bodies on top of each other. He makes love to me, and it's amazing as always. He's such a master at his craft.

"Don't stop!" I say.

He climaxes, and we lie there naked on the bed, arms around each other, looking into each other's eyes. Anyone could have seen us, since the curtains weren't up on the windows yet. The room feels so hot with the memory of the lovemaking I just experienced with Jack. Eventually, Jack says, "Come on. I need a ciggy. Get dressed."

He goes to put his clothes on in the bathroom—not in the bedroom where he just made hot passionate love to me—but I don't think anything of it, and I get dressed too. His voice calls from the living room. "Brayden, are you ready?"

"Coming, babe!" I shout back.

"I will meet you outside." I hear the sound of the front door opening and closing. I take one last look at our new home before we move in tomorrow. I wish it was today. I don't want to spend another minute apart from Jack.

I join Jack outside. He's on his phone, but when I walk over to him, he shoves it hastily into his coat pocket. "Oh, Jack, that sex was amazing. We've christened one of the rooms. Only four more to go!" I giggle, but Jack doesn't. Is he mad at me for interrupting him when he was texting?

I grab him in an embrace to show him I'm not angry at him. "Thank you for making all my dreams come true. I have never been this happy until the day I met you."

"Just think," he says. "Tomorrow, we will be moved in, and we will never have to spend one night apart from each other."

We walk back to the car, and I drop Jack home. He directs me to let him out by the park entrance—he will walk home to his parents' pub from there. We kiss goodnight in the car, and I hold on to him for several moments. I don't want to let him go. "I will see you in the morning," he says.

I kiss him again as he gets out of the car. He closes the door, and I wind down the window as he reaches inside his jacket and lights up a ciggy. "Can I have one more?" I ask.

We share one final kiss before our move into our new home tomorrow. As I am about to pull off, I toss a "Goodnight!" out the window. Jack waves and heads off into the park.

I drive home towards my last ever night of living with my family. I sit in my car in the driveway for a few moments. Just a few weeks ago, I was single and in a job which I hated, and my family didn't even know I was gay. Now, I have found the man of my dreams, we run a business together, and we're going to start living together tomorrow! Life is just great. I wish Mandy would have been happy for me and Jack, but I guess you can't have everything.

As I walk through the door of my childhood home, I hear my mum and dad talking. I hang my coat up and walk into the living room. My mum is on the sofa with Samantha, looking at catalogue full of new furniture. My dad is watching another one of those spy action films.

I say, "Evening, Mum. Dad. Sis."

They smile and say "Evening," back to me. My mum asks, "Everything all right, Brayden, love?"

"Yes, everything is perfect. Jack took me to see our new flat tonight."

"Ooh, tell me what it was like!" she says.

I nestle down on the arm of the sofa next to my mum, and my excited words flow out of my mouth. "Aw, Mum, it's gorgeous! Jack surprised me with all the equipment we need to decorate the flat. And best of all, the flat came fully furnished!"

"That's lovely! So when do you and Jack move in?"

I pause for a few seconds for the suspense, but it's no good—the excitement has got the better of me. I blurt out, "Tomorrow!"

A dumbfounded look appears on my mum's face. She says, "Oh, Brayden, I thought you and Jack would have waited at least a little bit."

I smile and say, "Why wait? Life is too short, and I am loving this whirlwind of a roller coaster I am on."

I say goodnight to my family and kiss my mum on the cheek. I don't want to disturb Dad or Sam—he is lost in the action film, and she is lost in one of those love stories in the mag she is reading. That reminds me—I still have the gay magazines in my wardrobe. With me moving out tomorrow, I have to get rid of them.

As I walk out of the living room into the kitchen, I look back and see my mum's face. She looks dejected at my news of moving in with Jack tomorrow. I give her a strained smile and close the door.

I loiter in the kitchen for just a moment, and my mum and dad's muffled voices start up in the living room. Their conversation is too faint for me to hear, but then my sister opens the door and I hear my dad say, "Well, Rose, he is old enough to do what he wants."

My sister closes the door and walks up the stairs to her bedroom without giving me a second glance. I open the wooden cupboard under the sink and take out a black bag to get rid of my gay mags. On my way out, I tiptoe past the living room and put my ear to the door. I hear only the sound of my dad laughing. Looks like the conversation about me was short-lived.

I walk up the stairs and enter my bedroom, closing the door behind me. I place the black bag on my bed and open my wardrobe to remove the pile of clothes covering the magazines. Once I've shoved the mags out into the open, I grab the black bag and toss the magazines inside, double tie it, and spend a few minutes arranging my clothes neatly back in my wardrobe.

I creep down the stairs with the black bag in my hand, hoping and praying my mum and dad don't hear me and come to see what I'm up to. I take care to be quiet as I turn the front door key and push the handle down. As I walk over to the recycling bin, I note that all the other neighbours have their bins out. It must be bin day. That means my magazines will be far, far away in no time.

I open the lid of the bin and pause to savor the moment. I have a chuckle to myself. This feels like a momentous event. Slowly, carefully, I place the bag in the bin. The moon beams down on me as I walk back indoors, but as I turn the door handle, a cat screams and almost scares me to death, somewhat ruining the moment.

I tiptoe back up the stairs to my bedroom. When I reach the top of the stairs, I hear the flush of the toilet, and I gallop into my bedroom to avoid being seen. I don't need nosy Sam asking what I was doing. I switch off my light and nestle down for a final night of sleeping in my bed. I set my alarm on my phone, place it down on bedside cabinet, and drift off to sleep.

Chapter Fifteen

The day I have been waiting for is finally here, and I am woken to the sound of raindrops tapping at my window as they fall. I walk over to my window open the curtains and look out at the rain pelting down. I do hope it's going to stop soon—I don't want to be moving my stuff in weather like this.

I turn away from the window, feeling a mixture of sad and happy. More happy on balance, because of the thought of me and Jack living together. Out of all the guys he could have been with, he chose me!

I hurry off for a shower and shave before the house comes alive, and before I know it, I am washed and dressed and back in my bedroom. I text Jack good morning with two kisses. A few minutes later, as I'm setting up some boxes to get packing, my phone pings with a text from Jack. *Good morning! I'm all excited about today*. He ends the message with four kisses.

I reply, *So am I!* and add four kisses. I then add another message telling him that I am going to start packing now.

He replies instantly with *Cool* and two kisses.

As I start to shove all my worldly belongings into boxes, my dad knocks on my bedroom door. I open the door and say, "You're up early."

He chuckles and hands me some boxes. "Morning, Brayden. I thought you might need these."

As a matter of fact, it's looking like I might need another box. A smile stretches across my face. "Thanks, Dad!"

He says, "You can never have enough boxes."

We both break into a chuckle. I say, "Is Mum still in bed?"

He pauses, and I can practically see the cogs going around in his brain as he tries to think of something to say. At last, he simply says, "No, she's up."

"Why don't you sit down, Dad?" I indicate the bed. As he follows my instruction, I think about Mum. It seems that she could not bear to be here on the day I move out. She told me I will always be her little boy, after all. But I wish more than anything that she could stick around to support me.

Dad finds the words. "Your mum had to go and help Shirley's sister with something, so she got up early this morning."

"Shirley's sister is more important than her own flesh and blood?" I say in a low voice.

"Don't be like that, son. This is a big shock to us all, you moving out. Especially for your mother. Who is going to take her and Shirley to bingo now?

"Dad, I am only moving to the other side of town, not to another country. Besides, I am thirty-five. How many other thirty-five-year-olds do you know who live at home with their parents?"

"Look at your sister. She is nearly forty, and she's happy here."

I giggle. "Yes, Dad, but Sam will be drawing her pension before she finds a man."

"Well, your mother and I want you to know this will always be your home. And if life doesn't work out with Jack, you know you're always welcome here."

"Thanks, Dad. But I think me and Jack will be together for eternity."

It's the first time in a long while I have felt so close to my father. I usually get along better with my mum. But Dad is acting so caring right now, and I can see he is sad about the thought of me leaving the family home. I clap my hands together. "Right, Dad, I better get packing."

"Yes, you carry on. I am going to make a cuppa and study the horses. But don't tell your mother."

I chuckle, and my dad goes off to the kitchen to place a bet on some horses.

A few hours later, most of my belonging are packed and moved to the boot of my car. I am nearly ready to leave. I take a box of items I no longer need to the rubbish bin outside. As I walk down the stairs, I call out to me dad to ask for his help with the last few bits and bobs left in my room.

I head down the drive, open the bin, and find it empty. Relief washes over me. The evidence of me hiding my secret all these years is gone.

As I walk back up the stairs, my dad waves to me from my room. I say, "Just a few more things to pack."

He places the final few items into the last couple of boxes I have left and helps me to load them into my car. I close the boot and go back upstairs, while my dad heads back into the living room to catch up with the horse racing.

"I won't be long, Dad!" I shout from the landing. "Just checking I haven't forgotten anything."

"Okay, son," he replies.

I stand in my empty shell of a bedroom, with just my bed and my drawer unit left. It's as if I've been robbed of all the possessions from my life with my family.

I sit on my bed and gaze out the window, which looks down onto the garden. My mind fills with all the happy summer days my family and I spent there. I remember sipping cold drinks on the lawn, and chasing my sister around the garden and soaking her with the hose pipe.

I shake my head and laugh. Those were fun days. But now it's time to go.

I text Jack to tell him I have all my worldly possessions packed up, and ask him to meet me at the shop. I get up off the bed. "Goodbye, bedroom. We have had good times in here."

I close the door and make my way down the stairs to say goodbye to my dad. He is so engrossed with the horse racing that he shouts encouragement at the TV screen as if he was there in person.

"Bye, Dad," I say.

"Bye, son," he says, not moving an inch.

I close my parents' front door and take one last look at the house as I walk down the drive. I glance over to Shirley's. It's so calm. Usually, Shirley is out in her garden every hour of the day, nosing—or what she calls "being observant." Chuckling at the thought, I make my way to the car and drive off to meet Jack.

By the time I arrive at the shop, Jack has already opened it up. He kisses me when I walk in, and I am all over him like a rash.

"Stop," he says, chuckling a little. "A customer could come in."

"I just can't help wanting you every time I see you," I say.

"Well, we will be seeing a lot more of one another now that we are living together."

I smile. "Excellent. Oh, my clothes and bits are in the boot of the car."

"Cool. Now, before I go off to help at the coffee house, I have something to show you."

I raise my eyebrows, and Jack laughs. "No, not my penis. This." He holds up a newspaper.

I examine the article. It's the write-up we had from the Kelford News about our opening day. We look elated in the picture, holding hands with radiant smiles on our faces. My mum and our first customers fill the background of the photograph. The accompanying text contains several quotes from me, though the reporter cut a lot of my gushing and rambling—probably for the best.

"I want to hang this on our living room wall! So see if you can find a frame for it on your travels," I say.

"Okay, babe, I will. I'll also drop your stuff off at the flat on my way to the wholesaler's."

Helen, Jack's boss, pops her head through the back door and asks Jack to add plastic plates, knives and forks to his shopping list for the wholesaler's. She wants to try marketing al fresco dining to the customers.

Jack and I have a little giggle. Helen bids us farewell, and Jack says, "I'd better be off." He kisses me goodbye. Just as Jack reaches the doorway, Harry from next door pushes his way, in holding what appears to be a copy of the Kelford News.

"Hello, Harry," Jack says.

"Hello, Jack," Harry grunts.

Jack looks at me and rolls his eyes. He mouths to me: *do what Harry wants.* I nod, and Jack smiles at me before leaving.

I say good morning to Harry, who shows me our grand opening article. He says, "Shame the photographer didn't catch my shop sign on the photograph. Now, what did I want to see you about? Oh yes, I remember. Look at this." Harry points to another article about the council wanting to move the Christmas tree from its usual spot, and starts complaining about the decision.

I pretend to listen. My mind is more focused on my first night with Jack in our new home.

The shop door opens and two more customers come in. Harry appears to be winding down his rant. "Let me know how you and Jack feel about this outrage," he says.

"Oh, we will," I say. "See you later!" As Harry leaves, I add under my breath, "I hope bloody not." All Harry ever seems to do is moan about stuff. Who cares where the Christmas tree is erected? I'm only worried about whether there's a tree at all.

I ring up my last sale of the day and clean the shop, ready to open again in the morning. A few hours pass, and Jack still doesn't arrive to pick me up.

I ring his mobile, but my call goes to voicemail, so I hang up. I walk over to the window display and pick up a toy which has fallen over. After rearranging a few things out of sheer boredom, I pick up my phone again and try Jack's number. Again, no answer.

He must have gotten held up, but why hasn't he rung me to tell me this? Or at least sent a text. Tapping my fingers on the counter, I try Jack's number yet again, but there's still no answer. I shoot him a text saying, *Babe, where are you?*

A few minutes later, to my relief, my phone buzzes with a text from Jack. *I'm parked by the clock tower. Come over.*

So I lock the shop up and walk over to meet Jack.

"Oi, wait for me!"

I turn to see Harry running up the street towards me. "Hi, Harry," I say wearily.

"So, how many sales did you make today?" He falls into step beside me.

I don't want Harry knowing my and Jack's business, so I quickly change the subject, even though it will bore me to death. "Bloody mess with this Christmas tree thing, isn't it?"

Harry goes off on his rant again, filling the rest of the walk to the car. When the clock tower comes into sight, I say, "Well, this is where my lift is."

Jack sits in the car across the road. He seems lost on his phone, and does not acknowledge me and Harry. I hope Harry doesn't cross the road to talk to Jack—I just want to get home to our new flat.

Luckily, Harry simply waves in the direction of our car before walking off.

I open the car door, and Jack smiles at me, mirroring my own expression. I lean over to kiss him, but as I do, I discover that the passenger seat is leaned all the way back. "Where have you been?" I say. "I have been waiting ages for you to pick me up. I've been ringing and ringing your phone, and there was no answer from you." I sway back on my heels.

He replies, "My battery went out on my phone."

"What has happened to the seat?"

Jack laughs it off. "Aw, I was balancing the stock from the wholesaler's on there, and I must have forgotten to move it back up. You can just do that now."

"Oh, yes, that's what it must be." I lower myself into the passenger seat and pull it up to the correct position.

Jack says, "So, how was business?"

I tell him about Harry complaining about the council moving the Christmas tree. We both giggle.

"I am starving," Jack says.

I rub his leg. "So am I." My hand wanders down to his groin.

He jumps. "What the fuck are you doing?"

"What I always do," I say, taken aback.

"Don't feel me."

"Oh, sorry … I thought, since it was okay before … but I'm sorry."

Jack says nothing and lights up a ciggy. His reaction made me feel like a child touching a hot surface for the first time. He must be tired—I bet Helen had him rushing everywhere today for her.

"No smoking in the car," I say.

"This is my car, too. If I want to smoke in it, I will."

The change in Jack's demeanour shocks me. This is the first time I've heard this nastiness in his voice. "Is there anything wrong, babe?" I ask.

"No. Should there be?"

"You don't seem yourself."

"I am fine. God, I'm starving. We'd better get some shopping in. The cupboards in the flat are like Old Mother Hubbard's—not even a bone in them. And we need fridge and freezer items."

"Let's stop off at the supermarket and do our first lot of shopping for our new home," I say.

As we walk around the supermarket, I get the impression Jack does not want to be here. It seems like it's me selecting all the food for the both us—he's distracted and playing on his phone most of the time.

After ten minutes of this, I decide to try and prompt him. "Jack, is there anything you fancy?"

"No. Just get whatever you want." He walks over to the newspaper section, picks up a magazine and brings it back to the trolley.

"Shall I get some strawberries and cream, or chocolate sauce? No, forget that—it will make too much mess on the bedding ." I grin and wiggle my eyebrows at him.

He doesn't say anything, but at least he smiles.

We proceed to the checkout with all the things we need. Jack pushes the trolley out of the store to the car. As we are putting the shopping into the boot of the car, Jack says, "Where's my magazine?"

"It's in one of the bags."

He searches through all the different carrier bags, unsettling most of the shopping, until he finds his magazine. He hands me the car keys. "You can drive."

I giggle. "Oh, thanks!"

He jumps into the passenger seat and unwraps the plastic on the front of the magazine, like a kid greedily opening a new toy. He starts reading all the celebrity gossip from front to back.

"The shopping trolley just needs taking back," I say, hoping Jack will oblige. Instead, he flicks through the pages and says, "Okay, babe," without raising his head.

At least he seems to be in a better mood. But to make sure he stays happy, I need to make our first night in our new home special and sexy. My strawberries-and-cream and chocolate sauce joke from earlier might just have to become a reality.

I head back into the store and walk on over to the fruit and veg counter for a pack of strawberries. Then, I go to the fridge and pick up a carton of cream. But cream will spill everywhere and make too much mess on our new bedclothes.

I glance around the supermarket to see what else I could use. A lady passes by me with her shopping trolley, and I notice she has a tube of squirty chocolate in her basket. That's it! Strawberries and chocolate—the perfect combination to eat off Jack's hot body later. Although I had my doubts about the chocolate sauce in the beginning, it will be much harder to spill—and worst comes to worst, I did buy some stain remover as part of our shopping.

I pay for the strawberries and chocolate. The sales assistant giggles to herself, as if she knows what I am going to use them for. She thanks me and says goodbye. I take a sly glance over my shoulder as I leave the store, and she's watching and chuckling as she talks to her colleague.

As I walk back across the car park, all I can think of is Jack lying in bed with the strawberries placed on different parts of his body, topped up with heapings of squirty chocolate. When I arrive at the car, Jack is still reading his magazine, glancing at his phone every few moments. He doesn't even ask me why I took so long. Maybe he didn't even notice I was gone, if the magazine is that interesting.

I sit in the driver's seat and awkwardly tap my fingers on the steering wheel. Jack lifts his head up. "What are you doing?"

"I am not sure of the way. I have only been to our flat once."

"You know where to go." He snickers.

"I really don't know, babe."

"Ugh." He passes me the magazine. "Swap seats with me. Hold on to this. I don't want to lose my place."

"Okay." I walk around to the passenger side, and he jumps over to the driver's seat. He starts the engine and turns on the stereo. We both sing along to the song playing on the radio as we travel towards our flat.

"I have a surprise for you after dinner," I say.

Jack keeps singing with his eyes trained on the road. I guess I am wasting my breath.

We arrive home. He reaches over and grabs his magazine, then heads off to open the flat door, leaving me to struggle with the carrier bags. "Oi, Jack, help me with the shopping!" I shout. "You can read your mag later! We need to get this food in the fridge and freezer before it defrosts."

Jack slowly walks back to the car. "It's your shopping."

"No, it's ours," I say.

He opens the boot of the car. "You bought far too much."

"Well, there are two of us."

We make our way up the stairs to the kitchen and place the shopping bags we managed to carry on the table. Jack hands me the car keys. "You can get the rest. Oh, and I forgot to tell you—I wasn't able to find a frame at the wholesaler's."

I deflate a little. I was really looking forward to having that article up on the wall. "Oh. Thanks anyway. Do you have any idea where to find one?"

"I'm sure there's a shop that sells them nearby." Jack goes into the living room and continues to read his magazine. I make my way back down the stairs to finish bringing in the shopping. There are another six bags left, and I struggle to lift them out of the boot. One carrier bag gets caught on something sharp, which pierces the bag and the pack of strawberries inside. One by one, the bright red fruits fall out and roll into the gutter.

"For fuck's sake." Now my dessert surprise for Jack is ruined. I don't attempt to pick the strawberries up. At least the birds will have something nice to eat.

I haul the rest of the shopping bags upstairs to the kitchen. I feel like I have run up and down a hill. I take a few seconds to catch my breath and glance into the living room. Jack still sits on the sofa, reading his amazing magazine, which he seems unable to put down for just one moment to come help me.

"Babe, come and help me put away the shopping," I say.

He just sits there. "In a minute."

I throw down the last remaining shopping bags on the table. Well, these things aren't going to put themselves away, Jack or no Jack. Just as I'm placing the final food items in the fridge, I hear Jack coming into the kitchen.

"Aww, I knew you would come and help me after I'd already put all the shopping away," I huff.

He pushes his body up against me. "Look, I'm sorry for the way I spoke to you earlier."

I am holding a loaf of bread in my hand, and I can feel his penis getting erect in his trousers, and mine reciprocating. We're pressed together like two slices of bread in a sandwich. I throw the loaf down on the kitchen worktop. I am so turned on. We start to kiss, and our tongues dance with one another. We can't resist it, and the next thing I know, we are ripping our clothes off in the heat of passion.

We slide down the kitchen cabinets to the floor, and Jack makes hot passionate love to me on the kitchen tile. We are both fully naked, and he takes full control, making sure he pleasures me every way he knows how.

All of a sudden, Jack's phone pings, and he jumps off me to get it. I remain lying there, wondering if he is going to continue where he left off, but he shatters my hopes within a few seconds. "I have to pop out for a while. My dad has texted me. He needs some help."

I jump up off the floor, still naked. "Shall I come with you?"

Jack races to get dressed. "No!" he shouts at me in a sudden vile tone.

"Okay, there's no need to bite my head off. I was only asking if you needed any help with your dad." I pick my clothes up and take them to the landing, where I get dressed. I peep through the kitchen door, and Jack is texting on his phone. I make my way into the living room, sit down on the sofa and flick through the TV channels. It feels a little surreal. We were just making love, and then he turned so nasty towards me.

Jack, fully dressed and with his phone in one hand, asks me for the car keys. I reach into my trousers and throw them at him. They hit his hand and tap the glass coffee table before falling to the floor.

Jack stares at me. His face seems to be carved out of stone. My stomach sinks. "Sorry," I say. "I didn't mean to throw them that hard."

Jack's eyes narrow to slits.

"Jack?" My palms tingle. Something's wrong. "Jack, please say something."

Then, Jack jerks into action, moving at the speed of lightning. He leaps over the coffee table. And smacks me in the face with the full force of his fist.

Chapter Sixteen

Pain explodes through my cheekbone, penetrating all the way to my heart. I choke out a gasp and place my hand on my face. Sparks dance in front of my eyes. Tears slowly well up. What just happened? Jack, my sweet Jack, would never…

I let out a couple of sobs before I dare say anything. "What was that for?"

Jack's jaw clenches, and he stands staring at me. "You hurt my fucking hand."

"I just threw them at you. I didn't know a little tap would hurt you! I am so sorry."

"Fucking fat pig." He grabs the keys and heads off to his dad's, slamming the flat door hard behind him.

I hug my knees and lie on the sofa, crying softly. My brain struggles to process. Jack would never hurt me. He loves me,

I know he does. Did I do something to make him act this way? None of this makes any sense.

Finally, I stand up from the sofa and look in the mirror. The left side of my face is as red as a strawberry, with Jack's faint hand print outlined on it. I go to the bathroom, turn the cold water on, and tear a few strips of toilet paper from the roll. I dampen the tissue and dab my face, hoping the pain will recede. It does, a little, but all the cold water in the world can't reach the ache inside my heart.

After I finish cooling my face, I walk into the kitchen switch the kettle on. Maybe a hot cup of coffee with a few extra spoons of sugar will help me calm down. I make my drink, head back into the living room and place the mug of coffee down on the table. I have to distract myself.

I text my mother to see how she is. I don't say anything about what just happened. I *can't*. I want to bury it deep down and forget it forever. The phone slips from my hand and clatters to the floor, and I don't bother picking it up.

I start to unpack the boxes of my stuff and place the items around the flat. I set up my old bedroom lamp on a table near the window. After I've gotten most of it put away, I lie down on the sofa, my face still throbbing with pain. The cup of coffee stands cold on the table—I'd forgotten all about it. Oh well.

My hand covers my sore face from the impact of Jack's blow, as if touching it will magically make it go away. Before I know it, I drift off to sleep.

I am awoken by a hand brushing over my head. It's Jack. I flinch. But instead of being angry, he caresses my shoulder gently. "I'm sorry," he says as he kisses my sore face and takes hold of my hand, pressing his lips to each of my knuckles.

I relax a little. Looks like the old Jack is back—the safe one, the one who cares about me. That incident earlier must have just been a one off

I look at the clock. "Oh my God, it's four o'clock! Where have you been?"

Jack stands up abruptly. "You know where I have been. At my dad's. I texted you a few hours ago. Look at your phone."

"Where is my phone?" I must have lost it in all the fuss.

"Here it is. On the floor." He picks it up for me as my eyes open fully from my sleep I see the mug coffee I made earlier and I didn't even drink it.

I can see from the screen that there are two text messages from Jack. The first one says, *Just arrived at my dad's. He's not in a good way—hit the bottle again. Won't be long.* The message ends with four kisses. The second text is timestamped two hours later than the last one. *Won't be long. Just talking to my dad,* plus six kisses.

I decide to take the kisses as an indication that everything is okay now. "How is your dad?" I ask.

"He's okay." Jack heads off to the bathroom.

"I'm off to bed," I say.

His voice drifts from the bathroom. "Okay. I'll be there soon."

I head for the bedroom and flip the light switch on. The bulb blinks and then goes dark.

I sit down on the bed. When Jack comes in, he says, "Why are you in the dark? And still dressed?"

"The bulb has gone." I quickly get undressed and jump into bed, pulling the duvet over me. I turn onto my side.

He goes into the living room and comes back with the lamp I set up earlier. "Babe, plug this in."

I reach over to his side of the bed and plug the lamp in for him. He undresses, with his taut, muscled body coming into view, looking like it was sculpted by a master's hand. I peep through the gap in the duvet, but soon he pulls the covers down and switches the light off. He wraps his arms around me and kisses my tender face, his manhood pushing into my back.

I turn over, and he starts to kiss me. I am getting turned on, although the memory of Jack hitting me still lingers in the back of my mind. But the pain is over now. Everything is okay. It has to be.

After just a couple of seconds of making out, Jack says goodnight and turns on his side. That's strange, but maybe it's some sort of test. I am so turned on. I want more, so I start to put my whole body against Jack, but I get no reaction back.

He must be playing hard-to-get. Like a soldier going into battle, I run my hand down his side and down to his groin.

"Stop," he says, removing my hand. "I'm tired."

I jerk my hand back like I've touched a hot plate. Embarrassment flushes over my face. "I'm sorry, Jack."

Jack scoots away from me a few inches. I feel a pang of hurt, but Jack's probably just having a bad day. Just a bad day.

I roll over on my side and fall asleep.

When I wake up on our second day of living together, Jack is still asleep. Half of his body lolls out of the duvet. I grab my phone from the bedroom cabinet, and it's displaying 6:00 a.m. Wow—I'm up early. I'd better not wake Jack just yet; the alarm won't go off till 8:00 a.m.

I place my phone back down and try to drop off to sleep. I turn onto my side, but it's no good. I shift to my back, but I just can't get comfortable. I carefully get out of bed, tiptoe into the living room and open the blinds. The sun's rays light up the whole space. What a lovely morning. We should have a busy day in the shop—the sunshine does bring out the customers.

I pick up the mug of coffee I did not drink last night, go to the kitchen and make myself a fresh cup. I consider cooking a full English, with some eggs and sausages, but I decide against it—the smell and the noise of the pan crackling would wake Jack up.

I settle for sticking some bread in the toaster, and I gaze out of the kitchen window while I wait for it to pop up. A magpie hops on the guttering of the building below. I gasp—seeing one magpie is a sign of sorrow.

The toast jumps up, and I jump with it. I struggle to spread it with the rock-hard butter from the fridge. After I finish my toast and sweep up all the crumbs, I wander back into the living room; my eyes are drawn to Jack's jacket, which hangs on the hook. He wore it last night, and it seems to be very dirty. I remember it being clean the last time I saw it.

I take a sip of my coffee. "Yuck!" I forgot to put sugar in it. I head back into the kitchen and add the sugar to my drink. I stand and stare out of the kitchen window. How would

Jack's jacket get so dirty? I sip some more of my coffee before throwing it down the sink. I really need to know what happened to that jacket.

I leave the kitchen, head on to the landing and take Jack's jacket off the hook with careful, quiet movements—the landing is not far from the bedroom, and I don't want him to hear. I take the coat back into the sunny kitchen. Jack's jacket smells like him, but I also detect hints of an unfamiliar aftershave. There is also a green smudge on the front—a grass stain.

I put the jacket over my arm, tiptoe out of the kitchen and hang the coat back on the hook, making sure it's placed exactly the way I found it. As I make my way back into the kitchen, Jack shouts, "Babe, bring me my ciggies and lighter!"

I freeze on the spot. I don't answer him at first He shouts again. "Babe, did you hear me? Bring me my ciggies and lighter!"

I reach into Jack's jacket pockets to find the requested items. "Okay, I have them!" At least it doesn't matter how his jacket is positioned on the hook now—I have an excuse for having moved it. But I would like to get some answers from Jack.

I bring the grass-stained jacket with me as I make my way into the bedroom. Jack is sat up in bed with half the duvet off him and his full package on display. His muscled arms rest on the duvet as he fiddles with his phone. He looks up at me. "Why have you brought my jacket? I only wanted the ciggies and lighter."

I shrug, handing him the coat. "I didn't really know what pocket to look in."

He looks at me in a strange way. "There's only two pockets in this coat. Why did you bring it, Brayden?"

I stammer for a couple of seconds. "I thought maybe there's something else in there you need?"

He snatches the jacket out of my hand. He reaches into the pocket, grabs his ciggies and lighter and throws the jacket across the room into the washing basket.

I take a deep breath to calm my rising temper. "How did you get that grass stain on your jacket?" I remember getting an identical stain on my own shirt when Jack made love to me in the park, back when we first started seeing each other.

"Get back into bed," Jack says.

I look over Jack's shoulder at his phone. The screen shows that it's 8:00 a.m. "We have to be at the shop before nine."

Jack lights up his ciggy, folds my side of the duvet over and pulls me back into bed. I don't refuse; I am like putty in his hand. I lie next to him, thoughts going around in my head like a merry-go-round. Why didn't Jack answer me when I asked about the grass stain on his jacket?

As Jack smokes his ciggy, he tells me cuddle into him, and I do, like a pussycat curling up to sleep. Jack kisses my forehead as he takes a puff of his ciggy. I start to feel Jack's hot body. He pulls the duvet back over him and tells me to go down on him. I slither like a snake under the duvet to the bottom and kiss every part of Jack's muscled legs as I make my way up them. I reach Jack's man tool and gently rub my hand over it. I can feel Jack is getting aroused, and so am I; I just want him to make love to me.

He moans with pleasure as I make my way back up his body. He finishes his ciggy and throws the duvet off us both, then rolls me over on my back with him on top, and our tongues lock in a passionate kiss. He runs his hands down my bare thigh until he reaches the band of my boxers and puts his hand inside to slowly release them from my waist. He kisses my rock-hard nipples. I do the same to him, and he flinches; he always finds it tickly.

He moves in and takes full control, as he always does when he is making love to me. I can see he is enjoying every moment as he pushes harder. I just love every second of it. He kisses me more, and then he climaxes.

Jack pants like a dog thirsting for water. "Did you like your morning surprise?" He reaches over to light up another ciggy. "Let's paint the rooms tonight, what do you say?"

I pull myself up to sitting and cuddle into Jack, trailing kisses down his shoulder. "I got to tell you, there will be paint everywhere." We both laugh, and I stifle a yelp as his hand brushes my face. "Thank you very much for the sex," I say, as if he was offering a service to me instead of enjoying a mutual pleasure with his boyfriend.

I look at my phone, which, in the heat of passion, has fallen on the floor. The time displays as 8:45 a.m. "Babe, we are going to be late for opening the shop!" I jump out of bed and rush to the bathroom to have a shower, still calling to Jack as I turn the taps on. "Come on, babe, get up. We are going to be late."

The water gushes over my body, and I think back to the lovemaking Jack and I just shared. I still want to make Jack tell me about the grass stain on his jacket, but it's probably best to leave it for another time.

I dry myself off with a towel and walk back to the bedroom, where Jack has only just gotten out of bed, his naked body on full display to me. He kisses me as he walks past. "I am just going into the shower."

I kiss him back, and my towel slips off and falls to the ground. My hands move down his body, which is still hot from the energy he used. He places my hand on his bum cheeks. Is he deliberately trying to make us late for work? "Jack, we can't have sex again!"

"Why not?" he says.

"We have to get to work."

He starts to kiss my neck and pushes me to the bed, and then he is all over me, caressing my body. My phone pings. I say, "Babe, we have to go!"

Jack's erected penis presses against mine. I push him off me, even though our tongues seem inseparable. "Quick, babe, get dressed."

Jack's face turns cold. "You're going to regret pushing me away."

As I stand gobsmacked at his sudden nasty tone, he walks over to the underwear drawer and picks out a white pair of boxer shorts. I don't reply to his comment, even though I desperately want to know what he meant. His man tool is soon hidden away in his bright white underwear.

Once we're fully dressed, I say to Jack, "Babe, have you got the car keys?"

"Yes. They are on the living room table."

I grab the keys off the tabletop, and we have one final kiss before we start our journey to work. We arrive at the shop and open up for the day just as the clock turns 9:05. A few moments later, the door opens, and it's Tyler and Aaron They have come to see us in our new shop, just like we visited them when they re-launched their club.

"Wow," Aaron says. "It's like being in Santa's toy shop."

Jack and I look at each other and have a little giggle. Aaron says, "Oh, Brayden, love, you could be Santa!"

Tyler looks at me. "My apologies on Aaron's behalf for comparing you to an old fat man."

Jack and I break down with laughter—not just at Tyler and Aaron's jokes, but at the happiness of being together with friends in our new shop. When we recover, Aaron says, "You must both come and see our new drag queen. Oh, she is the biz. She puts the G into glamour, loves."

I say, "What happened to Polly?"

Tyler nudges Aaron, and they grin at each other. Jack says, "Well? Tell us, then."

Aaron says, "Well, let's just say that she was caught with her knickers and tights down on the wrong side of the law. So we had to let her go from BillyJeans."

"The new drag queen, Dolly Rimmer, is so much better than Polly," Tyler says. "I think Polly has had her day, like those old ships they send to the knacker's yard. Or something like that. Mind you, Dolly does have a tongue on her—sharp as a knife!"

We all start to laugh. Aaron says, "Why don't you two come along tonight? There will be a bottle of champs on ice for you both."

Jack replies, "Now that's an offer we can't refuse."

Tyler and Aaron kiss us both on the cheek. "See you tonight!" Tyler says.

Just as they reach the door, Aaron halts and claps his hands together. "Oh, loves, I just realised what the BJ stands for!"

We all look at Aaron.

"Blow Job toys!" he says triumphantly.

We all burst into laughter. Jack says, "No, it's my and Brayden's initials, you loon."

Tyler says, "Come on, Aaron, let's go before you say anything else stupid."

After they leave, I turn to Jack. "Babe, we can't go to BillyJeans. We have some decorating to do. I want to paint the rooms."

Jack flaps a hand. "We can do the decorating another day."

"Okay. I suppose leaving it for another night won't hurt."

Jack heads outside for a ciggy, and a burst of customers walk through our door. One of them asks me if we stock a talking doll and action figures, and I point her in the right direction. My hands move like lightning as I check out item after item.

Jack returns and goes to rearrange the window display. The shop falls quiet when the last customer of the morning leaves, so I take the opportunity to restock the shelves. As I line up a row of teddy bears, I think of all the people who come to our shop to buy things not for themselves, but for their loved ones. Perhaps I should buy something for Jack to show him how much I love him. After all, it does seem like a while since we started going out with one another. I want to make him happy, so he won't get angry again and…

No, he wouldn't do that again. Everything is okay now. Still, I'm sure a present wouldn't go amiss. I place the last teddy bear in position and call to Jack. "I am just going to pop out for a minute, babe."

He grunts and says, "Okay, don't be too long."

As I walk down the high street, I scan the shops to try and find one that might have a suitable present. I spot Harry a lurking few doors down from the pound store, and I cross the road, hoping he doesn't see me. I really don't want to hear him complaining about that Christmas tree again.

I pass a jeweller's shop and peer in the window. A gold chain and two silver rings glisten in the display. If they're not too expensive, that could be a great present—a necklace and a set of matching rings for me and the love of my life!

I walk into the shop and ask the sales assistant, who is just placing a tray of rings back under the counter, if I can have a look at the pieces. She kindly takes them out of the window and lets me have a closer look. The rings have tiny words engraved inside: *I love you forever*. My heart melts. These will be perfect! It's almost like they were meant especially for me and Jack.

I ask about the prices. The gold chain's cost makes me wince, but the rings are only made of silver and are quite affordable.

The shop assistant places the rings into two gift boxes for me. I stow them in my coat pocket and make my way back to BJ Toys. When I walk in through the door, Jack is busy serving a customer. I'm desperate to give him the ring as soon as possible—I can't wait to see his face when I place it on his finger!

But then, an idea strikes me. Something this special should be presented in a special way. I will give him the ring tonight at BillyJeans, in front of everyone there. What a wonderful memory it will be when we're older!

I turn my face away from Jack to hide my grin as I walk to the back of the shop to hang my coat up. I slip my hand into the pocket and pull out one of the ring boxes. The beautiful silver sparkles inside. I trace the surface with my finger.

"Brayden?" Jack calls from the till.

I quickly snap the box shut and shove it back in my coat pocket. "Coming!" I hustle to the front, where a middle-aged lady is enquiring about where the jigsaw puzzles are.

The rest of the day brings wave after wave of customers, most of them shopping for Christmas presents. Christmas seems to have snuck up on me this year. I suppose the excitement about all these amazing changes in my life has drowned out my usual excitement about the annual holiday.

When the day ends, Jack counts the money in the till, and I go to the back of the shop to get both our coats. I press my coat's pockets tightly; the last thing I want is for the ring boxes to fall out and ruin the surprise.

Jack locks up the shop while I wait on the pavement for him. In my mind, I'm already at BillyJeans, presenting Jack with the ring and kissing him as the crowd applauds.

The town centre is winding down for the night as we walk back to the car. Jack lights up a ciggy, the smoke spiralling in the chill wind. His jawline is sharp in the dim light, his lips plump as he blows white mist between them. I really am lucky to have such a fit boyfriend.

We arrive at the car and Jack stubs out his cigarette. "Babe, I am hungry."

"Me too." I waggle my eyebrows. "But not just for food."

"Well, we can do something about that appetite of yours after we have some pizza."

I start up the car. "To the pizza shop, then!"

Jack's phone pings, but he doesn't look to see who the text is from. When I pull up to the pizza shop, Jack says, "I will go and order it What toppings do you fancy?"

"Any. Just so long as it has loads of meat on it." I nudge him.

Jack leans away from my touch. "Okay, got it."

Jack gets out and walks towards the shop door. He takes his phone out and appears to be checking it. As he enters the pizza shop, still typing on his phone, it suddenly occurs to me that he could just as easily have checked his messages while we were driving here. Why did he wait till he got out of the car before he replied to the text?

I rub a hand over my face. There's no point in being this paranoid. Everything is okay, and I need to get that through my thick head.

I reach inside my coat pocket, and my fingers close over the ring boxes. I pull one out to admire the piece of jewellery inside. I chuckle to myself. So simple, and yet so perfect.

I see Jack coming back with the pizza, and I quickly close the box and place it back in my pocket. I need to stop taking the rings out—it's too risky. I would hate to ruin the surprise.

I reach over and open the door for Jack, and he collapses in the passenger seat, lugging a ginormous pizza box. The smell of cheese, meat and sauce fills the car. I can feel my eyes bugging out of my head. "What size pizza did you get, babe? That box is huge!"

"A large triple meat surprise," he says.

"Well, it's a surprise, all right. We'll have pizza for days!"

I have to set a blast of air going on the windscreen to stop the pizza from steaming up the car. As I head towards our flat, I say, "Who was your text from?"

Jack opens the pizza box, and the wave of delicious smells hits me again. "Do you want a slice?"

Tempting, but it would be hard to drive with one hand. "No, babe, I will wait until we get home."

He shrugs. "Suit yourself." He stuffs a piece of pizza into his mouth.

I want to know why he seems so intent on avoiding my question. When he finishes chewing, I ask, "Seriously, who was texting you?"

"Oh, it was just Tyler checking to see if we're still coming to the club tonight."

"Right, okay." If it was just Tyler, then why did Jack try to hide it? Then again, maybe I'm making a big fuss over nothing.

Just a few minutes away from home, Jack puts his hand on my leg. "Kiss me."

"I can't. I'm driving."

"Come on, live dangerously for once."

Well, if he insists. "Hang on. I will find a safe place to pull over."

I park the car on the side of the road, and Jack and I share a hot, passionate kiss. Without the air conditioning, the steam seeping through the pizza box mists up all the windows. Our hands start to move all over each other's bodies, but it can't last. Jack gives me one last kiss and says, "Come on, hurry up and get us home."

I start the car. Jack devours another slice of pizza, and some of the tomato sauce gets smudged across his face. I glance over at him and start to chuckle.

"What are you laughing at?"

I point to his face, and he pulls his sunshade down to look in the mirror. He licks his finger and rubs the sauce off his face.

We arrive at the flat. As we hang up our coats in the hallway, Jack says, "I want to shag you, right now."

"What about the pizza?"

"Fuck the pizza. It will keep warm." He places the box on the stairs.

We strip right there in the hallway, our hands questing. Our tongues lock together. He strokes me with his soft touch. "Lie on the floor."

Like a solider taking an order from their higher officer, I do what he says. He lies on top of me and makes hot passionate love to me. It feels amazing; he knows his craft, and the size of his manhood leaves me breathless.

We climax at the same time, the tide dragging us both under. And then he's back to business, getting to his feet.

"Get dressed, babe. Remember, we are going to BillyJeans so we can see the new drag queen."

And so I can give him a fantastic present, but he doesn't know that yet. "Okay, babe."

Jack throws on his clothes and goes outside for a ciggy. I remain lying on the floor for a few seconds, getting my breath back after that steamy lovemaking. When I finally drag myself up and get dressed, I can't help checking my coat pocket again for the rings. They're still there, of course. I'm so tempted to give the ring to Jack now, but it will be much more special at BillyJeans.

Jack opens the door, and I quickly step away from my coat so he doesn't get suspicious. "Well," I say, "we may not have eaten the main course, but the dessert was divine."

"Indeed," Jack says.

We eat a few slices of pizza and store the rest in the fridge. Then, we share a kiss at the bottom of the stairs before I lead the way up to our bedroom. We both shower and get spruced up, and I phone a taxi.

As we get settled into the back seat of the taxi, I suddenly realise I put on the wrong coat when I left. With all the excitement about the club, and my leftover euphoria from the sex, I must have not been paying enough attention. The one I'm wearing is my blue jacket, while my black one is still inside on the hook, with the rings in the pocket.

"Fuck!" I say. "Um … babe, I think I forgot to turn the shower off."

Jack rolls his eyes. "Ugh. Go turn it off, then." He apologises to the taxi driver, even though the vehicle hasn't started moving yet.

I open the taxi door. "Do you want me to bring your coat too? It has gotten a bit cold out here."

"No, I will be okay. Just hurry up."

I dash inside and transfer the rings from my black coat pocket to my blue one. I smile as I look at the spot where Jack and I just had hot sex in the hallway. I could get used to having dessert there every night.

As I walk back to the taxi, I can see Jack talking on his phone in the back seat. When I open the door, he abruptly hangs up. "Now, you sure you haven't forgotten anything else?"

"No—everything apart from the fridge-freezer is switched off."

He snickers and tells the taxi driver to take us to BillyJeans. During the drive, it's all I can do to keep my hands out of my pocket. My instincts tell me to keep a tight grip on the rings to prevent them from falling out, but I can't risk making Jack suspicious. It would ruin the surprise.

The taxi pulls up outside BillyJeans, and Jack lights up a ciggy as we get out. He heads for the smoking area, and I wait outside and look at the posters outside the club. One of them advertises the new drag queen, Dolly Rimmer. I can't wait to see her perform. Tyler and Aaron said she was the biz. Then again, I suppose anyone would seem like the biz after Polly Easylay.

Jack returns to my side and says, "Come on, let's go in."

As we make our way to the bar, I say to Jack, "Please can we not sit in the Candy Lounge again? I felt like I was in Barbie's living room."

Jack laughs. Tyler comes to meet us and gives us both a kiss on the cheek. "So glad you came! Let me buy you both a drink. I insist."

"Very kind of you, Tyler!" I say.

"Anything for my friends. What would you like?"

"Pint of lager, please," I say.

"A vodka and coke for me," Jack says. Some irrational part of my brain is a bit annoyed that he didn't order a lager too—lagers are our thing—but perhaps he just didn't feel like having one today.

Just then, a loud booming sound comes from behind the bar. Tyler says, "What the fuck is Aaron doing now?"

Aaron appears by his side. "Hello, everyone!"

"What was all that noise?" Tyler asks.

"I was just connecting one of the speaker leads into the bar area. Did you hear it?"

"Yes, I did. And so did the rest of Kelford. You nearly deafened us all!"

"Well, it bloody did not work." Aaron smiles at me and Jack. "Darlin's, welcome back!" He snaps his fingers to get the barman's attention. "Cocktails all round, please!" He turns back to us. "What would you girls like?"

"Sex on the beach, please, Aaron," I say.

"Oh, sex on the beach, is it, love? I remember when I had sex on the beach. I got sand in places where the sun don't shine, I can tell you that much."

Jack and I laugh. Tyler pulls a face. "I am sure Jack and Brayden don't want to hear what we get up to on the beach."

When we finish laughing, Tyler says, "Shall we go and sit down?"

I brace myself for Barbie's living room again, but luckily Aaron has a table reserved just three rows back from the stage, perfect for viewing Dolly Rimmer's show. We all sit down. Tyler says to Jack, "Do you fancy a ciggy before Dolly comes on?"

Jack says, "Why not?"

The two of them head off to the smoking area, leaving me alone with Aaron. Aaron begins to talk about his and Tyler's sex life, half-complaining about how Tyler keeps asking him to try the wheelbarrow position. "I just don't have the core strength, you see. Honestly, it's like he thinks I'm a gymnast or something!"

I nod and smile, feeling inside my coat to caress the ring boxes. It's the perfect time to put my plan into action. Pushing away my nerves, I say, "Hey, Aaron, would you mind helping me with something?"

Aaron smiles as he takes a sip of his cocktail. "Anything for you, love!"

I glance around, then pull the ring boxes out. I open the lids to display the gleaming silver pieces. "I'm planning to give one of these to Jack tonight. As a sign of my love."

Aaron presses a hand to his chest. "Oh, that's so lovely! When is the big day? I'll need to buy a new hat. Oh, love, you're going to make me cry!"

"No, no, we're not getting married," I chuckle. "Well, not yet. For now, I just want to show Jack how much I love him." I slip the rings back into my pocket and take a deep breath. "So I want to ask you a massive favour. Before you announce Dolly's show, would it be okay for me to go up on the stage and give Jack his ring in front of everyone?"

"Oh, of course you can! Anything for true love."

A huge smile spreads across my face. "Thanks, Aaron! You're a star."

At that moment, Jack and Tyler return. Jack squints at me. "What are you two grinning about?"

"Oh, Aaron just made a funny joke," I say quickly.

"Really? Let's hear it, then," Jack says.

Aaron glances at his watch. "Oh my, is that the time? I need to go check on Dolly Rimmer." He leaps up from his seat and heads off backstage.

Nerves build up in my stomach as I sit in silence next to the man I'm about to publicly confess my love to. People begin to congregate around the stage. Tyler says, "You're going to love Dolly! She's a class act, I'm telling you."

"I bet she is," Jack says.

My hand shakes as I take a sip of my drink, willing Aaron to hurry up. I want to get this over with before I vomit from nervousness.

The intro music starts, and Aaron walks onto the stage. My heart pumps as if it is going to jump out of my skin. I don't think I've ever been this apprehensive in my whole life. Deep breaths, Brayden.

Aaron taps the microphone. "Good evening to all you wonderful guests of BillyJeans! I hope you're enjoying yourselves here tonight."

A chorus of cheers echoes around the room, and Jack and Tyler join in. I clench my hands into fists to try and stop the shaking.

Aaron continues. "Before I welcome our very own queen of BillyJeans onto the stage, we have a guest in the club tonight who has something very special for someone very special!"

A few chuckles flutter around the room. Aaron says, "No, I don't mean a quick shag in the lane! There's true love blossoming in BillyJeans tonight." He looks at me and beckons. "Come on up, Brayden!"

Chapter Seventeen

I force myself to stand. I look at Jack, whose forehead is creased in confusion. "What's going on, Brayden?" he says.

I give him a shaky smile. "You'll see." I take a sip of my drink and walk towards the stage.

Cheers and whoops reverberate in my ears. Behind me, I can hear Jack's voice saying, "Do you know what this is, Tyler?"

By some miracle, I manage to walk up the steps without falling over. Aaron moves aside to let me stand in front of the mic, and I clutch it with both hands, squeezing it for comfort. Dozens of pairs of eyes gaze at me. I clear my throat. "H-hello, everyone."

"Hello!" a few people say back. One man in the front row gives me a nod and a thumbs-up.

I suck in a breath. It's okay—these people are on my side. I try to draw strength from their encouragement. Time to speak right from the heart. "A short time ago, I fell in love with the hottest, fittest guy in Kelford. Yes, Jack Holiday, that's you, and I want everyone to know just how much I am in love with you."

Jack stares at me, his face an unreadable mask. My stomach sinks, but there's no going back now. I let go of the mic, put my hand inside my pocket and bring out the two gift boxes. "Jack, could you come and join me up here, please? I have something I want to give you."

Jack just sits there like a statue. Tyler reaches across and pushes him, and he finally stands up and makes his way to the stage, his movements jerky and robotic. The club cheers as he mounts the steps. He makes his way over to me, smiling awkwardly, but his tight jaw betrays his displeasure. In a soft voice that no one but me can hear, he whispers, "What the fuck are you doing?"

My breath hitches. I thought Jack would be happy, that he'd appreciate my confession, but he seems to be angry. It's too late now, though. I have to go through with this if I don't want to embarrass myself in front of everyone.

I open one of the gift boxes, and the silver ring catches the light. "I got this to show you how much you mean to me, babe," I say into the microphone. I pluck the ring from its case and slip it onto his finger.

As the audience goes nuts, Jack replies in the same quiet voice, "I don't need a ring to show how much I love you. You fucking idiot. You have shown us right up now. Look at everyone gawping at us!"

His words are like swords stabbing into my heart. I swallow. I don't want to cry in front of everyone.

Mercifully, Aaron comes to reclaim the microphone. "Oh, loves, I am going to cry and all my makeup is going to run! Poor Dolly Rimmer—she's going to have to try and top that!"

I scurry back to our table as fast as I can, with Jack at my heels. I drop into my seat, swallowing down the lump in my throat. I won't cry.

Jack knocks back his drink in one go. He looks at me with a dark expression and shakes his head. Tyler looks a little confused, but he has the good sense to say nothing.

When Aaron's finished introducing Dolly, he dashes over to see what's wrong. He whispers in Tyler's ear, his face concerned. Tyler lightly pushes Aaron back into his seat, ready to watch Dolly's show.

"I need a ciggy," Jack says.

"And I need the toilet," I say. That's not true, but I need a place to break down without anyone seeing.

Unfortunately, the smoking area at the back is right next to the toilets, so Jack and I end up walking together. His jaw is locked tight, and a vein stands out on his neck. I must have really upset him.

As we pass into the deserted corridor that leads to our destinations, I say, "Babe, what's wrong?"

Without warning, Jack grabs hold of me and pushes me against the brick wall of the club, pressing one hand into my throat. Blood roars in my ears, and my hands scrabble to make Jack loosen his grip. "You're … hurting me!" I choke out.

"What the fucking hell did you humiliate me in front of everyone for, then?" His spittle hits my face.

No, this can't be happening, not again. It was just a one-off. It can't be happening again. "I didn't … humiliate you. I wanted to prove … how much I love you … now please … let me go!"

Jack pushes more, and I gag. His twisted face blurs as my eyes fill with tears. "Stop!" I scream.

Jack lets go, and he heads out to the smoking area. I sag back against the wall, massaging my aching throat, sucking in huge gulps of air. I take my phone out of my pocket to call my mum and tell her what's happened, but my fingers freeze two inches from the screen. In the end, I shove the device deep into my pocket. I know she will only worry, tell me to leave Jack or something horrible like that.

Tears pour down my face. But … Jack loves me! I know he does. So why did he do that? I must be going insane.

When my legs start working again, I run into the toilet, unable to contain my sobs any longer. A couple of guys stare at me as I flee into a cubicle. I lock the door and sit on the toilet seat, hugging my legs, rocking back and forth as I cry. How did my plan to show Jack I love him end up going this wrong?

At least the two guys I saw on my way in leave pretty quickly. Everyone wants to see Dolly's show, so I'm left to break down in peace.

A few minutes later, the main toilet door opens and I hear someone walking across the floor. Someone unzips their fly and liquid tinkles into a urinal. "I know you're there, you fucking fat bastard."

A buzz goes down my spine, and I raise a hand protectively to my throat.

"Oi, fatty," Jack continues. "I know you're there."

I remain quiet. His footsteps walk over to my cubicle, and a pair of black shoes stops outside. He bangs on the door, making it rattle. "Why the fuck aren't you answering me?"

I whimper, fresh tears welling up. "Jack, please don't."

The door flies open with a crash, and Jack's standing there, glowering at me.

I let out a cry. I must not have locked the door properly! He raises his hand as if he's going to hit me, and I curl into a ball, my back pressing into the toilet cistern. "Please, Jack, don't hurt me!"

Jack grabs hold of my shirt and tries to pull me off the toilet seat. I put my feet on the floor to keep from falling over onto the tiles. "Stop! You're going to tear my shirt!"

It's too late—I hear the noise of the cotton material ripping. Jack grips my arm and manhandles me to my feet. He takes the ring off his finger and shoves it in my face. "What the fuck do I want a ring for? I am not going to marry you! Do you really think I want to spend the rest of my life with an overgrown fucking beached whale?"

My whole body shakes. Jack's going to hit me again. I need to get out of here, but I can't with him holding on to me and blocking the doorway.

Jack says, "Here's what I think of the ring you gave me." He flings it behind him, and I hear a *ting* as it rolls across the floor. His spit flies in my face as he shoves me into the toilet cubicle wall and screams, "Now fuck off away from me!"

I whimper some more and finally gain enough control to say, "Why are you being like this? I only wanted to show you how much I love you. Why, why, Jack?"

"You fucking showed me up, is why!"

"I love you, Jack! I wanted everyone to know, that's all."

Jack raises his hand, and I cower away from him. He's going to hit me! But instead, he punches the door of the toilet cubicle and says, "Well I don't love you. Now, fuck off." A glob of his warm saliva hits me in the face. He undoes his fly and wiggles his penis at me before doing his zip up again. "Don't expect to ever see it again!" With one final shove, Jack storms out of the toilets.

I sit there trembling until I can make my limbs work. I have to get out of here. I have to get safe.

I stumble out of the toilets, bumping into several men on the way out. I barely register them. A mixture of Jack's warm saliva and my own tears runs down my face. I wipe my cheeks as I return to the club area, heading for the exit as fast as I can. I glance over at our table, but there is no sign of Jack—just Tyler and Aaron enjoying the show. The air seems to suffocate me. Dolly Rimmer is on stage, and she must have spotted me leaving because her voice booms over the speakers: "I know my nipples are the eyes of my face, but do you have to stare at me like that? Why are you rushing? Got a date on Dick Finder?"

Laughter echoes around me. The club door bangs against the wall as I push it open. Once outside, I run and run until I can't any longer. I collapse on a bench just opposite the clock tower and sit there bawling my eyes out.

A pair of workmen glance at me as they string Christmas lights across a shop front. Many of the other shops already have their decorations up. The cheery twinkling bulbs seem so random and out-of-place in this nightmare that I almost laugh through my tears. The man I love just turned into a monster, but life goes on for the rest of the world.

In the depths of my mind's confusion, I have a vague notion that I should call a taxi. I take my phone out of my pocket, but then I put it back. I don't want the taxi driver to wonder why I'm so upset. Or worse, ask me about it.

I raise myself from the bench and automatically head in the direction of the flat. As I walk, I almost remove my ring and throw it in a nearby rubbish bin, but the sparkling silver doesn't deserve that. I take its box out of my pocket and nestle the ring inside with shaking hands.

I pass the coffee shop where Jack and I first set eyes on one another, and memories crash into my brain. If only I had a rewind button for my life so I could turn back time to a happier moment, before things got this complicated, back when it was just me and a hot man looking at each other across a counter and dreaming of what could be.

I reach the flat and race up the stairs like a rat up a drainpipe. Once in the bedroom, I peel my sweat-soaked shirt off. My face looks puffy and red in the mirror. I brush my fingers over the purple bruise forming on my neck. Oh, shit—what will my family say next time they see me? This looks like it'll take a while to heal. They will think the worst, for certain. And they'd be right.

I crawl under the covers and lie there shivering, tears and snot running down my face. God, I feel disgusting. This can't be happening. But maybe it'll be all right. I'll just wake up tomorrow and everything will be back the way it should be. Jack will love me. The bruise will be gone. Everything will be okay.

Despite my exhaustion, I lie awake for hours. Dread creeps up on me as I realise that Jack will be back soon. I don't want him to hurt me again. I should've gone to my parents' house instead, but I just wasn't thinking straight. Now I curse my own stupidity.

Just as I'm considering whether I should go home now, I hear a car engine outside. I get out of bed and hurry over to the window. Jack is getting out of a taxi on the road below, his face illuminated by the streetlamps. He looks up at the bedroom window. A stab of fear goes through me, and I jump back into bed, pulling the duvet over me. The soft blanket provides a small sliver of comfort. I feel like a little child, hiding under the covers to escape the monster under the bed. Except now I know that a duvet isn't an impenetrable shield.

I hear the front door open. I glance at my phone's clock. It's 4:00 a.m.—over three hours since I left BillyJeans. It feels like much longer than that.

The stairs creak, and Jack's shoes thump on each step. I curl into a ball, but he doesn't come into the bedroom straight away. I hear him moving around, from the kitchen to the living room to the bathroom. His footsteps fall silent.

After about twenty minutes, I creep out bed and peep through the crack in the door. No sign of him. He's taking an awfully long time in the bathroom.

I keep watching, waiting to see when he'll emerge, my body taut as a puppet's string. At last, the bathroom door opens with a thud. I dash back into bed. I can hear Jack muttering to himself, and a few scuffling noises like he's dumping his shoes and jacket on the floor. I can't make out his words, but their slur indicates that he's quite drunk.

The bedroom door opens. I close my eyes tight, my body stiffening. Maybe if I pretend to be asleep, he'll leave me alone.

The mattress sags as he sits down. "Oi, you awake?"

I fight to make my breathing steady. *I'm asleep, I'm asleep, I'm asleep.*

He slaps the duvet cover. "Oi, fat bastard, are you awake?"

I remain quiet, silently begging him to go away.

The duvet cover whips off my body, dousing me in cold air. A hand closes around my shoulder and wrenches me onto the floor.

I cry out as my body crashes into the carpet. "What the fuck are you doing, Jack?"

He sits on the bed and scowls down at me. "Get the fuck out of my bed. I don't want you in here. And by the way, I am not working in that stupid toy shop anymore. You're on your own."

I gasp as I pull myself back up off the floor, standing on shaky legs. Despite my fear, a burst of anger builds up inside me. "Why are you still being so nasty to me? I said I was sorry about tonight. You're overreacting about something so tiny! It was only a ring, for crying out loud. And even if I did upset you, you're way too drunk to have a proper conversation about this now. We can talk about it in the morning."

Jack shoots to his feet. "No! I want to fucking talk about it now."

I climb back into bed without a word. He's not going to push me out of this flat that I'm helping pay for. I find the courage inside me to say, "Well, I don't want to talk about it now. Goodnight, Jack."

Jack gets into his side of the bed, and his hands push into my back as he tries to shove me out again.

I roll over so that I'm face-to-face with him. "Will you stop? I am trying to go to sleep."

His palm crashes into my face, and an explosion of pain rips through my jaw. I scream, fire racing across my cheek. His knee collides with my shin and he pushes me over the edge of the mattress and onto the floor. My body aches, and tears well up in my eyes. I just want this nightmare to end; I want my Jack back.

"That does it," I say, trying to inject some venom into my voice with the dying embers of my earlier rage. "I have had enough, Jack. There was no need to hit me again."

Jack does not say anything. He just lies there, still as a statue.

I grab my pillow and head out to the living room, where I make a bed for myself on the sofa. Now, I am wide awake. I consider switching the TV on, just so I can feel less alone, but I decide against it. I don't want Jack to hear it and get angry.

A glance in the mirror shows a red handprint on my cheek, overlapping with my existing bruise. What have Jack and I become? I lay my head down on my pillow and the tears start to fall again as I cry myself to sleep.

Chapter Eighteen

The next day, I am awoken by Jack's soft voice. "Brayden, I am sorry, babe."

I look up at him and hold my pillow in front of my chest like a shield. Soft morning light frames his silhouette, but I haven't forgotten his devilish actions last night. "Jack, this can't go on. I am not a human punching bag."

"No, I know that, babe. I was just shocked that you gave me a ring, that's all. And I think I may have had too many vodkas."

"I don't think any amount of shock or vodka merits hitting me and spitting in my face. No, Jack, I have had enough. I don't think you love me half as much as I love you. If you did, you wouldn't have acted like you did last night, let alone thrown away the gift I got for you."

Jack laughs nervously. "I am truly sorry, babe. I picked the ring up after you left."

I glance at Jack's finger. "Oh really? Then where is it?"

"In my coat pocket. Where's yours? You're not wearing one either."

"In the box in my jacket pocket."

Jack dashes to the pocket of my jacket to fetch my ring and places it back on my finger. Our fingers brush a little, and I flinch, but nothing comes of it. His touch doesn't come with pain today.

He smiles. "Come back to bed then, and when we get up, I will put my ring back on. Okay, babe?"

"Well…" He seems to be sorry. Do I dare hope that Good Jack is back? "Okay."

He gently takes my hand and places it down his boxer shorts to feel his penis, which is starting to get erected. I quickly jerk my hand back. I'm not sure I'm ready for that yet when he's only just started being nice to me again.

He bends down and kisses my head and face. My bruise is still tender from last night, but I can almost ignore the lingering soreness as a tingle runs across my skin at Jack's touch. He presses his mouth to mine, and our tongues start to dance. He pulls away. "Come on. Come back to bed, so I can show you how sorry I am."

"Okay. I will be there in a minute."

Jack heads back to the bedroom. "Don't be long!" he calls.

I stare out of the living room window at the bright blue sky outside, my mind racing. If I'd been more sensible yesterday, I could have gone and moved back in with my family. My dad did say I could come back any time. But now

Jack seems to be good again. Maybe his bad behaviour was just growing pains, and now everything will be okay.

I can't be alone again.

"Brayden, come on!" Jack calls.

I reply, "Coming now." As I stand up to go back to the bedroom, I hear a ping from a phone. Mine is lying on the living room table, but there aren't any notifications on it. So it must be Jack's phone.

Another ping sounds, and I'm pretty sure it came from Jack's jacket, which is still crumpled on the floor from last night. I don't know quite when I got so paranoid, but I cross to his coat and take his phone out of his pocket.

There are two text messages displayed on the screen—one from a guy called Cory, and another from someone called Jorden. My body judders. I want to know what the messages say, but the preview doesn't show the actual text—just the names. And Jack's phone is locked.

Could Jack be…?

No, he wouldn't cheat on me. He's a good person.

Just out of curiosity, I check all of the coat pockets for the ring. It's not there.

A shiver goes down my spine. Jack lied to me. My heart pounds as fast as a terrified rabbit.

I turn the key in the front door as silently as I can, and the hinges creak slightly as I open it. The morning sun pours into the dark hallway, and the light blinds me for a moment as I step outside. I feel in my coat pocket for my car keys and fish them out. The cold wind doesn't help the pain from

Jack's ferocious attack on me last night—it just makes it worse.

I climb into my car and place the key in the ignition. Twisting my wrist makes the pain flare up again, and I yelp. My hand hovers near the radio—some morning tunes may take my mind off the aches, even just for few minutes—but I decide against it. Silence would be more fitting right now.

I slide down into the seat, and my mind wanders back to last night at BillyJeans. How could Jack, my lovely Jack, be the perfect lover one minute and then turn into an evil monster the next?

I pull the mirror down from its holder and gaze into it. The redness on my face doesn't seem as bad as I thought. I touch my injuries and let out a yelp—my face is still tender and swollen. The last few hours have engraved Jack's temper all over my body. I feel an ache on my left shoulder. Pulling my T-shirt collar down and glancing in the mirror, I see a cascade of bruises spilling over my shoulders—too tender to touch even to rub cream on them.

I fix my T-shirt so my injuries are not exposed and fold the mirror back into its holder. It's going to be Christmas season in a few days. My family would believe me if I told them I merely missed them and wanted to come and visit, but how am I going to explain these bruises to them? My mind floods with excuses—stock fell on me, a door hit me in the face, I tripped on the pavement.

But they would be able to tell I'm lying. I've never been good at lying.

As the clouds start to gather and the sun's rays dim, I open the car door and place one foot on the concrete kerb. The paper boy slows his bike down as be approaches me, copies of the Gossip of Kelford lying limp in his bag. "Hey, mate, are you all right?"

I nod my head. "I'm fine."

The boy looks sceptical, but he shrugs and rides on. I heave myself out of the seat and close the car door, my body kicking with pain all over as if I just went six rounds with Mike Tyson.

The door stands ajar when I arrive back at the flat. I step inside and close it quietly, then tiptoe back up the stairs, pressing a hand to my aching chest as though that will stop my heart from breaking.

I can't go back home. But I don't know if I'm safe here.

Jack calls my name as I step onto the landing. I reach into his jacket and fish his phone out. Jack shouts from the bedroom, "Babe, what are you doing? Get in here!"

I take a deep breath and head into the bedroom with Jack's phone. "Here, babe. You have some text messages. From two guys."

"Oh." Jack snatches his phone from me and places it on the bedside table face down. "Thanks. But never mind that. Come back to bed." He grins and flashes his erected penis at me.

"Um ... I'm not sure that's a good idea. It's a bit late. The day will be gone soon." Truth be told, I'm still a bit wary of him. Especially since he seems to want to hide his phone from me.

Jack laughs. "You won't be wasting your time, trust me."

"Aren't you going to see who your text messages are from?"

"Later, later. Get back into bed."

"No, Jack. I need to sort out the Christmas decorations. When I was walking through the town last night, I saw some people putting up lights. Made me realise Christmas is closer than I thought. We need to get into the festive spirit."

Jack laughs again. "So you're not in the mood for sex."

"No, not yet."

Jack's smile drops off his face. "Well, okay then." He grabs his phone and flops back on the bed. "Go make me some coffee, babe."

I go to follow his order, fuming a bit that he didn't even say please. But at least he's not hitting me anymore.

As I create the brew just the way Jack likes it, I can't help thinking about Cory and Jorden. They could just be friends of Jack's, but would he hide his phone from me if it was really nothing to worry about?

When I walk back into the bedroom, Jack is still on his phone, but he is quick to place it face down on the bed. I hand Jack his coffee and snatch his phone up in one swift movement. To my elation, it didn't have time to lock itself. Jack's home screen spreads out before me, the messages app right within my grasp.

"What fuck are you doing?" Jack's coffee sloshes onto the duvet as he dives for the phone.

I back up, holding the device out of his reach. "Who are Cory and Jorden?"

Jack blinks at me, and his mouth opens and closes a couple of times before he says, "They're just some guys who used to work at the Coffee House. I haven't seen them in months."

"So you're not sleeping with them behind my back, then?"

"N-no, of course not. Now please, give me my phone back."

I slam my finger onto the messages app. Cory and Jorden are right at the top. The latest message from Jorden, sent just a few minutes ago, reads, *Yeah, last night was amazing as always! By the way, you forgot your ring. I found it on my bedroom floor.*

The most recent text from Cory says, *So we're still on for meeting today at mine?* With a winky face and an eggplant emoji.

I feel like a whole set of knives has been stabbed into my heart. I look up at Jack just as he grabs the phone from me and drives his fist into the side of my head. My ears ring and I stumble to the floor, my head spinning.

"They're lying," Jack rasps from above me. "They're just jealous of me being with you, that's all. I swear nothing happened."

Tears squeeze out of my eyes. "Those didn't seem to be jealous messages, Jack. I don't even know them, but you sure do."

"You're so fucking paranoid!" Jack's voice suddenly escalates to a yell. "Why can't you just believe me? Why do you have to question everything I do?"

"Because you're a liar!" I shout back, my head throbbing. "And you know what? I … I am going back home to live with my parents!"

"Fuck off, then!" His spit sprays over my face.

"I will!" I walk out of the bedroom and slam the door behind me, wiping Jack's hot spittle from my face.

I text my mum to tell her I am on my way over, my fingers pushing the keys so hard that I'm surprised I don't break my phone. My ear and head pulse with pain, so I wet a facecloth in the bathroom and hold it over the injury to ease the soreness. I do a mental run-through of the bare minimum I need to bring with me to my parents' house—change of clothes, wallet, laptop. I don't want to stay here any longer than necessary.

The bathroom door flies open, and Jack enters wearing only a shirt. His expression is unreadable as he grabs my arm, sending my phone clattering to the floor.

"Let me go!" I struggle, but he's too strong. He rips the button off my trousers as he pulls them down.

My throat goes dry.

Jack drapes me over the side of the bath. I squirm and wriggle, whimpering, but it's no use. "Get away from me!" My chest squeezes, restricting my airflow. I don't know what's going on. I can't breathe.

Jack pulls down my boxers, ripping them down the side seam, and forces his penis into me. Pain rips through my entire body, and I scream. "You're hurting me!"

"Shut up," he growls in my ear. "This is what you wanted, and now you're getting it. Happy now, you fucking fat bastard?"

All the air has fled my lungs. My hands scrabble against his grip, but the pain makes me even weaker; I might as well be wrestling a tiger. Tears drip from my eyes and fall into the bathtub. The pain stretches on and on and on. I gasp for air. *Please, make it stop, make it stop, make it stop.*

Finally, after what seems like an eternity of torture, Jack pulls out. "There," he pants. "Did you enjoy that?"

I let out a breathy sob. "No, it hurt, and it still does."

"Get up. Get dressed."

I collapse on the bathroom floor. My body has no energy to move. I hurt all over.

"I'm going to have a ciggy," Jack announces, stalking out.

The button of my trousers rolled under the sink cupboard, and I stare at it, trying to process what just happened. Did Jack make love to me, or did he rape me? Jack, my Jack, would never do anything as horrible as that.

But is he really my Jack anymore?

I finally find the strength to pull myself off the cold bathroom floor and sit on the toilet seat. It's a small victory.

Jack pokes his head in through the door. "Why are you still in here?" Without waiting for my reply, he says, "I wanted to let you know I have to go see my dad. He just called me."

I say nothing.

"Babe, come on, get dressed. I won't be long, and I thought you wanted to sort out the Christmas decorations."

"Yeah. I do." My voice comes out hollow and dead.

"Well, I can help as soon as I get back." He grins. "I know you really enjoyed that shag just then."

I take in a shaky breath. "Is that all I am to you now? A shag? A piece of meat?"

Jack laughs. "Nothing wrong with a little rough sex once in a while. Now, I have to go and see my dad."

I don't reply, and he leaves. A few seconds later, I hear the front door slam. He's off to visit his dad, or to call on one of his lovers, or to get his ring back. Putting up Christmas decorations seems like the most stupidly trivial thing ever. Who knows what he's really going to get up to while I'm hanging tinsel and sorting through ornaments?

I head into the bedroom, still shaking and crying. I grab a suitcase from inside the wardrobe and start to throw all my clothes into it. I think back to the day Jack and I first met. He seemed so nice, so handsome. The kind of person who would never dream of doing all the horrible things he's done to me.

The words Mandy said during our last conversation drift back to me with startling clarity. *Jack might not be the person you think he is.* Well, it turns out, she was right. Jack was hiding behind a mask. And cheating on me with other men is the least of the ways he's hurt me.

I pace the floor, turning those thoughts over and over in my head. Fact is, despite all the things Jack has done, I still love him. I can't imagine life without him. Am I giving up too easily by packing up and leaving? Am I doing the right thing?

The bedroom door opens, and I gasp and turn around. Jack smiles and waggles his hand at me. "There you go! My lovely ring is back on my finger, where it belongs." He approaches and plants a kiss on my mouth.

I push him off—I don't want to deal with him right now. Almost wearily, I watch his mask slip off yet again. He raises his fist and, as a tornado on target, it crashes into my face, knocking me onto the bed.

Pain erupts and expands all over my face like a nuclear mushroom cloud. I yelp and start to sob into the patterned duvet cover, pressing the blanket over my nose and mouth to protect myself.

Jack stands over me as I lift my head off the duvet. My body shakes. What is he going to do next? *What is he going to do next?* The thought ricochets around in my mind, echoing over and over again.

He sits down beside me and pulls me into his slender torso. His eyebrows draw together as he looks at the suitcase on the bed. "You're not going anywhere."

"You have hurt, me, Jack," I say. "More than you will ever know."

He shoves his hands in his pockets, the mask sliding back into place. "I am sorry, babe. I am truly sorry. I haven't cheated on you, I swear. They were just old school friends I used to work with and they had a party at their house last night—kind of a school reunion. That's where I went after we left BillyJeans, I promise you."

"Okay." I don't even have the energy to argue with him anymore, or consider whether he's lying or not.

He takes the suitcase off the bed and starts to put my stuff back in the drawers. I text my mum again. *Actually, I guess I'm not leaving after all.*

Jack sits on the bed and pats the spot next to him. "Sit down."

I obey. He begins to kiss me, but I pull away. He says, "What's wrong?"

"I want to sort out the Christmas decorations," I say. I can't be around him right now.

"Okay, babe. I thought you were going to do that while I went to visit my dad. I am sorry, though." He kisses me again, and this time I let him.

When he releases me, I get up. Time to get to work. I set some Christmas music going, and the next few hours are consumed with tinsel, lights and decorations. Despite his words earlier, Jack doesn't lift a finger to help. He puts his feet up on the table and turns the TV on to flick through the channels.

I notice a decoration on the Christmas tree that does not look placed right, and he clearly isn't going to help fix it, so I'll have to do it myself. I try to climb over his legs, but pain shoots up my body from where Jack pushed me out of the bed. I won't be able to lift my foot high enough without hurting myself.

I clear my throat. "Babe, I need to get to the tree, but you have your feet stretched out."

"Jump over them," he grunts.

My eyes widen. He has become a human barrier, for no other purpose than to make things harder for me. As I climb over his legs to reach the Christmas tree, groaning through the pain, he turns the TV off. I reach the tree and fix the decoration. Jack snickers behind me. I turn to see him smiling at his phone, typing something back to whoever he's texting.

I climb back over his legs, gritting my teeth against the soreness, and he turns his phone over as though he doesn't want me to see who he's texting. I almost ask him about it, but it could be a Christmas present he's ordering for me. I don't want to spoil the surprise. And I certainly don't want to seem paranoid.

With the flat decorated like Santa's grotto, I walk over to the window and look up at the sky. A single, shining star smiles back at me. I glance at Jack, who is still on his phone. "Jack, there's a star in the sky."

He replies without lifting his head. "There's millions of the stars in the sky."

"You know what I mean. Come here and make a wish with me."

Jack stands up. "I'm off to bed."

My heart sinks. The old Jack would be leaping off the sofa to come and join me.

Before I follow him to the bedroom, I make my wish quietly under my breath. "I wish the old Jack will come back to stay." But I guess he's gone, and now I have to get used to the new Jack. I sound like a broken record, repeating myself, hoping and wishing the old Jack will return.

We both head into the bedroom, and all I can think of is what tomorrow will bring. We lie down on the bed. He turns the bedroom light off and rolls onto his side, his body pressing into mine. I feel his penis erected in his boxer shorts. He starts to kiss my neck, but I lie there as stiff as a board. I can't do this. Not tonight. Not unless the old Jack comes back.

"Babe?" he mumbles into my shoulder. "Brayden?"

I don't answer him, and he retreats.

The following morning, golden rays of sunlight spill into the bedroom, waking us both up. We get dressed and washed. My body aches—all the battering it's received has taken its toll.

Jack says, "Why don't you stay home for a while, and I will open up the shop?"

I smile. "No, it's going to be far too busy for just one of us to handle. It's nearly Christmas."

Jack places his hand on my shoulder. "Relax. I got this, babe. Now, stay home, and if you feel up to it, you can come to the shop later."

I nod. "Okay. I suppose a little bit of daytime TV with Phil and Holly will take my mind off my aches."

Jack chuckles awkwardly as he reaches over and picks the car keys up from the table. I suppose I was hoping for another apology, but he just leans into me and kisses me. He is so jolly this morning—maybe my giving him the cold shoulder last night has made him think. He kisses me one more time before leaving to open the shop.

A few hours pass as I sit on the sofa. I am burdened with guilt, sitting here while Jack is working hard at the shop. Around lunchtime, I decide that's enough daytime TV, and I slowly move to the bathroom for a shower and shave before I leave.

BJ Toys is very busy when I arrive. I smile at Jack, who is serving a customer. I throw my coat over the chair behind the counter and get to work.

A steady stream of customers flows through the shop throughout the afternoon, and we get lost in the routine of working. After what has been another busy day, I count the money in the till. Jack says, "Babe, I am just having a ciggy, and then I'll be ready to go home. Hurry up."

I smile faintly and place the money in the safe. After a few other final tasks, I lock the shop up and meet Jack outside, where he is on his phone. He places it back in his pocket when he sees me and hands me the keys.

As we drive home, Jack is strangely silent. I try to start up a conversation about how busy it was in the shop today, but it seems to fall on deaf ears. Jack stares out the window of the car, grunting vaguely in response to my statements. I consider asking him what's wrong, but I don't want him to start a row, so I choose not to.

We arrive home, and Jack says, "I am shattered. I am going to go and have a lie down." He kisses me and heads off to the bedroom, closing the door behind him.

I walk into the kitchen. The light of the moon shines bright through the window. I flick the kettle on, open the fridge, and think of what can I cook for tea. I turn around to check the pantry and end up knocking my shoulder on the fridge door. The zap of pain shoots up my arm, and I yelp so loud that I'm surprised Jack doesn't shout across the flat to tell me to be quiet.

I'm not hungry anyway. I close the fridge and make myself a coffee. I walk into the living room and switch on the Christmas tree, and the cascade of colours lights up the room.

I sit down on the sofa and switch the TV on to flick through the channels. After what seems to be two hours, Jack walks into the living room. "I am starving, babe. What are we having for tea?"

I say, "Well, we could have had fish and chips, but it's too late now. They are closed."

Jack laughs. "Wow, I have been asleep for ages!" He then suggests we have a takeaway.

"I do fancy a Chinese takeaway," I say.

"Deal," he says. "So do I."

I order the takeaway, and Jack goes to collect it. While he is gone, I walk into the kitchen and prepare the plates and cutlery. As I ferry our eating utensils into the living room, I start to wonder why Jack was so quiet on the journey home. He seemed preoccupied. With his dad, perhaps? Or with the men he swears he isn't seeing behind my back?

I hear the door close. Jack is back with our takeaway. I dish out the food onto our plates, and we devour it as we settle down to catch up on the week's soaps. After a few hours of soapland, we decide to call it a night and head off to bed.

A nice, normal ending to a nice, normal day. I just hope this lasts.

Chapter Nineteen

The following day, it's Christmas Eve. The town is alive with festive cheer. Jack has to go and work at the Coffee House, so I run BJ Toys on my own. It's a very busy day, with lots of people buying last-minute presents for their family, so I call my mum in to help me serve everyone.

I smile and wish each customer a happy Christmas, but inside I am cold. I haven't bought Jack's Christmas presents yet, so during a brief lull I tell my mum I'm going to pop out.

"Okay, Brayden love," she replies. "Don't be long, though, will you? I have shopping to do too."

I grab my coat. "I'll be back soon, Mum."

I walk at a fast pace through the town, scanning the shop windows for something that Jack might like. I spy a pair of nice shoes that are just his style, and I buy those for him, along with a couple of stylish shirts and a pair of jeans.

When I return, the toy shop is heaving. I almost panic at the thought of my poor mum trying to serve all these customers by herself, but then I spot Jack, back from the coffee shop, helping her at the counter.

I sigh with relief, though I'm a little sad that my few hours of freedom away from him are over. I should hate him, but I love him with everything I've got. And that scares me.

I drop my bag of shopping in the back and relieve my mum at the till. Jack says, "Where did you go, Brayden?"

"I just had to pop out to buy some last remaining presents. You finished work early."

"Yeah, we closed early. Helen has to travel up to London and she didn't want to get caught up in the Christmas traffic." He smiles at a customer as he scans her items. "But that reminds me, I have to go buy some things too. Are all the shops still open?"

"I think so. All except for the Coffee House, apparently." I wink at him.

My mother grabs her coat and kisses me and Jack. We both thank her for helping us today. "See you both for dinner tomorrow!" she says, walking out the door.

Jack leaves with her. I gaze out the window as my mother walks up the street with him. The light outside is fading, and the rush of customers will be fading to a trickle soon.

At about four o'clock, the last customer leaves, and I decide to close up for the Christmas season. I'm just changing the 'Open' sign to 'Closed' when Harry appears at the door. "Closing already, Brayden?" he says.

"Yes, Harry. It's Christmas."

"Well, merry Christmas to you both, I suppose. Where's the other half?"

"Gone to buy some last-minute gifts."

Harry snorts. "I bet all the good stuff will be gone by now."

"Well, we can only hope there'll be something nice left."

I shake Harry's hand, and he leaves. I go to the back room of the shop and wrap Jack's presents on the table. We have some very nice black carrier bags to use for gifts, so I select one and put the presents inside. As I grab my coat, there's a knock on the door.

I return to the front to see Jack standing outside, clasping three carrier bags in his hands. I open the door. "Just closed up, babe." I try to have a sly peep at the contents of the bags.

Jack leans forward and kisses me, holding the bags close to his chest. "No peeping until tomorrow. Come on. Let's start our Christmas."

I say, "Yep."

We lock up the shop and walk up the street, me with my large black bag and Jack with his shopping bags. Most of the shops are closed, but the pubs and restaurants are alive with people. We pass the Christmas tree, and I giggle. "Remember when Harry was complaining to us about where they were putting the tree?"

"Yeah," Jack says. "Looks like he got his wish after all."

We drive home and settle in for an early night. Jack pushes me onto the sofa. Our tongues dance with one another, and my heart sings—has the old, kind, sweet Jack returned?

He runs his hands down my body, kissing every part, and I'm in heaven until he touches a bruise still hasn't fully healed. I wince at the pain, but he kisses it tenderly. I unbutton my trousers and wrench them off, tossing them and my underwear on the carpet. Jack wastes no time in stripping himself, and he lies on top of me, the warm tip of his penis touching my thigh.

Jack makes love to me on the sofa for the first time since the bathroom incident, but this time he is gentle as a teddy bear. Why couldn't it be like this all the time? Why did Jack have to hurt me to get what he wanted? And why did he sleep with other men when he could've just stuck with me? He said he didn't cheat, but I'm not convinced.

It hardly matters now. I don't know that I could leave him if I tried.

Afterwards, we lie on the sofa, hugging and kissing one another, our skin damp with sweat. Jack says, "I just need to go and have a ciggy."

"Okay. I'm going to bed."

"Keep my side of the bed warm for me."

I reply, "I will."

I hide Jack's presents underneath the tree by covering them with branches and tinsel. I switch the living room light off, walk back to the bedroom, and get under the covers. Not very long after, Jack joins me and kisses me goodnight. "I love you."

"I love you," I echo as we drift off to sleep.

*

It's the dawning of Christmas Day, and I am wide awake the second my eyes open. Jack is still fast asleep, so I slowly get out of bed, careful not to wake him. My thoughts go back to how Jack made love to me last night on the sofa, and how amazing it felt. I feel so blessed to have the old Jack back. I'm sure he's sorry for the hurt he has caused me, and it was all just a flash in the pan that won't happen again. This is going to be the best Christmas of all time!

I make my way into the living room and switch the Christmas lights on. The bulbs join with the morning sunlight to brighten up the entire room. I bend down in front of the tree and bring Jack's presents forward. Some of the baubles catch the light and cast rainbow patterns on the carpet and ceiling. It's perfect.

My phone pings with a text from my mother. *Merry Christmas to you and Jack! The turkey is in the oven. Don't be late!*

I text her back, wishing her, Dad and Sam a merry Christmas too. I flick on the telly and watch Christmas specials for a few hours. When the clock hits ten, I decide to go check on Jack and get dressed.

I find him sitting up in bed, typing on his phone. He turns it off and throws it face down on the bedside table. "Merry Christmas, Brayden."

I'm expecting him to try and kiss me, but he doesn't. I push all the strangeness aside—I can't spend Christmas Day worrying about who Jack might be texting. "My mum wants us there for dinner at twelve."

"Okay."

"Are you getting up to open your presents?"

"Yeah, in a minute." He fiddles with a loose thread on the duvet.

"Well, don't be long. There's less than two hours till we have to leave."

He says, "Yes, Brayden, I know."

I return to the living room and get back to the Christmas specials. An hour later, Jack joins me, already dressed for Christmas dinner. He kisses me, and our tongues lock together. His hands start to wander, but I stop him. "We won't have time to open your presents."

"I'll open them later."

"Well, I still need to get ready for dinner."

"Okay, fine." He grabs the remote and flicks through the channels on the TV.

I head to the bathroom to get ready. As I catch sight of the bathtub, my memory flicks to that horrible morning when Jack bent me over the side. The pain is still fresh in my mind. I've been in the bathroom a couple of times since, and managed to successfully ignore my surroundings, but it's like my brain has run out of energy to do that anymore. The memory comes back with a vengeance, and I bend over, taking deep breaths to avoid passing out.

I barely manage to avoid cutting myself with my razor as I attempt to shave with shaking hands. As I straighten my tie, the door opens. I jump with fright and let out a squeak.

Jack pauses in the doorway. "Are you all right, babe? Did I scare you?"

"Yes." I drop my eyes to the washbasin. "Sorry, babe."

He lifts my face and kisses me. I try not to think about him forcing himself inside me in this very room. "Can you get my family's presents?" I ask. "They're under the tree."

"Sure." He gives me one last peck and leaves.

I try to breathe easy again. But as I leave the bathroom, my eyes wander over to the bathtub again. My mind suddenly flashes with the memory of Jack raping me, my lungs squeezing with panic, my body convulsing in pain. I dart from the bathroom and slam the door, the trapped breeze floating out. I gasp, trying to compose myself. It's Christmas. I should be happy!

I force myself to dance down the stairs with a Christmas tune in my head. I open the front door, and Jack has the engine running. The radio blasts a festive song as I slide into the front seat. We both sing along on the journey to my parents', and I pretend that maybe, just maybe, everything is normal.

When we arrive at my parents' house, my dad greets us at the door with a hug. My mother is busy dishing up the dinner in the kitchen, but she pauses to give me a kiss and wish me a merry Christmas. I'm helping her arrange the finger sandwiches on a plate when I realise Jack has disappeared.

I poke my head out of the kitchen to see Jack talking on the phone in the hallway. I hear him say something that sounds like, "You know I like your lips around my cock."

My blood runs cold. Jack glances up when he sees me, opens the front door and continues the call outside. I stand there, swaying in shock. Maybe I completely misheard him. After all, who would call someone to talk about sex during a Christmas party at their boyfriend's parents' house?

There's no time to worry, though, because my mother calls to me to help her bring the dinner into the dining room.

Jack comes back inside and sits down at the table just in time. My mum bends over to kiss him on the cheek. "Merry Christmas, Jack!"

"Yeah, merry Christmas." He smiles at her, but it doesn't reach his eyes.

My sister bursts through the concertina doors and takes her place at the table. "Merry Christmas, Brayden! Merry Christmas, Jack!" Her eyes go wide as she looks at the food. "Wow, Mum, you've really outdone yourself this time!"

"All right, let's eat!" my dad says.

I watch Jack as the rest of us tuck into Mum's delicious spread. Aside from nibbling on his turkey, he leaves his food untouched. My mother tries to make conversation with him, but he only answers with one-word responses or grunts.

After dinner, we head to the living room to play charades, pull Christmas crackers and tell jokes. Jack sits in the corner of the sofa the whole time, refusing to participate in any activities. What's the matter with him? Could it be something to do with that phone call he didn't want me to hear?

My mother catches my eye. "Brayden, love, I want to start washing a few dishes before the evening is over. Would you come and help me?"

"Sure, Mum." I follow her into the kitchen.

Mum leans against the counter, blatantly ignoring the dirty dishes. "Brayden, are you and Jack getting along okay?"

For a second, I almost tell her about everything. But it's only recently that things started going downhill. Things were perfect before then—and maybe with time, they'll be perfect again. They have to be, because I can't live without Jack. "Yes, Mum, we're fine. I think he's just worrying about his dad, and his mum not being around for Christmas."

She studies me for a few seconds and then seems satisfied. "All right, then. Let's open presents."

We return to the living room, where I hand my parents and my sister their presents from me and Jack. Just as they're ripping the wrapping paper off, Jack looks at the time on his phone. "Brayden, we have to be going," he mutters. "I want to go and visit my dad."

"Okay, Jack. In a few minutes."

"No!" His lip curls slightly. "Now, Brayden!"

Shock flits across my mum's face, but she composes herself enough to say, "Okay, boys, if you have to leave then you have to leave. You both have a lovely Christmas." She chuckles. "What's left of it, anyway? All this build-up for one day, and then it's gone. See you both for dinner tomorrow!"

My mum hugs me and kisses me on the cheek. Jack walks off to the car with his ciggy and his phone, not even waiting for my mum to say goodbye to him.

"Are you sure everything is okay, love?" my mum whispers to me.

"Yes, Mum. I think he is just worried about his dad." I wish I felt half as confident as I sound.

My mother and father wave me off, and I head to the car with our still-wrapped presents from my family under my

259

arm. I slide into the passenger seat. Jack grips the wheel, a nasty expression contorting his face. How can someone who's usually so beautiful become so ugly? And what did I do to make him this angry?

As we drive back to our flat, Jack's phone rings. I say to him, "Shall I answer it for you?"

He grunts, and the silence stretches out for several seconds before he says, "Yeah."

The number is withheld. I accept the call and put the phone to my ear. Music plays in the background, loud and upbeat, and the voice at the other end says, "Oi, Jack, it's Ben. We still on for our shag tomorrow night?"

The breath flies out of my lungs, and I couldn't answer even if I wanted to. I jab my finger into the "end call" button.

Jack glances at me as tears start to fill my eyes. Something wet trickles down my cheek. I gasp for air, the walls of the car closing in on me like a vice.

Jack slams on the brakes, so hard that my seatbelt almost winds me. "What's the fucking matter, Brayden? I said, what's the fucking matter?"

I can't find the words to speak. My voice fled the second I heard the words of the guy on the phone. His answer still reverberates in my mind.

As I glance out the window, I see Jack pulling his arm back in the reflection of the glass, and I've barely processed what he's doing when his fist smashes into the side of my face. My head hits the passenger door window and my brain fills with clouds for a second. I burst into tears, a burning sensation filling my skull. "What was that for, Jack?" I scream.

Jack presses his lips together and speeds onwards, tyres squealing on the road. By the time we arrive home, I am still trembling in my seat. Jack leans over and wraps his arms around me, pressing a kiss to my aching temple. "I am sorry, Brayden."

I reply, "Are you, Jack?"

He does not say anything. He gets out the second he turns the car off, leaving me to carry all the presents.

I climb the stairs and enter the living room to find Jack ripping the paper off one of the presents I bought for him, balancing his phone on his shoulder as he listens to someone talking on the other end. I set the gifts from my parents on the coffee table. "Okay, we can open presents now. Good idea. Where are mine?"

Jack points to a carrier bag under the tree. I glance inside it to find a few cheap-looking presents, none of which are wrapped. For some reason, all I can fixate on is the lack of wrapping paper. Funny what your mind focuses on when you're slowly falling to pieces.

"Why didn't you wrap them?" I ask him.

Jack takes the phone from his ear and hangs up his call. "I never had time. Just fucking have them, or don't bother." He shoves his now-opened present—the pair of shoes I bought him—underneath the coffee table.

"Jack, what's wrong? You've been in a funny mood all day. Even my parents noticed it."

Jack stands up. "I'm going for a pee." He places his phone screen-down on the coffee table as he leaves.

I quickly pick his phone up before the screen locks. A message thread is up from someone called Ben. As I scroll, my eyes get wider and wider, taking in vivid descriptions of all the dirty things Ben wants to do to my boyfriend—and things that my boyfriend wants to do to him. The most recent messages confirm that Jack has arranged to meet Ben tomorrow night on the bench in the park.

The toilet flushes, but my muscles have frozen me in place. I stare at the screen, tears blurring my vision, until the phone switches off on its own. Jack's footsteps sound behind me. My voice quavers as I say, "Who's Ben?"

"No one." Jack snatches the phone out of my hand with a scowl.

"You've been cheating on me again."

"What the fuck are you on about? You're crazy."

I struggle to keep speaking around the lump in my throat. "It's all on your fucking phone. You have been sleeping with him behind my back. It's written right there." I place my finger on the screen and point at the message on Jack's phone. "And there was that call I answered while you were driving. You can't deny it!"

He looks away, but not before I see a truly furious expression erupting across his face. His jaw tics. Jack wheels around, and his fist crashes into my head, once, twice, three times. My head rings, and I flail my arms, trying to fight him off as the blows keep coming. What is happening? The world slips into a strange surreal state. This can't be real. Any of it.

Something warm trickles from my nose. I crumple under Jack's onslaught. That's it; I'm going to die here, killed by the man I love.

No, I can't let that happen. I can't die. I let out a yell and shove Jack as hard as I possibly can. He stumbles back, sitting down hard on the sofa. I get to my feet, pinching my nose shut as blood stains my fingers.

Jack snarls and dives for the shoes under the coffee table. He grabs one and launches it into the side of my head.

"Fuck!" I scream, pressing my other hand to the site of the new blossoming pain. I stagger to the armchair and sit down, bracing myself for another round.

Luckily, Jack just gets up and storms off to the bedroom, slamming the door behind him.

Chapter Twenty

I remain frozen in the chair, shaking, waiting for Jack to return. After an eternity, I realise he's probably gone to sleep. I should too, but as exhausted as I am, I can't relax even when I settle down to sleep on the sofa. The hands on the clock revolve with military precision as I lie there. Boxing Day dawns with a weak, watery light. I gaze out the window. What will today bring? Good Jack, or Bad Jack?

The sun's golden rays light the street. I stretch my arms, and my head throbs. I get up and gaze at my reflection in the mirror. More bruises, a small cut above my ear, and trails of blackish dried blood. The horror hits me all at once. Jack, my Jack, the man I love, threw a shoe at me, beat me with his fists until I was sure I would die. It seemed like a horrible dream, but as I search the bathroom cabinets for something, anything, to put on my battered face, I realise that this is reality. My bitter reality that stares back at me, bruised and bloodied, from the mirror.

My injuries might heal, but I can't erase the emotional wounds of a Christmas spent in fear and tears. There's nothing useful in the bathroom, but there might be something in our bedside drawers. I make my way silently to the bedroom and slowly open the door so I don't wake Jack. He's all wrapped up in the duvet and he looks like he is still sleeping peacefully.

I hold my breath so as not to wake him as I kneel beside the bed and quietly open the first drawer. Nothing there, so I ease the second drawer open. Success! I take the ointment and slip it into my pocket.

"What the fuck are you looking for?" Jack roars.

I am glued to the spot, frozen in fear. How can I feel like this about a man I love so much? I blubber out a few apologies, but I realise I have to tell him the truth. Maybe then he will see, just once, how much he has hurt me. "I needed some antiseptic cream for my head. You threw shoes at my face yesterday. I'm all cut and bruised."

I wait for an apology, any sign he is sorry, but instead Jack picks his phone up and looks at the screen. "It's nine fucking a.m.! Are you nuts?"

I cower. "It's not that early, babe. I have been awake for hours. But I was just leaving anyway." I laugh weakly.

But Jack can hear weakness. He strikes, raising his arms and hitting me in the face. All the blows last night made me feel empty, but somehow this one completely shatters my world. The floodgates open, pouring more tears than I ever thought possible out of my eyes. I gaze up at Jack, begging, pleading. "Why? Why would you do this?"

But I could be talking to a stranger in the street. The face before me belongs to the man I love, but that's where the resemblance ends. The person behind it is not my Jack. Instead, he's a wicked, cold, unfeeling void. I have never felt so alone.

Trying to gather myself from the floor, I fumble for words to say. Words to make him hear me, hear my pain, understand that my heart is breaking. "You hurt me. I am sorry I woke you, but I was just trying to find something to put onto my face."

Judging by his unfeeling mask of an expression, I might as well be speaking into a bottomless well. I swallow. This is truly the worst Christmas ever in the history of Christmases.

I get up on shaking legs. I have to get out of this room. But before I can go, Jack slides out of bed and raises a fist. I shrink against the wall, but the blow never comes. Instead, he snarls, "Get the fuck out of my room, you overgrown fucking fat whale!"

Every word is like a dagger to my heart, shattering me beyond repair. I slip away and sprint to the bathroom. Behind me, he shouts, "Wake me up again and there will be another bruise to match the one you got yesterday!"

A small object whooshes past my head, and the bedroom door slams. I stand in front of my bathroom mirror, wincing as I apply the cream to my face.

Who am I? How did this happen? Why? The simple questions race around my mind, their simple answers eluding me. My mind simply refuses to work the way it's supposed to. Jack has broken me, and yet I can't fathom the idea of leaving him.

A ping from my phone drags me back to reality. It's my mum, asking if Jack and I are still coming for our family's traditional Boxing Day meal. I can't let her down, so I reply that we shall see her at 1 p.m. sharp. I'll make sure to wear clothes that cover my bruises, and I can make up some excuse for the obvious cut on my face.

I hear another ping, but it doesn't come from my phone. I head out into the living room to see Jack's device on the carpet. I remember when I was fleeing the bedroom and he threw something at me—it must have been his phone. The notification on the screen is a text from Ben.

I pick up the phone and press the home button out of habit. To my surprise, the screen unlocks. Jack must have turned the passcode off. Why would he do that?

My mouth falls open as I look at the nude photo that Ben just sent. As I watch, another one pops up. It slowly dawns on me—Jack removed his passcode because he doesn't care about secrecy anymore. He wants me to know what he's getting up to with other men, just to torture me. How could he be so brutal to me?

The phone slips from my fingers and thumps back onto the carpet. I wander to the sofa and pick up a magazine. I need to do something to stop myself thinking about all the horrors of the last twenty-four hours.

I hum a little tune, flicking to an article that might interest me. But before I can even start pretending that everything is okay, the bedroom door flies open. Jack walks towards me, half-dressed, and I can see from the look on his face that he is furious. My stomach ties in knots; I think I'm going to be sick.

"I told you to be fucking quiet!" he rages. I fumble for words, half-formed apologies dying on my lips, but Jack continues his rant. "I'm sick of having to share this fucking flat with you. You make me miserable. I am heading to BillyJeans tonight and getting drunk. I don't want to see your fat fucking face there."

"Okay." I try to smile. "I … I mean, you've seemed stressed lately, and I'm sure some relaxation will do you some good."

"I don't fucking care what you think. I don't want to relax; I want to forget. Forget you and your pathetic shit." He punches me in the face and I crumble to the floor, the pain from the blow taking me to my knees.

I press my hands to my head. Again, the tears come, and I don't stop them. In a rage, Jack lifts the Christmas tree from its stand and throws it against the wall. The coloured baubles smash and shatter into pieces on the living room floor. He picks up a Christmas figurine and stamps on it until it's broken into bits. It feels like he's stamping on my heart. I worked so hard on those damn decorations. They made me happy. I sob harder, my breaths wheezing from my lungs.

He walks back into the bedroom, leaving me to sit there amid the wreckage of our Christmas decorations. Jack comes back into the room fully dressed a few moments later, and for a second, I entertain a sliver of hope that he will apologise. But this is the bad, new Jack; not my Jack. He looks down at me as I hold my head. "I can't do this anymore. I need to get out of here."

I look up at the face I love, which somehow manages to be beautiful and ugly at the same time. "What do you mean?"

"Be with you! I have to get out of here. I never really wanted to be with you; I just took pity on you because you're a complete fucking idiot. Even Tyler and Aaron said I could get better. I needed someone to cook, clean and iron for me, and you were an easy option."

Through my tears, I beg to know what I did, beg him to tell me how this happened, but my words just enrage him. He kicks me in my leg, and my ribs explode. I gasp for breath and curl into a ball, crumpled and broken on the floor.

He sneers. "Oh yeah, and when I was making love to you, I had to pretend I was making love to all those other guys who were a better shag than you could ever be. I'd never be able to get off otherwise." His spittle hits my face. "That's right, Brayden. I never really cared about you—you were just a safety net. But I don't need you anymore. Have a good lonely life, you fat bastard."

Jack turns and strides out of the room, down the stairs and out the door, slamming it behind him. I try to stand, but my body is too damaged to move. I slowly gain the strength and drag myself across the living room, towards the landing. "Jack? Jack?" My voice comes out weak and pathetic.

It's no use; my plaintive words just echo in the empty hallway. I look at my phone to check the time. It's 9:30 a.m. We'll have to start getting ready to go to Mum's in a few hours. Funny what your brain focuses on when you're falling apart.

I make my way into the bedroom. All of Jack's clothes are still there, including the Christmas presents I gave him yesterday. But the Christmas cards from mine and his family, which contained gift cards and money, are gone.

My heart sinks with shock. Maybe he hid them somewhere just to spite me. As I search through the drawers full of my and Jack's clothes, I find a large pile of papers stuffed under a pile of his trousers. I turn them over, and they're not just papers— they're photographs. The first one shows Jack standing in BillyJeans with his arm around the waist of a handsome man I've never seen before.

My throat constricts as I shuffle through the rest of the pictures. The background of BillyJeans remains the same, but each one displays Jack with a different guy—holding him close, kissing him on the lips. One photo, of Jack making out with a thin dark haired man, makes me do a double take—that woman with the blond hair in the background looks a lot like Mandy, and the man she's talking to is definitely Enzo.

I choke back a sob. Mandy was right all along about Jack. Maybe she even saw him making out with that man, and she tried to warn me. And I refused to listen. In the end, she might have been my only real friend.

I drift back into the living room. It's started to snow outside. I stare at the white flakes, my body hurting, tears rolling down my face. With every bit of strength I have left in my aching arms, I remove the ring Jack placed back on my finger a few days ago and place it on the table next to a photograph of us both in happier times. I keep staring out of the window as the snow falls lightly and dusts the cold stone pavements and roads.

My phone pings. Maybe it's a long-overdue message from Jack to say he's sorry. I unlock the screen, and it's a text from my mum asking if Jack and I are on our way.

I place my phone down on the coffee table and take a few deep breaths to pull myself together. I look at the broken Christmas ornaments scattered across the living room floor, dotted around the severed branches of the Christmas tree. I can't leave the flat when it's in this state.

I hobble into the kitchen, take out the dustpan and brush, and start to sweep away the pretty-coloured fragments. Every swipe of the brush sends an ache all the way to my shoulders, but I need to clean this mess up. I'll also need to think of an excuse to explain why Jack isn't coming to the family meal.

I dispose of the broken ornaments and go to splash some cold water on my face, hoping the cuts will lose their redness before I arrive at my parents'. I wait an extra hour in the hope Jack will return, but there's no sign of him. The street has become a winter wonderland. Where could he have gone off to? How long is he planning to be out?

Well, I can't leave my family waiting any longer. I leave the flat and dust the covering of snow off the windscreen of my car, my hands becoming numb from the cold. As I sit down in my seat, a sharp pain shoots up my body as if I was stabbed by an invisible sword. I'll have to be careful not to seem like I'm moving stiffly at my parents' house.

On the way, I keep scanning the pavement, hoping I might see Jack. The streets are mostly empty—everyone's spending Boxing Day indoors with their families. But there's no sign of him.

When I arrive at my parents', I park on the road instead of on the drive, just to give myself a few extra moments to prepare. My face looks surprisingly normal for the amount of pain it's gone through, but there's an obvious cut near my eyebrow. I'll say that a glass Christmas ornament smashed and a shard of it hit me. Mum will believe that without question.

As I get up out of my seat, the front door opens to reveal my mum. I start to slowly walk up the drive to the front door, pasting a grin on my face. She waves at me and glances over my shoulder. "Where is Jack?"

I say the first thing that comes to mind. "Oh, Jack has a dodgy stomach. Thought it would be best for him to stay home and rest."

"Well that's a shame," my mum says, standing aside to let me in.

I enter the living room, where my dad and sister are sat watching TV. My mum repeats my lie to them: "Jack won't be joining us for lunch, as he has a upset stomach."

I paint a paper smile across my face. My sister frowns. "That's a shame. I was looking forward to seeing Jack today."

"What happened to your face?" my dad asks. I tell him my prepared excuse, and that seems to satisfy him.

My mother claps her hands and tells us all to go into the dining room, as dinner is served. Once again, she has outdone herself, with beautiful table decorations and a banquet fit for royalty. In a normal year, I would inhale my entire plate of food within a few moments and beg for seconds, but this year I have to force down every bite. I manage to eat almost the whole plate until I announce that I am stuffed. In reality, my stomach feels like a bottomless pit, but just the thought of eating more makes me feel sick. "I don't feel well myself, actually. I might have caught Jack's stomach bug. I am going to head off home."

My mum smiles. "Okay, love. Before you go, I have put together a plate of dinner for Jack, so make sure to bring it to him and give him our love."

I kiss my mum on the cheek and say my goodbyes to my father and sister. My mother walks me to the door, the cold evening breeze catching my face as I open it.

I say goodbye to Mum one last time before walking back to my car. The dusting of snow from earlier has melted away, but there's still a chill in the air. I turn to see if she is watching, but the door is closed—it must have been too cold for her, so she decided to go back into the warmth of the house.

I arrive back at the flat, hoping for and dreading Jack's return. I call his name, but my voice echoes around the hallway with no reply. Closing the door, I hobble up the stairs, every step hurting. The living room looks exactly as I left it.

I call Jack's name again, but there's no sign of him. In the bedroom, the pictures I found of Jack with the other men are still spread out on the duvet. He's not back yet. And I wonder if he ever will be.

I crash onto the bed with tears streaming down my face. I push the photos onto the floor and I sob into the pillow, my only comfort.

Chapter Twenty One

The next morning, as the sun's golden rays pour into my bedroom, I wake up and glance at Jack's side of the bed. He's not there.

I stand up, still dressed in my clothes from yesterday, and the pain from my leg shoots up my body. I take my trousers off. There's a huge bruise on my leg from Jack's Boxing Day onslaught. I put my jogging bottoms on and walk into the living room, wondering if Jack came home and slept on the sofa, but he hasn't.

I sit down on the sofa and place both hands over my face as I burst into uncontrollable crying. My mind spins like a merry-go-round, all those nasty words Jack said to me yesterday flooding my mind. If he's gone, that makes it more likely he meant them. And that means I'm not lovable. I'm just a tool.

Did Jack have this whole thing planned? Did he intentionally use me for cooking and washing and ironing right from the beginning? After all, he did say I was his safety net.

I can't pretend there's any hope for us any longer.

I walk into the bedroom and text my mum to tell her the truth about Jack. My tears blur the words I'm typing, and I hit send without even proofreading the massive wall of text. But apparently she understands perfectly well, because she writes back almost immediately. *I'm on my way, love.*

A few minutes later, she arrives at the door. I sob in her arms, and she just lets me, making a few concerned noises but not trying to push me into talking.

When my crying fades to a few sniffles, she says, "I knew there was something not right with you and Jack on Christmas day. Your face yesterday just confirmed my feeling. I didn't think you were telling the truth about cutting it on an ornament."

"How did you know, Mum?"

She hugs me closer. "Just call it a mother's intuition." She kisses the top of my head. "Come on, son. You will be all right. And you're welcome to stay with us if you want."

I shake my head. "I think I need some time alone. And I'm safe now. Jack isn't coming back here."

A few days later, it's New Years Eve. I text Jack, but I don't receive a reply. I try to ring him, and an automatic message tells me that his number is not available anymore.

I have to face it. Me and Jack are over.

I have to face the new year sad and single once again. What started out to be the best year ever for me has turned into a living nightmare.

My mum texts to invite me to the family New Years Eve party. I shoot her a text back. *I am not going to come. I have a headache.* Which is true, but I would probably decline her invitation even if it wasn't. I don't want to see anyone right now.

She replies, *Okay, love. Take care of yourself, please. Happy New Year!*

I text back, *Yeah Happy New Year to me*, with a tear emoji. And three kisses.

She does not text back, and I assume she's worked out I just want to be left alone.

As the evening drags on, I hear people shouting "Happy New Year!" to one another, even though there is still one hour to go. I don't think I want to stay up and hear the celebrations, so I turn in to bed. I wonder where Jack is now—if he's celebrating, if he's happy.

A more pressing consideration what will happen with my and Jack's shop. Well, maybe it's only my shop now. Can I even bring myself to open it again in the new year? Will the whole thing be ruined for me after this whole ordeal?

On New Years Day, I am woken early by a sound from my phone. I reach over and grab it, wondering if it's a text from Jack, but to my dismay it's just an alert telling me that the phone battery is about to die. I plug the charger in to top up my phone.

That's how lonely I am now. My only phone notifications these days are from my mum and the phone itself.

I get out of bed and walk into the living room. The clock shows eight a.m. as I look out of the window. It's only just starting to get light, and the pavement slabs sparkle from the touch of frost they received last night. Streamers and deflated balloons lie forlornly on the pavement. I know exactly how they feel.

The next day, my mum and Shirley arrive to help me pack Jack's clothes and possessions into bags. I say to my mum, "What am I going to do about the shop? I can't run it on my own."

My mum says, "Don't worry about that now. Your wellbeing is more important than a shop'."

After placing the last piece of Jack's clothing into a bag, my mum says, "Right, Shirl, it's time for a cuppa. You want one too, son?"

I am crying inside, but I know she is just trying to cheer me up. I nod and give her a weak smile. "Milk and three sugars, please."

*

The days and weeks pass, and Jack does not contact me. I can't stay in the flat where I still sometimes flash back to Jack raping me every time I look at the bathtub, so I find a new flat at the other end of the town at a very reasonable price. There are only two downsides to my new home —it's not far from the park where Jack made me love to me, and it's just down the road from BillyJeans. I wish I could enjoy being near BillyJeans, since it was my introduction to the gay scene, but now it just reminds me of Jack and everything that ended up breaking me.

BJ Toys is a little harder to let go. I pay a whole new month's rent for the shop, trying to work out how I can keep it going, but in the end I just can't. Aside from the shop being another reminder of Jack, I'm in no state to run a business successfully. At least my parents don't expect me to pay back their loan any time soon.

Add that to the list of dreams Jack took away from me.

I find a new job working at the Kelford train station. I've always liked trains. It's not the most exciting job in the world, but it gives me a reason to get out of bed every day.

One night, I finish my shift at the train station, and the road I usually take to go home has been closed, so I have to take a detour past BillyJeans. There is a crowd of people dressed in formal outfits milling around outside the club. I recognise one them as Tyler, with what seems to be a vivid tiny box in his hand.

I pull over across from BillyJeans out of morbid curiosity. A car pulls up to the club entrance and two men emerge from the back seats, kissing one another as they stand on the pavement. My heart sinks, and I feel like I'm going to be sick.

One of the men is my Jack.

I don't know who the other man, is but he is all over Jack like a rash, and Jack's reciprocating very hungrily. They look totally in love with each other. As they pull apart and gaze into each other's eyes, there's a light in Jack's face that I never saw when he was with me.

Just then, the club door opens, and I catch site of a printed banner hanging just inside. The words JUST MARRIED are written across it in enormous letters. And below it, in slightly smaller letters: JACK AND BEN HOLIDAY.

I gasp, and I feel like my neck is being crushed by a boa constrictor. I don't want to see any more. I swerve out of the parking space, tears flowing from my eyes. It's a miracle I make it home without crashing from my blurry vision.

I collapse on the sofa and phone my mum, and she picks up right away. "I just saw Jack!" I get out between sobs.

Her soothing voice answers me. "Oh, love, you mustn't worry about that. Jack's in the past, and that's where you must leave him."

"No, you don't understand." I hiccup. "I saw him having a party. A wedding party. He's just got *married*, Mum!"

The line goes quiet for a few moments. Then, she says, "Wedding or no wedding, he never deserved you anyway. And one day, you'll find a man who will love you properly. But until then, you always have us to take care of you."

I don't know if I'll ever be able to trust anyone enough to try again. I don't know if a man who will love me properly even exists. But as my mum's words sink in, I can't help but smile. She said a man. Without hesitation, she said a *man*. Which means she accepts me for who I am.

I suppose that's one good thing Jack gave me. The push I needed to come out to my family. And whether I'm dating a man or not, being gay is a part of who I am. I'm gloriously, wonderfully gay. And not even Jack can take that away from me.

I never did see Jack again after his wedding day. BillyJeans closed down a few days after Jack's wedding reception and got replaced by a block of flats. It's a huge relief to not have to see that awful reminder anymore, but at least I'm not so daunted by the idea of going into a gay club anymore. Maybe if I manage to save up some money, I'll travel to a big city to check out the gay scene there and party the night away.

I don't know if I'll ever find the kind of love or trust I thought I had with Jack. But I do know that one day I'll heal. I have a family who accepts me, and that's all I need right now. Mandy once said that if I fell in shit I'd come out smelling of roses, and I'm determined to prove her right.

There's one other thing I know for sure. I will never forget the evil Jack Holiday concealed behind his masks.

The End